Cluelessly *Yours*

max
monroe

New York Times & USA Today Bestselling Author

Cluelessly Yours

Published by Max Monroe LLC © 2023, Max Monroe

All rights reserved.

Editing by Silently Correcting Your Grammar
Formatting by Champagne Book Design
Cover Design by Peter Alderweireld

Dedication

To solo cups of Froot Loops and their fueling capacities.

To our crazy boys and their inspiration for all things "kid."

And to those who loved Matthew Perry like we did, we have some words from Michael Scott for you… "Well, this is gonna hurt like a motherfucker."

Author's Note

Cluelessly Yours is a full-length, action-packed romantic comedy stand-alone novel that's chock-full of unexpected surprises that will consume you. (We'd like to say we're sorry for the wild turns this book is going to take you on, but yeah, we're not. LOL.)

As usual, this book is hilarious, but it's also filled with the kind of excitement that will keep you on your toes.

As such, we suggest you heed the following warning:

Due to the hilarious and addictive nature of this book's content, the following things are *not* recommended: *reading in bed next to a sleeping spouse, reading on a first date, reading while you're in the lobby of the doctor's office, reading on your wedding day, reading during the birth of your child, reading at a family dinner, reading while eating and/or drinking, reading at work, reading this book to your boss, and/or reading while operating heavy machinery.* It might seem like a long list of places not to read, but we assure you, if you do it in the right setting, it'll be worth it.

Happy Reading!

All our love,

Max & Monroe

Prologue

Tuesday, May 31ˢᵗ

Sammy

"It's been two days. When is she going to wake up? Is she going to wake up? I don't—"

"Brooke, baby, take a breath. Don't get yourself worked up."

"Take a breath, Chase? How am I supposed to take a breath when my sister is—"

"Shh, baby. I know."

I can hear my sister. And her fiancé. I want to go to them. I *need* to go to them. But murky water surrounds me. It mutes the light and feels thick like swampy sludge against my skin. I struggle against it, but my fight is futile, and I drift deeper and deeper beneath the surface, despite my sister's crying.

"I know this is hard, but you have to give her time. Her body and her brain need to rest."

"But for how long? I need to see her eyes. I can't have this baby without her. I need... God, Chase, I need her."

Soft sobs echo around me, and my head swims with a throbbing vibration.

"The impact she took was significant, and honestly, she's lucky her injuries aren't *worse than they are. We have to be patient.*" A third voice sounds familiar, but I can't seem to place it right now. I can't make sense of anything, really.

"*But what about him?*"

There's a pause of some sort. It's weighted, but my thoughts are too sloppy to understand why or how.

"*As you know…his injuries are a little more severe. Now, we're just watching and waiting.*"

"*Can't you at least put them in a room together? I feel like they need to be in a room together.*"

"*Let me see what I can do.*"

The voices fade. Time skips a beat and drifts to blackness. I don't even see the water anymore. The world is a concept rather than a reality.

Roaring pain in my side seems like it should make me jump, but I can't feel myself doing anything.

"*You shouldn't be here!*"

"*I need to be here.*"

"*Are you kidding? Look at my sister. Look at him!*"

"*Brooke, baby, let's step out of the room for a minute, okay?*"

Everything fades away, and I fall back into nothingness. It's such a peaceful contrast to how I normally feel. And yet still, it doesn't feel quite right.

Everything is…missing.

Beep-beep-beep drifts into my subconscious, and I fight the pull of fatigue as hard as I can. My brain feels fuzzy, and I can't remember what day of the week it is.

Were the kids supposed to be dressed up as something today? Or wear a special color?

I have the most nagging feeling that I've already forgotten something, and I'm not even awake yet.

Ugh. It's getting harder and harder to make mornings happen, but I'm a mom. I don't have the option. It's time to get up for work. Time to get the boys to school. Time to start the day.

But damn, I'm struggling to open my eyes.

Did I finally try to use that new lash serum I bought off Amazon months ago? Surely I did it wrong if I've lost the function of my eyelids.

It feels like ripping a stuck Band-Aid off a fresh scab, and my vision could easily be described as legally blind, but I've done it—I've forced the hard start and woken up. Everything is muddled and mashed together, and light forms glowing orbs that distort my surroundings.

I blink what feels like one thousand times to clear the warped fog so I can get my ass moving, only to find that I'm not in my bed...or my bedroom, for that matter.

I'm not anywhere that I recognize at all.

Okay, scary.

I take inventory.

Stark white walls reflect unforgiving fluorescent light, and a scratchy white sheet rubs like sandpaper on my body. There's an incessant beeping from somewhere to my right, but when I go to slap it like I do my alarm clock, a painful cord tugs at my arm.

Ow.

Shit. Is that...an IV?

Am I in the hospital?

I move my head to the left, and pain shoots down my side and around, right into the length of my ribs.

Ow, jeez. Okay, maybe it's good that I'm in a hospital. That really fucking hurts.

More carefully this time, I continue my perusal of the room. My heart lodges itself in my throat when I see *him* in a bed a few feet away from mine.

An onslaught of tenderness, of adoration and affection, floods into my veins.

I want to go to him. But I can't find the strength to move a single one of my limbs.

But wait…his eyes are closed, and there's a white bandage stretched across his head.

Is he okay?

My ribs pull again, and I wince.

Are *we* okay?

Footsteps fill my ears, and I slowly turn my head to the right again. A woman walks inside. Her belly is rounded with pregnancy, and it reminds me of my sister, Brooke.

The woman doesn't look at me. She goes straight to his bed and sits down in a chair beside him. But when she looks across the room, her eyes meet mine and she startles.

"Oh! *Oh!* Oh my God!" She hops up from her chair and grabs something, tapping her fingers against it maniacally.

In a few seconds, a voice fills the room.

"Can I help you?"

"Uh…hello? Uh…hi…Uh…I think she's awake," she fumbles to answer. "The woman…the woman beside my…boyfriend is awake. Her eyes are open."

Boyfriend?

"I'll send the nurse in," the voice replies, but all I can think is, *boyfriend?*

How could he be her boyfriend when I'm in love with him? When he's told me he's in love with me?

"Hu—" I try to speak, but my throat is so dry it's like my vocal cords are stuck together. I swallow against the blockage and try again, but all that comes out is a rough, squeaky sound—one that doesn't sound like anything at all.

The woman stares at me with longing in her eyes as she grabs his hand and squeezes. *She's* holding *his* hand. Everything inside my body wants to revolt against the gesture.

With her free hand, she nervously rubs at her rounded belly, and that movement triggers a memory to break the surface of my consciousness…

We laughed and smiled and kissed as we walked toward his apartment. We stumbled down the hallway, anticipation coursing through our veins, hands greedily grabbing at each other's clothes. We couldn't get close enough.

Everything felt like bliss.

Everything felt perfect.

Until we reached his door, and she was there.

"I'm pregnant," she told him.

Agony rips through every part of me as it all comes flooding back, and I let out a scream I didn't know I was capable of. Doctors and nurses and what feels like a million people flood the room at once, and right in the middle of my cries, everything, once again, goes black.

It feels like a metaphor for my life.

Where Sammy Baker goes, disaster and chaos follow.

Over a month earlier

PART ONE

Sammy

Chapter One

Friday, April 22nd

I tuck my big tote tightly beneath my arm, trying to ignore the fact that it's boasting the smells of Italy to everyone within a one-mile radius, and churn and burn my legs like a lady on a mission.

After a quick check-in at the front desk, I smack the visitor sticker to my chest and push through the lobby doors of Calhoun Elementary. Immediately, I spot the sign that reads **Career Day** in a bold but playful font, pointing toward the auditorium, and I haul my skirt-covered ass as quick as my nude heels will take me.

Surprise, surprise, I'm late to something *again.*

In my past life, I was a time-management beast. I made it where I needed to be five to ten minutes early, and I never, but never wasted anyone's precious time.

But since the moment my birth canal opened its mouth and shot out my first baby *two full weeks after my due date,* I've been perpetually behind.

I think it was a sign. Or an omen. Or fortuitous, at the very least. And unless they change the way clocks work, I'm pretty sure it's my forever destiny. At least, it will be until my two boys are grown.

My phone pings from my garlic-scented bag—trust me, it's a *long* story—and I pull it out to find a text message from my sister. As I read, I power walk so hard I'm just short of a jog. My mall-walking grandma would be so jealous if she were alive to see me now.

Brooke: Where in the hell are you???

Me: Relax. I'm in the building.

Brooke: I'll relax when you deliver the goods.

Ten seconds later, two more texts chime in.

Brooke: Actually, scratch that. I won't get behind the mic UNTIL you deliver the goods.

Brooke: PS: Spoiler alert: Noah gets better looking every time I see him. Just WAIT until you get in here and see him too.

The Noah she is referencing is *Dr. Noah Philips*, a man who is a good friend of my sister's because their dogs are the HEA version of Romeo and Juliet— *also, incidentally, a long story.*

And unfortunately, over the past six months, Brooke has become a broken record on all things *Dr. Noah Philips and me.*

Noah and I would look so good together and he's such a good person and our souls are the *perfect match*—blah, blah, blah. Far too much of her energy is fixated on finding a way to be my unauthorized matchmaker.

Don't get me wrong, I *know* Noah is good-looking. Everyone in his vicinity knows he's good-looking. The man has a head full of shiny, thick, dark brown hair and the kind of blue eyes that make your bones turn to butter. Not to mention, a straight, white smile that could light up a dark room and muscles that make the quartz countertops in my New York apartment look soft.

He's *illegally* attractive, a screaming success in his career, and kind. The real-life, unscripted, cheese-less version of *The Bachelor.*

But just like on the show, he's not short on opportunities with the opposite sex. At any given moment, twenty-five women are undoubtedly vying for their chance to bag him.

The mere idea of him and me actually working out without carnage, catastrophe, and heartbreak? My sister is cray-cray.

I roll my eyes as I type out a response she most definitely doesn't deserve, and I don't have the time for.

Me: You do realize you're pregnant and happily engaged, right? Seems like maybe you should focus on your fiancé's nuts instead of Noah's, you little squirrel.

Brooke: Like Chase would get mad that I'm noticing the male form. Pfft. Just yesterday, he told me what a great job I did of describing my new character's penis. Plus, I'm not gawking for me. I'm doing this for YOU.

Chase is her fiancé and baby daddy—*aka my soon-to-be brother-in-law*—and her editor at Longstrand Publishing.

And he's completely obsessed with her. Though, I guess you'd have to be to live with a person *and* work in the worlds they create in their books. His whole life is Brooke Baker, and in all the time I've known him, I've never heard him complain.

Chase Dawson would one hundred percent understand the ogling of Dr. Noah and, if given the opportunity, would probably help her position her chair to get a better view if she requested it.

Another text from a different sender pops onto the screen, and I close out of Brooke's cockamamie imaginings to find a message from the one person I actually couldn't live without. And believe me, it's no man.

It's Zoe Bannon. My nanny.

Zoe: I had to keep Grant home from school. He threw up right before we left the apartment. But don't worry, he's just running a low-grade fever now and the only casualty is my shoes.

Son of a bitch.

Running late to my eldest son's Career Day event while my youngest son is at home puking on my nanny? You'd think this would take the cake for chaotic in my life, but sadly, it's just another day in the life of Sammy Baker.

I groan out loud as I hurriedly type out a response—while I continue to speed walk toward the auditorium doors that are now in sight.

Me: Oh my God. I'm so sorry, Zoe! He didn't show any signs this morning that he was feeling bad.

Zoe: It's okay, really. Have no fear, I'm good at getting vomit out of shoes.

Me: Ugh. I can't believe he's sick again. Kindergarten is going to kick him out at this rate. And seriously, I'm so, SO sorry.

With my attention still on my phone, the front of my shoe snags against an uneven tile on the floor, and I barrel through the auditorium doors with all the grace of a herd of antelope falling off a cliff.

The sounds of a song from the *Frozen* soundtrack fill the air—*yes, I recognize it*—and I'm sent immediately into embracing my Anna era.

I am awkward. I am sometimes desperate. I am hopeful and brave.

Though, if I'm completely honest, I'm still convincing myself of the last two.

Thankfully, aside from three snickering girls in the back row, no one appears to notice my falling faux pas. I even manage to hold on to my phone instead of sending it careening down the aisle.

Am I…better than everyone? *Ha.* Kidding.

I glance down at the screen to double-check that I haven't cracked it with my newfound superhero abilities, and instead, find that the digital clock showcases a whole seven minutes after the time I was supposed to be here.

Thankfully, chatter is ever present among the kiddos that fill the Calhoun Elementary auditorium, and by all indications, the presentations have yet to start. Brooke and Noah are already up on the stage, poised in folding chairs while they chat with my eldest son Seth's teacher and the organizer of this event, Ms. Katy Dayton. I make a beeline straight for them.

My phone buzzes with another reply from Zoe, but I trust that she has Grant handled for now and focus on the present.

Brooke spots me as I approach, just as Ms. Dayton runs down the stairs located on the opposite side of the stage. We make eye contact briefly from across the room, and I nod hello to the woman I've had enough parent-teacher meetings with this year to be on a first-name basis.

Ms. Dayton offers a smile, but her attention is on something behind me as she moves on quick feet toward the back of the auditorium.

I don't waste any time jogging up the stairs located stage right and head for my heavily pregnant sister. My eyes survey the roundness of her belly under her maxi dress as I close the distance between us. She's completely adorable and about seven months along, but for a woman as clumsy as her, she might as well be a year into this pregnancy.

The big ball of fur curled up at her feet—otherwise known as her German shepherd Benji—is dressed up like Batman and has a vest on his back that's labeled with "Service Dog" and "Do not pet me, please." Unlike me, he really is a superhero.

"Do you have the goods?" Brooke asks immediately, not bothering with the pleasantries of a greeting.

"Yes, I have your chicken parm. Vinny went in early just to make it for you so I could fulfill my end of the bribe."

"I'd say I'm sorry for Vinny's and your trouble, but I'm not sorry. Signing someone up to speak to a room full of elementary kids without checking with them first has consequences," Brooke says with a shrug.

Real talk: My seven-year-old Seth is a bit of a troublemaker, and because of all the class distractions he's caused Ms. Dayton this year, I felt compelled to find a way to repay her. Too bad for my famous author sister, I volunteered her as my personal tribute.

"You're lucky that Vinny is your soon-to-be brother-in-law and that you're one of his wife's favorite people. He doesn't make special batches of chicken parm for just anyone."

Truth be told, I'm incredibly lucky too. Vinny and his wife, Mo—short for Maureen—are such great bosses. I met them through Chase—Mo is his older sister—and I've been working as the general manager at their restaurant La Croisette ever since I moved my boys and myself from a house—where I could hardly take a shit with the doors on—in midwest Ohio to New York City.

Make that thrice we've landed on the whole *long story* thing.

Brooke just grins and shamelessly takes the purse off my shoulder, opening the takeout container inside to get a whiff.

"Jeez, Brookie. Tell me you're not going to eat that right now, on this stage, in front of all these kids." My voice melts into a whisper. "Anarchy will ensue, and quite frankly, I'm probably already on this school's no-fly list, thanks to my son trying to earn Class Clown MVP for the year."

"Relax. I just needed a little hit."

Noah chuckles, and for the first time since I've arrived, I allow myself to look at him directly.

Of course, like always, he looks damn good. Thick dark brown hair, intense blue eyes, strong jaw, and the kind of full lips that could serve as Webster's definition for "kissable," the attractiveness that is Noah Philips is impossible to miss.

It's for the best that he's an anesthesiologist for *pediatric* patients. Any adult woman who would have to look up into his eyes during surgery would be at risk for heart palpitations, and the hospital would no doubt be dealing with litigation from insurance companies over too many unnecessary surgeries as women tore themselves up for a chance to have him put them to sleep.

Despite what my sister thinks—and has pushed on me to the point of annoyance—I have *no* business trying to date someone like him.

His magnetism rivals the intensity of the sun, and I'm nothing more than a messy mortal.

"Hi, Noah," I greet, but my voice comes out a little self-conscious. I involuntarily tuck some of my wildly escaping hair behind my ear as a distraction. "Thanks again for doing this for me."

"Of course." He smiles up at me, bright and beaming, and I try not to let it go to my head. "I just wish I'd known we were allowed to ask for La Croisette food bribes. I could really go for some white-wine-soaked mussels right now."

Brooke kicks at my ankle, knocking the bone with the least funny of thuds. "Ow." I wince, picking it up to rub at it.

Her expression is a fraud of apology. "Sorry, my reflexes have been super freaky this trimester."

Super-freaky reflexes, my ass.

"Yeah, well, I'll only be accepting bribes from pregnant people at this time, and even my generosity with that is starting to dry up." I shoot Brooke a glare—she just smiles, hugging the container of chicken smugly.

"Damn. That's too bad." Noah's smile deepens, and I have to look away from the blinding light. His perfect features are a solar eclipse, and thanks to a shitty ex-husband, young kids, and a tough divorce, I don't own any of those special glasses. All my defenses are dried up. If I let myself succumb to Noah's charisma, everything inside me—that's barely hanging on by a thread, mind you—is sure to shrivel up.

Plus, there is *no way* this is the type of man who is looking for a woman with my kind of baggage. He's perfect. His life is perfect. And my life is...a well-contained dumpster fire on a good day. On a bad day? That fire has spread to every building within a one-mile radius, and the world's best firefighters struggle to get it under control.

But seeing as he is smack-dab in the middle of doing me a giant favor, I don't leave him hanging. "Come by the restaurant one night when you get a chance, and I'll make sure to slide you some mussels to-go at no charge."

Noah smiles again, but this time, I hold it without looking away. *And what a fucking mistake that is.* "A chance to see one of my favorite Baker sisters and free food?" He shakes his head just slightly—playfully. "That's one hell of a good deal. Count me in, Sammy."

I force myself to smile through the blush I can feel tingling in my cheeks and strongly caution my tongue against its growing urge to stutter. "Well, I do owe you. Seriously, thank you for showing up for something some crazy woman just signed you up for in the name of making amends for all of her kid's sins."

"No thanks necessary," Noah says through a soft chuckle.

"Get real, Noah," Brooke chimes in. "Thanks are definitely necessary in this scenario. Maybe a little groveling too."

"Ignore your sister. I'm happy to help." Noah reaches out to gently squeeze my wrist for a beat. "Promise."

His touch, while completely platonic and minor, feels way too good.

I chance a small glance at Brooke, although, I don't linger. I can only imagine she's feeling like a pig in shit right now, watching this interaction. She's been trying to push us together for *months*, undeterred by my repeated and certain decree that a fleeting romance with eligible bachelor Noah Philips would be the end of me.

"I really do appreciate both of you coming here and doing this."

"Yeah, yeah. We're the best," Brooke replies with a teasing wink. "Now, I see Ms. Dayton heading this direction, so why don't you duck and cover and find somewhere to hang out while we get this over with?"

I nod, picking up my bag and jetting for the side of the stage in a hurry. I have nothing against Katy Dayton—she's a super teacher and an even nicer human being—but with my son being a recurring thorn in her side, I don't necessarily feel like making small talk with her today.

Plus, I've got a text message about my other son's projectile vomit to get to. *Yay!*

I watch as Katy jogs up the steps and stops at Brooke and Noah, asking them some sort of question that makes both of their heads bobble up and down.

As she talks to them, I read the final message from Zoe.

Zoe: I talked to his school, and they understand. They'd rather have him home if he's sick, and they said something's been going around. We'll tuck in and watch a movie until you get home. Seriously, no worries and no need to rush back. Grant is doing well.

Zoe truly is the best. I don't know what I did right to end up with her as our nanny, but I'll pay penance forever if I have to.

The first thing I see when I look up from my phone is Katy heading in my direction, and I meld even farther into the shadows. She does something that turns off the joyful music from the *Frozen* soundtrack that's playing over the speakers and changes the lighting to highlight the stage directly.

She's quick, and before I know it, she's back over to the podium, tapping the mic to test it and then speaking directly into it. "Good afternoon, everyone!"

"Good afternoon, Ms. Dayton," the whole auditorium responds in unison.

She reminds the kids to be on their best behavior—most of them nod in agreement—and moves right along to present the first speaker.

"I'd like to introduce you to Brooke Baker," Katy continues, looking back at Brooke and Benji. "Brooke is a number one *New York Times* best-selling author. She is loved by many readers, and Netflix recently made a series based on her Shadow Brothers Trilogy. Please give her a round of applause as she comes up here."

The students clap their hands, and Brooke makes her way to the podium, Batman Benji following right behind her and settling at her feet when she comes to a stop behind the mic.

Several years ago, a diagnosis of vasovagal syncope and a multiyear struggle with the fainting it causes brought Benji into my sister's life, and the superhero costumes she dresses him up in pay homage to the protective role he plays. Without him, I don't know where she'd be.

"Good morning, students," my sister greets into the microphone. She's nervous; I can hear it in the faint tremor of her voice, but I can't say that I blame her. Neither one of us was ever fond of public speaking. It's ironic, really, since our father will boom his banter at anyone who will listen. "I am so excited to be here with you guys today."

"That's my aunt Brooke!" a child's voice yells from the crowd, and all the blood in my veins instantly turns to ice. Because that's not just any voice— that's *my* Seth's voice. "She's awesome!"

"Thanks, Seth," Brooke says into the microphone on a laugh, and my stomach clenches around the hope that this is where his little public display of affection ends.

"Seth Brown, you need to sit down," Principal Dana Harris whisper-yells, already slowly moving toward him, but Seth just keeps talking.

"She writes books that have s-e-x in them! My mom says I can't read them, but I've heard my mom talking about them!"

Oh no.

"Oh God," Brooke mutters, but it's right into the microphone, and her words echo throughout the entire auditorium. I jump from the side of the stage in sheer panic, but it's too late. Seth is already on a roll that can't be stopped.

"I don't know much about s-e-x, but my aunt Brooke does because that's how you get a baby in your belly!"

"Seth Brown! Sit down!" Principal Harris is practically climbing over kids to reach him at this point, and my chest is seized into painful arrest.

I start to head toward the stairs to take control of my child, but the sound of my sister's voice echoing through the speakers stops me in my tracks.

"I think I need a minute," Brooke announces, and the softness of her voice is frighteningly foreboding. Benji is on his feet, nudging her legs persistently with his snout, and Hot Dr. Noah is already moving toward her with concern on his face. *Oh shit.*

"You okay, Brooke?" I hear him ask her, and all she can do is shake her head.

Brooke's knees buckle, and Noah just barely reaches her before she faints. He catches her in his arms and gently lays her on her back, and Katy Dayton streaks across the stage to help.

After that, everything moves at a rapid-fire pace.

"Oh my God, she's died!" one student yells, and that makes the rest of them scream in horror.

More kids start shouting from their seats.

"Call 9-1-1!"

"Call my mom! I want to go home!"

"*I'm so scared! I've never seen a dead woman before!*"

"*You think they're gonna make us look at the body?*"

"*I'll puke!*"

"*My mom loves to listen to smodcasts about people dying!*"

Teachers bounce around the room like pinballs, trying to bring calm, but it's too late.

The entire auditorium is in pandemonium, a crowd on the stage is on the phone with 9-1-1, and Principal Harris is clutching her chest in abject horror.

And *my* kid is the one responsible.

Something tells me I'm about to find myself in the principal's office, suffering the consequences of what will be yet another *long story.*

Chapter Two

"We're not in the business of suspending seven-year-olds, Ms. Baker, but it's safe to say we need to find a resolution here."

Bone-chilling words from Principal Harris spin through my head as Seth and I rush from our meeting in the head honcho's office at Calhoun Elementary to St. Luke's Hospital, where my sister is located after being carted there in a freaking ambulance.

The guilt I feel for putting Brooke in this situation is clawing at my nerves, and one thousand pounds of stress sit on my shoulders as I try to navigate my eldest son and myself through the crowded New York sidewalk traffic.

Truthfully, I don't know whether to laugh or cry or go fetal right here on the concrete.

The only thing that's preventing me from having a full-on breakdown is knowing that Noah went with Brooke and they're heading to *his* hospital, where his Chief of Pediatric Anesthesiology title ensures my sister will get the best care. He was kind enough to ride in the ambulance with her so that I could collect Seth *and* get an earful from his principal.

It goes without saying that Principal Harris's words weren't ones I was happy to hear, but without a shadow of a doubt, they're words I was expecting. Not only has Seth been a constant distraction for his class, his teacher, and himself this year, but today, he told his entire elementary school and its Career Day guests that my sister writes sex books for a living while her seven-months-pregnant, frequent-fainting, vasovagal syncope-suffering ass was on the stage.

Forget suspension. I was considering strangulation.

I love my son, *obviously*, but my patience is half past tried.

I've been through the wringer since my shitty ex-husband Todd underwent a pathetic midlife crisis and decided he wanted a life that didn't include his wife and kids. In an instant, I went from being a stay-at-home mom to a forty-one-year-old *single* mom trying to find her way again with two young boys in tow.

Before my sister's generosity and vacant apartment made it possible for me to move myself and my kids to New York, I was living in Hometown, Ohio, with my parents and had no career prospects to count on. Between my complete and utter lack of direction and my dad's shock and horror every time my children acted like children, it was a nightmare. And while relocating to the Big Apple has helped me find my freedom, it's still been hard.

And I know that Seth must be suffering too, but I'm trying with everything I have to give him—and Grant—the kind of life they can be proud of. I want to be supportive and easygoing and loving, but my God, most days I feel like I'm on the brink of collapse.

Since the moment he started to toddle, Seth's been hell on wheels. And my ex was a walking, talking red flag from the moment I met him, but I was too young and naïve to notice.

Basically, I've been the primary parent every step of the way. Todd barely knew his kids existed even when they were right under his nose, and now, I have full custody—that he didn't even fight me on. And while he does have visitation rights, he's pretty much MIA from their lives and off doing only God knows what in Cincinnati, Ohio.

"Mommy, when am I supposed to see Ms. Sandy Rose?" Seth asks, and I gently grab the back of his jacket to guide him away from a huge puddle on the sidewalk.

"You're going to hang out with her for about an hour, twice a week, for the rest of the school year."

Counseling sessions with Ms. Sandy Rose, the school's psychologist, are what Principal Harris and I settled on for Seth in lieu of strangulation.

It's the best answer when I consider that maybe his acting-out is deeper rooted than I can imagine. Divorces can be hard on kids. And while Grant appears to be taking it all in stride, he's only five. Seth is seven and far more aware than his little brother.

Plus, a little therapy can't hurt, no matter what's causing Seth's wild behavior. Hell, I'm pretty sure I could use some of my own.

"Do I get to miss school for it?" he questions further. "I want to skip science."

"No, buddy. You'll talk with her after school."

He groans, but his attention is otherwise diverted toward a taxicab driver who is loudly honking his horn at a delivery truck illegally parked on the street.

"I want to drive a taxicab. Or a big truck like that," he announces, pointing toward the scene. "And I definitely want to be able to honk my horn like that too! I bet it's fun!"

Pretty sure neither driver is having the time of their lives right now, but I keep that information to myself. Just because adulthood has broken me, doesn't mean it should break him. He still believes in Santa and fairy tales and that being a grown-up means you get to do whatever you want—just like I did when I was a kid.

It doesn't even matter, though, because before I can even finish my thought, Seth is already on to the next thing. Abruptly, he bobs and weaves on the sidewalk, fake-punching the air like he's some kind of ninja, and it takes everything in me not to roar at him like the Indominus Rex from *Jurassic World*.

I hate to be this way as a mother—it's literally the least flattering image of myself I can visualize—but some days, I swear it's all I can do to survive.

"Seth! Watch out!" I shout, just as an older man stumbles because my child juked in front of his trouser-covered legs. Instantly, I grab Seth by the shoulder and pull him back in front of me. He has the decency to look sheepish, but if someone were staring at me the way I'm staring at him, I'd tuck my tail too.

"I'm so sorry," I tell the innocent bystander and usher my wild child forward on the sidewalk, trying hard to keep my cool. As we walk, I bend at the hip to speak directly into his ear. "Please, for the love of everything, I need you to relax and pay attention, buddy. There are a lot of people on the street today, and we're in a hurry to check on—*Umph.*" I groan as the impact I've just made with a stranger radiates throughout my shoulder, down into my arm, and ends in a tingle of my fingertips.

We hit hard, and this time, it was *my* fault.

"Oh my gosh! I'm so, *so* sorry," I start to apologize as the irony of lecturing my kid about paying attention while *not* paying attention pinkens my cheeks. Seth's small smirk says he noticed.

It also says that he might be a sociopath, but I'm kind of in a one-problem-at-a-time phase.

Dressed in one of his sleek, signature suits, I quickly find that the stranger I bumped into, as it turns out, isn't a stranger at all. He's actually one of my most regular customers at the restaurant. As our gazes meet, his green-hazel eyes and strong jaw melt from a grimace into friendly recognition.

"Sammy!" Gavin Evans greets warmly, as though I didn't just body check his abs hard enough to cause an internal bleed. "What a nice surprise, running into you out here in the wild."

"That's really sweet of you to say, but I doubt you can appreciate being *bumped* into this literally, Mr. Evans. I normally try to keep maiming people off my list of services."

"Running into you is always a highlight, even if I have to endure injuries. But…*Mr. Evans?*" He groans dramatically. "Sammy, I think we've more than reached the point where you can call me Gavin. Plus, Mr. Evans sounds genuinely terrifying." He winks, and his simple kindness in the middle of my stress is enough to bring my shoulders ever so slightly away from my ears.

I laugh, disarmed even more as he makes a kooky face at Seth that makes him giggle.

"I only hear it at my office, and even then, I can barely stand it. My father is Mr. Evans, and I like to think I'm still too young to be anything but Gavin."

"Okay." I swallow hard to wet my now-dry tongue. "*Gavin.*"

"Much better."

I know from the many professional dinners I've organized for him at La Croisette, Gavin Evans is midforties and incredibly successful. He's an important man in the information technology side of the business world, and his company is based in New Jersey and consults with a lot of companies in New York—hence the business dinners in the city.

He's an incredibly attractive guy—confident and tall, with the striking features to match. His sharp black hair has a barely there sprinkle of gray at the temples, and his clean-shaven, strong jaw gives way to a genuine smile full of healthy white teeth.

His personality is both dynamically self-assured and friendly, and truth be told, every interaction I've had with him has been pleasant—even playful and flirtatious on his end from time to time.

And for someone who was wearing a crop top and low-rise jeans the last time she felt attractive, the positive attention is refreshing.

But beyond that, I know absolutely nothing else about him.

Gavin eyes me closely for a long moment before lowering his voice to a soothing murmur. "Listen, I was going to call you to set up another business dinner at La Croisette soon, but I also wanted to call you for a dinner…with you."

My head jerks back in confusion. "With me?"

"With you. And me. You and me, to be specific."

"And, like, someone else?"

"No," he says through a small chuckle. "No one else, actually. Two is the magic number."

"Y-you want to take me to dinner? Like, on a date?"

"I would say that's an apt description of what I'm trying to do," he answers without the slightest hint of nerves or awkwardness. "What do you say?"

A flutter in my chest says *I'm flattered*.

But…no. No way. I have no business dating anyone right now. I wouldn't even know how to fit a date with a man into my current hectic schedule.

Are you sure? the woman who's somewhere deep inside me, the one with wants and needs and desires that don't revolve around her two boys and career and daily responsibilities, questions.

But not even a second later, a shooting pain radiates up my calf, and stars find their way behind my eyes as the bottom of Seth's foot makes hard contact with the top of mine on an energetic jump. With a grimace, I grab Seth by the shoulders and gently relocate him to my side as all thoughts of considering bringing more chaos into my life fly off with the wind.

I mean, I'm on my way to the hospital to see my sister, for God's sake. I have enough going on.

"Are you all right?" Gavin questions, concern wrinkling the corners of his eyes.

"Sorry, Mom," Seth apologizes at the same time.

I swallow past my discomfort and meet Gavin's eyes again, a few tears surely glistening in mine from the sting in my toes. "I'm okay."

"Are you sure?"

I nod. "I'm really fine. But…"

"Oh no. Not the but," Gavin comments good-naturedly, his back arching with the gentle blow of rejection.

"I'm sorry. But my life is absolute chaos on a good day. I…just…I can't go to dinner. Not right now."

His reaction is surprisingly—thankfully—relaxed. And his smile is even charismatic as he looks down at Seth. "Looks like I struck out, huh, bud?"

Seth looks defensive, his brow flexed in a harder line than normal. Given the impulsive state of his brain-to-mouth coordination, I pull him directly to my front and wrap my arm around his chest in warning. "Sorry," my son says simply, and I let out the breath I was holding in terrified anticipation. "But my mom doesn't like losers."

"*Seth!*"

Gavin laughs it off, waving at the air in front of him, and my whole body catches on fire, I'm so humiliated.

"Apologize to Mr. Evans right now."

Seth rolls his eyes, and once again, I consider doing something to him that would land me on an episode of *Law and Order: Special Victims Unit.*

I settle for squeezing his shoulder a little tighter instead.

His voice is disingenuous, to say the least, but he does apologize. "Sorry, Mr. Evans."

Gavin has the decency to accept his pathetic apology with a smile. "No worries. A son's job is to be protective of his mom. That's how I know you're a good kid."

"I'm bad to the bone," Seth counters. "I almost got kicked out of school today."

Oh, for the love of everything.

A genuine laugh jumps from Gavin's lungs. "You know, Seth, the instant I saw your light-up Captain America shoes, I knew you were not to be messed with." He flashes a discreet smile in my direction. "Only real tough guys can pull off sneakers like that."

I snort, but I also let out a deep sigh. "You'll have to excuse my son, but it's been a long day. For both of us. Mr. Bad-To-The-Bone here got in a bit of trouble at school this afternoon, and if he keeps this attitude up—" I pointedly squeeze Seth's shoulders again "—he'll certainly be facing more trouble when we get home."

Seth straightens his back and keeps his little mouth shut, and Gavin's smile turns knowing, even a little entertained.

"Looks like you've had quite the day, huh?" he asks, his eyes softening toward me.

"That's an understatement." I blow out a breath. "And sadly, the day is still young."

"Well, how about you just think on the dinner thing? No rush. No deadline. Just…keep it in the back of your mind, and I'll silently hope you'll reconsider at some point." He winks, and I'm surprised when a smile actually finds its way onto my face.

"Okay. I can do that."

"Good. I know you've got my number. So, call me if you change your mind, or hell, call me if you don't. If you want someone to talk to. Whatever, Sammy. Just use it."

I nod. He's called me about business dinners enough times for me to have his number programmed into my phone.

"I really don't mean to cut this short, but we better get moving," I hedge carefully. "My sister is in the hospital, and we're heading there now to visit her."

"Oh no. Is she—"

The sound of my ringing phone interrupts Gavin midsentence. One look at the screen, and I hold up a finger to apologize. Though I'm so anxious to hear about my sister, I don't do much else. Truth be told, I'm not even sure if I say anything before answering the call and turning away so I can hear better.

"Is everything okay with Brooke? I'm on my way now."

"She's doing great, Sammy." Noah's voice is in my ear. "I just wanted to update you that they're going to run a couple of tests to make sure it wasn't something outside of her normal episodes. Benji alerted but not nearly as quickly as normal, so they just want to make sure she doesn't have something else going on with her blood pressure that might mask warning signs."

"What kinds of tests?" I ask, concern for my sister and the sweet baby growing inside her belly making my whole body tingle. "They don't think there's anything wrong with the baby, do they?"

"No, no, the baby's fine. Ultrasound showed the baby's heart rate is excellent and amniotic fluid is at a healthy level. But they want to rule out every possibility for that reason, specifically. Anything that might be underlying would be a bigger risk with the pregnancy, so we're not taking any chances."

"Wait…are you still with her?"

"Yes. Of course. I've stayed with her the whole time, and Chase should be here any minute," he confirms, and there's a part of me that's taken aback by his kind gesture. "Dr. Cummings is actually running her care since he's the OB on call, but rest assured, I'm keeping my eye on things."

"Thank you so much, Noah." The urge to get to my sister as fast as humanly possible makes my nerves grate at the edges of my raw stomach. "I'll be there as soon as I can."

I hang up the phone quickly, and before I can even say anything, Gavin is shaking his head. "No, no. Don't worry about me or let me keep you. You obviously have somewhere you need to be. I hope everything works out and your sister is okay, and if you need me at all, just give me a call. Yeah?"

I nod, clutching Seth's shoulder and pushing him forward. "I will. Thanks, Gavin."

He turns on his heel, heading in the opposite direction from us, and I guide my little troublemaker back toward the hospital.

But not even thirty seconds later, Seth starts asking questions.

"Who was that guy, Mommy?"

"Just someone I know from work."

"Does he want to marry you?"

I laugh outright. "No, buddy. He just wanted to go out to dinner. Sometimes adults do that with other adults."

"That's what Aunt Brooke wants you to do with Noah."

That pulls me up short, and it takes a Herculean effort not to stop right here in the middle of the sidewalk.

"*What?* Where'd you hear that from?"

"I heard Aunt Brooke talking about it to Uncle Chase. She said you and Noah are lobsters. What does that mean? How can people be lobsters?"

Good grief. My sister needs to stop watching *Friends* reruns. She also needs to mind her own beeswax when it comes to the love life I don't have time for.

"It means your aunt Brooke is silly." *And* lucky she's already in the hospital.

Because if she weren't, there's a good chance I'd put her there.

Chapter
Three

Benji is perched at the foot of Brooke's hospital bed, his snout resting between his paws. Her eyes are closed, and her mouth is slack as Seth and I shuffle quickly into her room on the fourth floor of St. Luke's.

The line to check in at the front desk was long, and the haul to the OB unit wasn't much shorter. My nerves are shot, and it's not even four p.m. yet.

My sister shifts just slightly, causing a moan to roll from her lips. Panic freezes me at first, but when a second groan rents the air, I take off to her bedside with concern.

"Brooke," I say gently, shaking at her shoulder to wake her from her painful slumber. "Brooke, are you okay?" I ask as her eyes struggle to open. She looks pale and completely exhausted, and the guilt of being at the center of causing her hospital admission multiplies exponentially.

I can't believe I thought mixing her condition with a bunch of loose-cannon elementary school kids was a good idea. I mean, I live with two of them. They're practically terrorists.

"*Brooke*," I say again, this time with more vigor than gentleness.

She finally stirs, and I cup her cheek with love and worry. "Oh, sis. I'm so sorry. Are you..." My voice breaks. "Are you okay? What did they say after running the tests?"

She scrubs at her eyes and sits up a little straighter, confusion rampant. "What? What's going on?"

"Oh my God," I whisper. *Is she delirious? Did she somehow hit her head and cause some sort of amnesia?*

Real, raw panic is settling into my bones now. "I can't believe I did this to you. I can't believe—"

"Sam," a familiar and warm male voice interrupts, his gentle hand on my shoulder.

I turn to meet Noah's eyes, tears plainly falling from my own now. His face startles as he takes in the distress I'm currently drowning in. "Sammy? Are you okay? What happened?"

I dive forward and bury my face in Noah's chest, not thinking of how awkward that must be for him—not thinking of anything, really.

"What's wrong? Talk to me," he urges, pulling my body away just slightly to meet my eyes.

"Brooke," I manage on a cry. "I can't believe I did this to her. She looks awful and run-down and—"

"Whoa, whoa, Sammy. Hold on a minute," Noah interrupts, his tone gentle but undeniably firm. "We got the tests back, and everything is fine. Her iron's a little low, so we're giving her a supplement in her IV, but other than that, Brooke is good. The baby is good. I swear."

"But…" I turn to glance at her ashen pallor again before whipping back to Noah. "She's sluggish and hardly responsive and—"

Noah smiles, a tenderness in his face I can't even fathom. "Oh, Sam. She's sleepy from gorging on Italian food. She just pounded that chicken parm you brought like no tomorrow."

"She…she what?"

"Man, it was good," Brooke says from behind me, her voice devoid of the agony I heard mere moments ago. Without a second thought, I spin on my heels and thump her on the forehead with a flick of my index finger.

"Ow!" she yells, and Seth laughs immediately, each peal rife with the hysteria only a seven-year-old can pull off. Brooke, however, is aghast, rubbing at her forehead furiously. "What was that for?"

"For scaring me! I thought you were on your deathbed!"

Brooke groans. "Oh jeez."

"Oh jeez? *Oh jeez!* I was beside myself!"

"Mom, what's this do?" Seth asks, tugging at one of the wires plugged in behind Brooke's bed.

"Don't touch that!" Brooke and I yell in unison, and he jumps back like we've shot him in the hand before twirling so fast he bumps into the wall.

Brooke sucks her lips into her mouth and then turns to me with wide eyes. "You ought-bray the iminal-cray to the hospital with you?"

I grit my teeth. "I had to. The anny-nay is at home with ant-Gray uking-pay all over everything I own."

Brooke scrunches her nose and gags. "Ugh. Gross."

"How about I take Seth with me for a little while?" Noah interjects, stepping up beside me. "Show him around the hospital? Sneak some snacks from the lounge?"

"Yeah!" Seth yells excitedly. Which, considering his little ass's penchant for trouble, shrivels the very soul inside me. *Dear God, I pray for the safety of those within these walls.*

"Are you sure? I don't know if that's such a good idea…"

Noah waves me off. "No worries, Sam. We'll be fine."

"Can I, Mom? Can I? Can I?" Seth begs excitedly. I consider him for a long moment. It would be good to get a chance to talk to Brooke alone, but with my child, a hospital is one giant disaster waiting to happen. And I definitely don't have the money lying around to pay several doctors, patients, and visitors restitution. "I promise I'll be good, Mom! I promise!"

I point at Seth sternly. "You better be on your best behavior."

"Yes!" Seth cheers, jumping up and doing a spin, and even going so far as to high-five Noah.

I close my eyes briefly, only to open them at the feel of Noah's hand on the small of my back. It's so freaking warm and comforting. I don't know if he keeps a space heater in that thing or what the deal is. "It'll be fine, Sam. I promise. Just text me when you're ready to find us."

A few seconds later, before I've even given confirmation of permission, my little troublemaker and Noah are out the door together, destination unknown.

"Are you sure you don't want to date him?" Brooke asks straightaway. "That hug between the two of you looked mighty cozy…" My head swivels faster than the girl in *The Exorcist*.

"*Brooke!*"

"What? I'm just saying. He's hot. He's smart. He's successful. He's thoughtful. And the fact that he's not afraid of your eldest son should be enough to earn him a little heavy petting, you know?" She jerks her head toward my special place without shame. "The old coo-coo-cachoo could use a touch or two."

My head falls back on an exhale. "Do we really have to go through this right now?"

"Of course we do!" Brooke affirms. "Because if not now, when? I mean, let's be real, Sammy. You're into each other. And don't give me some bullshit excuse that you're not because I see the way your face turns red when he touches you."

"*Into each other?* Ha." I suppress a laugh. "I think you're seeing things, Ms. Romance Writer. He's never even asked me out."

"Well, no freaking kidding, Sam!" She slaps both of her palms down onto the bed hard enough to startle Benji's eyes to open for a brief moment, but as soon as he takes stock of the normal drama, he drifts back to sleep. "You're about as open to that kind of invitation as I am to a quick trip on an airplane."

The last time Brooke was on a plane, they had to make an emergency landing in Buffalo *because of her*. Thanks to a twenty-thousand-dollar medical bill, she still can't stand the sight of the friendly skies.

"Look at my life," I counter on a sigh. "You think I have time to be seductive and sexy? To worry about getting myself ready and flirting and showing avid interest in someone else's life? I'm barely afloat, Brookie. I don't have the energy for sex on top of it. Falling into bed at night to go to sleep is the only escape I have."

"But you could be on the bottom."

"Brooke!"

I pointedly avoid telling her about the Gavin situation that occurred on my way here. I can't decide if that would fuel her constant push to get me to date Noah or make her mad that someone who isn't Noah asked me out. Either way, I'd never hear the end of it.

Brooke frowns. "I know it seems like it'd be more work, I do. But Sam, the right guy helps your life…not the other way around."

Almost as if on cue, her fiancé Chase Dawson comes strolling through the door, his head craned toward the haul of goodies in his arms. "Okay, I got pickles, ice cream, cookies, some animal crackers, and they even had those mini-Oreo snack packs you love, so I got some of—"

He looks up midsentence to see me standing there, and his face melts into a smile. "Oh. Hey, Sam." He sets Brooke's snacks down on her bedside table and, after a quick look around and a dust of his hands, looks back at me. "Where are the boys? Do you need me to watch them while you hang with Brooke for a bit?"

Brooke grins pointedly in her best *I told you so*, but I ignore her and smile gratefully at Chase instead.

"Thanks for the offer, but Seth is with Noah, and Grant is at home sick with Zoe."

"Oh shit. Is little G okay?"

"Yeah, he'll be fine. Probably just a twenty-four-hour bug." *I hope.*

"How is Zoe, by the way?" Chase asks conversationally. "Did she get into that master's program at Vanderbilt?"

Zoe is actually a friend of Chase's family. When I started working at La

Croisette, his sister Mo put me in touch with twenty-three-year-old, money-needing, college student Zoe, and it's been a match made in heaven ever since.

"Nope." I frown. "Wait-listed."

"Damn, that sucks."

"I couldn't agree more." Selfishly, though, I'm secretly a little—*okay, a lot*—grateful.

Zoe is in her senior year at NYU and currently figuring out her next big plan. One of which was to move to Nashville, Tennessee, and attend grad school at Vanderbilt. I swear I want the best for Zoe, but the mere idea of her not being in New York is terrifying for me. I don't know what I'd do without her. Right now, she's my lifeline. The sole foundation of how I keep things afloat.

Of course, I don't dare say any of that out loud. It sounds *awfully selfish* even inside my own head.

"Are you getting released today?" I ask Brooke instead. "Or are they keeping you overnight?"

"I'm pretty sure I'm going home today, but the doctor is supposed to come in shortly to give me the rundown," she answers around a mouthful of mini-Oreos.

I glance at my watch, trying to decide how much more time I can hang around here before I need to relieve Noah of his Seth duties *and* stop at home to drop Seth off with Zoe and check on Grant before I head into work.

"Sammy, you don't have to stay," Brooke adds, silently sensing my dilemma. She's a pain in the ass, but at the root of it all, my sister cares about me deeply. "I completely understand if you need to leave. I'm good. The baby's good." She grins down at the insane number of snacks on her bedside table. "And I have enough snacks to last my pregnant ass for at least another hour or two."

"I know, but I want to stay. Let's just see how long it takes for the doctor to come in."

The door swings all the way open, and a pretty brunette in purple scrubs walks in with a clipboard in her hand. "As luck would have it, he'll be here in about five seconds."

I smile awkwardly, but she just grins. "Hi. I'm Melody, Brooke's OB nurse. I'm guessing you're her sister, right?"

I nod. "Guilty."

"Knock, knock," a tall, fit doctor with a vivid smile says as he steps through the door.

"Hi, Dr. Cummings," Brooke greets cheerfully.

"Looks like you're feeling better, huh?"

"Much better." My sister sits up straighter in her bed and drops the empty mini-Oreos wrapper onto the bedside table. "It's amazing what some fluids, food, and a nap can do."

"Thrilled to hear it. Let's go over all your tests and get you discharged."

Nurse Melody clears her throat, and Dr. Cummings's head swings to her. All he has to do is look at her, and, instantly, he's smacking himself in the forehead.

"Oh. Yeah. Protocol is for one more fetal check before you go, too, and you have to finish the iron IV."

Melody smiles, and Brooke promptly starts investigating. "Okay, I have to know. How long have you two worked together? You seem pretty in tandem."

Nurse Melody laughs, but Dr. Cummings smiles proudly as he walks toward her and pulls her into his side. "Not only is Melody your fabulous nurse today, and the best help I've ever worked with, but she's also my wife."

"I freaking knew it!" Brooke exclaims through a giggle.

"Uh-oh…are we that transparent?" Melody asks with wide but playful eyes.

"Let's just say that we know a little something about mixing fun in with the job," Brooke answers and pulls Chase toward her with an affectionate tug of his arm.

"Oh yeah?" Melody questions with interest. "Do tell."

"I'm a writer, and he's my editor," Brooke expands. "Technically speaking, I wrote an entire book about my crush on him—without his knowing—before we got together."

Chase beams down at my sister. "And I had the pleasure of editing it."

"And falling in love with me," Brooke adds and Chase winks.

"That too."

My sister and her fiancé smile at each other with lovey-dovey doe eyes as they recount their real-life romance story to the good doctor and his nurse wife. And before I know it, the two couples are laughing and smiling and joking about what it's like to work with their significant others.

Of course, all I can do is stand there feeling completely out of place while my solo-dom makes my stomach roll to the side in discomfort.

Gah, this is so awkward.

I'm officially the fifth wheel, and it doesn't take long before the urge to make my exit is too strong to deny. Without much grace or explanation, I excuse myself. "Shoot. You know what, guys? I better get out of here before I'm late for work."

Brooke's head jerks in my direction, and I don't like the expression on her face. It's way too knowing. But instead of facing it head on, as I make my way to the door, I deliberately pull my phone out of my purse and look down at it as I type a text.

This situation doesn't need Dorothy. *Oh no.* This calls for the Cowardly Lion.

"I'll see you tomorrow, okay, sis? I'll stop by to check on you." With a wave over my shoulder, I'm out the door and heading in any direction my feet can carry me while I hit send on the message I have typed out.

Me: *Time for me to head out. Assuming you're still alive, where should I meet you to get Seth?*

His response comes in promptly.

Noah: Alive and well, just like I promised. You can find us in the cafeteria, behind the wall of shrubbery and out of sight of our enemies.

Me: I'm sorry…what?

Noah: You'll see when you get here. ☺

On that note, I double the speed of my walk and follow the signs down to the cafeteria.

When I arrive, it's mostly full of hustling medical personnel, with a few patients and their families sprinkled throughout the massive space.

I scour the room for Noah and Seth, but I don't see their faces anywhere. Suddenly, a balled-up napkin comes flying from behind a wall of faux bushes, out into the cafeteria, where a male in baby-blue scrubs and a white lab coat blocks it with a lunch tray.

"Ha! Blocked!" he shouts, and the sounds of Seth's belly giggles fill my ears.

"We're gonna get you, Scott!" my son exclaims.

"Yeah, Scott!" a voice I know is Noah's adds. "You're going down, bro!"

Now Noah's message is starting to make a little more sense.

Marching cautiously through the firing zone, I make my way around the wall of bushes until both Noah and my hugely smiling son come into view. They're hunkered on the far side of a table, Seth rolling napkins, and Noah setting up their medical-supply-made launcher with one from the pile.

I clear my throat, and Noah's warm eyes come to mine.

"Hey, Mom!" Seth shouts.

"Hey, Mom," Noah repeats cheekily, his voice more of a whisper.

I put a hand to my hip. "So…what…um…exactly are we doing?"

"We're playing Cafeteria Battleship with Dr. Shepard!" Seth explains excitedly as he looks over at Noah with the biggest smile on his face. "And we're beating him!"

"Oh, really?" I ask through a soft laugh. "And whose idea was this?"

Noah chortles, shaking his head with a false crease in his eyebrows. "Scott Shepard. He's a real kid at heart, you know?"

"Are you sure he's the only kid at heart?" I tease, and Noah's grin grows.

"Seth might've also loved the idea."

I quirk one eyebrow at him. "And what about you?"

"Oh, I'm just happy to help Seth take down Shepard."

"Mm-hmm," I murmur. "I see. Very magnanimous of you."

A raspy chuckle jumps from his throat, and I have to jerk my gaze to the floor to avoid staring at the bob of his Adam's apple.

"Well, I really hate to be the bearer of bad news, but I need to get Seth home."

"Ah, man!" Seth groans. He looks over at Noah like the man walks on water, and it makes my chest crack with discomfort. *This, right here, is the kind of fun he should get to experience with his actual father.*

"I don't want to go, Mom!" Seth exclaims, and his shoes light up when he stomps his right foot to the floor. "I'm having too much fun!"

"I'm sorry, baby. I know you're having fun, but we have to get going. I have to drop you off with Zoe and get to the restaurant."

"But, *Mom!*" Seth whines, and Noah places a hand on his shoulder.

"You gotta listen to your mom, bud," he says, but his voice is soft, and his face is friendly. "But thanks for helping me beat Scott today. No one else has been able to take him down."

"Game's over, Scottie!" Noah shouts toward the other doctor before my son has a chance to protest. I'm instantly thankful. "Seth has to go home, and since we're currently in the lead, it's safe to say victory is ours!"

"Ha! Yes! We beat you, Scott!" Seth fist-pumps the air.

"Ah, man!" the other doctor shouts. "I'm not letting you have Seth on your team anymore, Noah! He's too good!"

I can't remember the last time I saw my son smile this big.

"See ya around, buddy," Noah says, and Seth jumps up to high-five him.

"C'mon, Mom! Let's go!" My son takes off around the shrubbery and straight into the rest of the cafeteria, and any chance of lingering and talking to Noah is gone.

That's probably a good thing…

"Looks like I better head out," I state as Noah stands to his feet. "Thanks again for entertaining him."

"It was no trouble at all. To be honest," he says on a bit of a whisper, "it was a lot of fun."

For some strange reason, after one last wave to Noah, I have to force myself to turn on my heel and jog after my son so I can start the process of facing the rest of my busy night that includes a full shift at the restaurant.

But as I walk, my sister's words bounce around inside my head…

With the right guy, life gets easier.

Yeah, right.

I grab Seth's hand and guide him toward the exit doors of St. Luke's, but just before we make it outside, a text vibrates my phone. I glance at the screen to see who it is.

Gavin: *I really hope your sister is okay. Don't hesitate to reach out if you need anything.*

I don't think any man, anywhere on this planet we call Earth, can make *my* chaotic life easier.

But I have to admit…I've sure as hell never had two of them try at the same time.

Chapter Four

Saturday, April 23rd

"Wasn't Noah so great yesterday?" Brooke asks, mooning up at me like a lunatic. White sugar from the powered donuts she just ate mixed with a new lipstick color has her looking suspiciously like the Joker.

She's currently perched in her bed—while Benji lies on his dog bed a few feet away—and I fluff the pillow behind her back a little harder than I probably should. Her upper body jostles somewhat violently, but the motion isn't hard enough to stop her. Evidently, being a pain in the ass is shaking-proof.

"He's kind of like a doc-tor sup-er-he-ro, you know?" She keeps going, her voice becoming staccato with the motion. "Stepping up in a crisis and all."

"He's a doctor," I mutter. "Stepping up in crisis is literally in his training."

The regret of coming over to her apartment to check on her this morning is strong, but I don't think I could have skipped it without feeling guilty.

Plus, I had zero excuses to utilize.

Since Grant turned the virus corner like a typical five-year-old and is fully back to his normal self, both of my sons are with Uncle Chase, Uncle Vinny, and Aunt Mo. The five of them are spending the day hanging out before heading to the night baseball game of their dreams—Yankees versus the Cleveland Guardians. And while the restaurant is normally only closed on

Sunday and Monday, Vinny added today into the mix so that they could get a few renovations done.

Right now, at this very moment, I have nowhere to be but here. Which is probably why I've stayed to listen to my sister's romantically inclined water-boarding for two entire hours of my day so far.

Don't get me wrong, I love my sister…when she's not being annoyingly manipulative, that is. Hanging out with her is always a witty and engaging time. If my love life weren't her fixation, but rather the romantic activities of some other innocent schlub, I'm sure I'd enjoy the tenacity of her hounding.

"Yeah, I know he's a doctor, but he's, like, a world-renowned pediatric anesthesiologist, Sammy. Some people really just excel, you know? If he told me to dance right now, I'd do it."

"Well, then…" I pause and push a gritted-teeth, overtly sugary smile to my face. "I guess that means you're feeling good, huh? I was worried I might need to stay longer just to make sure you're feeling up to being alone, but since Noah's a Marvel character and you're ready to impress Fred Astaire, I guess I can be on my way."

"Fine, fine." Brooke eyes me with annoyance. "You can relax. You don't have to leave. I'll quit, I swear."

"Thank you." I sigh appreciatively. "Let's just…have some sister time. Please. In case you haven't noticed, I don't really need any other pressure-cooker situations in my life."

Brooke looks half-baked on her way to saying something else about how *the right person helps your life*, but she stops herself. Evidently, my face is correctly conveying how capable I feel of rage.

"Okay. Sister time, it is." She fiddles with the edges of the quilt over her lap. "So…uh…seen any good movies lately?"

"Seriously, Brooke?"

"What? I'm rusty when it comes to everyday conversation! I spend most of my time alone with my characters! You know that."

"You live with Chase. That doesn't help?"

She shrugs. "He finds my psychobabble cute and endearing."

I snort. "Of course he does."

"Whatever. At least tell me you're going to do something when you leave here. This has to be your first Saturday off—sans kids—in ages. You should go out. Get your nails done. Go for a walk in the park. Take yourself to dinner. Something, for Pete's sake."

"Yes. Yes, *obviously*, I'm going to do *something*."

She stares at me for a good five seconds before a barking laugh barrels out of her lungs. "Oh my God! *Liar!* You have nothing planned, do you?"

"I'll do something, I swear!"

"What? Tell me right now."

"No. Stop being pushy. I'll figure it out for myself and do something. Fun. I promise."

Brooke hums. "O-kay."

"I will. I'm not going to waste the night to myself. That would be dumb."

Sure, I most definitely *was* going to waste it on takeout and a Netflix binge on my couch, but now, all thanks to my nosy-ass sister, I feel like I *have* to go out and do something.

"All right, Sammy." She waves her index finger in my face. "Just know, I'm counting on you to get out there and get spicy. I'm an engaged, pregnant, frequently fainting woman. I can only cause so much excitement for myself."

I pick up the remote and turn on the Soap Channel, where a full day of drama will play out right before my sister's eyes. If she wants action, I'll give it to her… It just won't be coming from me. "There," I say, nodding toward the TV and setting the remote beside her. "I'm sure there'll be plenty of excitement as mafia bosses live and die and resurrect their one true love on here. Maybe it'll be enough to keep you entertained for a while."

She huffs out a sigh. "I don't even understand why I'm on bed rest in the first place."

"It's not really bed rest, Brookie. Just a day where Dr. Cummings suggested you stay off your feet. Apparently, your iron levels being in so much flux yesterday could make you a little weaker and unsteady. It's just a precaution. And I *know* you're going to do what you need to do to protect this baby, aren't you?"

"I liked it better when I was the annoying one."

I laugh. "Yeah, I'm sure you did."

Brooke's eyes start to look heavy as she stares at the TV, Carly and Sonny and the whole *General Hospital* gang lulling her into a state of twilight.

A few minutes later, I rise from my chair beside her bed and lean down to kiss her on the temple. She startles slightly, but I whisper, "I'll talk to you later, okay? Get some rest, and call me if you need anything."

She nods and settles back into the pillow, her soft lips curving into a small smile as her favorite mafia-style enforcer—Jason—comes on the screen.

I scoot out the bedroom door, pulling it closed behind me, and walk down the hall of Brooke and Chase's casually modern apartment. It's both homey and trendy in a really cozy way. I might feel badly about my own decorating skills if I didn't know they had to hire someone to pull it off.

As it is, I'm still functioning in a lot of Brooke's leftovers in her old place. I'm happy, though. After living with my asshole ex-husband, and then my parents, her old place is the Taj Mahal.

A vase with fresh flowers sits front and center on her kitchen island as I go to pick up my purse, the delivery card still attached and sticking in a plastic fork at the top. Even though it's none of my business, I peruse the typed message.

"Pretty flowers for the most beautiful girl. Love, Chase," I murmur aloud, trying not to choke on the bubble of saliva filled with longing that's lodged itself in my throat.

Never in my life has a man said something so simplistically beautiful to me just because. Never.

My sister really did something when she wrote a whole-ass book about this guy.

With a sigh, I pick up my phone and scroll through my contacts. I don't know that I'm looking for anything in particular, but I'll admit to pausing a little longer on two specific numbers—Gavin Evans and Noah Philips.

Could one of them be my Chase Dawson?

No. Don't even think about it.

Shaking my head, I close the phone app and lock the screen, grabbing my purse and my keys and locking the door behind me as I leave.

By the time the elevator reaches the bottom floor of Brooke's building, I've decided on a plan. With the week—hell, the last several years—I've had, I think I deserve it.

I'm going to go home and take my time getting ready. I'm going to fix my hair and my makeup and put on something that makes me feel good. Sexy, even.

And then, I'm taking myself out for a drink because I am a strong, independent woman who doesn't need—*or have time for*—a man.

Bailey's, a little bar in Midtown, is more vibrant and more crowded than I ever imagined it'd be. I've heard about it from enough La Croisette customers that I probably should have realized it's a beacon of Manhattan popularity, but when your personal life is as dry as mine, I guess you tend to think it's the same for everyone else.

Are we not all sitting at home just trying to survive?

It takes a bit of patience, but eventually, a seat opens up at the bar, and I fling my ass into it with stunning immediacy. There's one thing I'll fight for in this life with consistency, and it's a place to sit down.

It only takes a few minutes after that to order my drink, and before I know it, I'm sipping on white wine like I know what the fuck I'm doing.

Spoiler alert: I do not.

Being at a bar, by myself, for the first time in many, many years is way out of my comfort zone and a true lesson in humbling oneself.

I glance around a bit, feeling nervous about being on my own and the small talk I might have to make with strangers. Outside of work, I spend an astonishing amount of my time talking about poop, pee, not touching either of the two, and in a startling third place, dinosaurs. I think it's a boy-mom thing.

Eventually, though, after I've managed to drink half of my glass of wine, I relax into my barstool a little more. I even find myself taking inventory of all the people in this joint, pointedly picking out the men who appear to be couple-less and aren't showcasing a wedding ring on their hands.

But it's all pointless.

It's not like I'm going to try to talk to any man I deem eligible. Hell, Gavin Evans, one very eligible and successful man, asked me out yesterday, and I told him no. When he texted me something super-sweet and comforting, I didn't even respond.

I'm a social pariah.

The only thing I can count on getting out of this evening is the enjoyment of a glass of wine and experiencing the feeling of being on my own, without kids. Which, I'll admit, is a welcome change of pace.

And, hell, I guess I can also *silently* suss out the best-looking men in the bar. There's never any harm in looking, right?

Right.

One sip of wine at a time, I let my eyes continue their inventory down the massive bar, passing swiftly over a few men who look to be midseventies and then pausing on a woman who seems to be wearing every piece of jewelry she owns. She's animated with confidence, and those around her laugh as she tells some kind of joke. Another drink of wine, and I stop on a dime when the sight of dark hair and strong shoulders fills my view.

Okay, he definitely *has potential…*

Even from behind, there's a calm strength about his posture that inclines me to keep looking. I put the glass to my lips, willing him to turn his face a little—just enough to give me a peek at what he's working with from the front.

Cool liquid touches my tongue just as he does the same to my eyes, and I nearly choke on my wine when I realize the attractive man in question is someone I know.

Oh my God. Noah is here. *And I'm gawking at him.*

All I can hear is the sound of Brooke's annoying voice in my head. *"Out of eleven billion bars in the city, you picked the one where you run into him? This is a sign, Sam!"*

I shake my head against the incessant power of her mental takeover, but the Brooke of my imagination keeps pushing just like the nasty old devil would if he were sitting on my shoulder. *"I'll freaking kill you if you waste this opportunity. You know that, right?"*

I nearly laugh. My imagination isn't far off the truth. Brooke Baker will definitely murder me if I let the opportunity to chat up Noah Philips in this bar go unused.

Okay, fine. Fine! I'll do it.

It takes a hot minute for me to gather some courage, but ultimately, I do. I slide off my stool with my wineglass in hand and weave my way through the crowd toward the other side of the bar where Noah sits. He's mostly keeping to himself; though he does exchange a few good-natured hellos with people he's probably seen before in his immediate vicinity.

I press on, excusing myself as I have to physically push in between people to close the distance between us.

I approach from behind, and I steel my nerves against the quaking power of how strong he looks in his suit.

I've just lifted a finger to tap him on the shoulder—I'm so close, I can smell the scent of his woodsy, fresh, amber-warm cologne—when a redheaded woman ten feet in front of him affectionately shouts, "Paging Dr. Philips!"

Her smile beams, and I rock to a stop as he jerks his head up from his drink.

Not even a second later, his feet kick into motion, and he's off his barstool and heading straight for her.

They embrace in a warm hug, and the visibly attractive woman presses a gentle kiss to his cheek.

My whole chest deflates. Of course he's not here alone. *I'm such an idiot.*

It's all I can do not to lose my feet, the surge of adrenaline from the moment taking over my body. Suddenly, these five-inch heels seem like an even worse idea than they did when I put them on.

My flight instincts are officially engaged.

Abort! Abort!

Slinking carefully backward, I discreetly round my way to the other side of the bar again, drop my nearly empty glass on the mahogany top, and head straight for the door. Being here…it's just not right. I know it's my first night alone in ages, but I'm not ready for this kind of thing. The hope. The fear. The unknown. I can't do it.

As quickly as I can, I make my way out to the sidewalk and then pause briefly to look up at the sky and take a much-needed deep breath. It's chilly out, so much so, it feels like I should be able to see my exhale, but I can't.

Regardless, I cross my arms over my chest and walk.

The nip in the air starts to dissipate the farther I get into the three-block trek to the nearest subway station, but the piercing cold of reality's knife in my chest doesn't ease a bit.

Halfway into my journey, my phone buzzes in my hand, and desperate to distract myself from the warring feelings inside me, I lift it to look at the screen. I know the caller, and for some reason—some itchy feeling deep inside the darkest part of me—I put it to my ear.

"Hello?"

"Hi, Sammy," Gavin's voice trills, the friendliness in it soothing something I can't explain. "How's your sister doing?"

"*Oh…she's good. Already home from the hospital,*" I answer and lean one hip against the cement block that separates the subway stairs from the sidewalk. "Thank you for asking, and thank you for texting yesterday, too. Sorry I didn't respond. Things have been a bit crazy."

"No apology necessary," he says, and his voice sounds completely genuine.

"So…uh…is that why you called?" I ask. "To check on my sister?"

"Well…that was part of the reason," he answers through a soft chuckle.

"Okay…"

"I know it's a long shot…but I'm in the city and I thought of you, and I'm wondering if there's any chance you're free for dinner tonight? I'm finishing up a quick meeting right now, but I'll be done in about an hour."

"Dinner? Tonight?"

"Only if you want to, Sam," he interjects quickly. "Consider it a friendly reminder that my offer is always on the table. Of course, there's still no deadline. Or pressure. But you know what Wayne Gretzky says…*you miss 100 percent of the shots you don't take.*"

"Wait…was that Wayne Gretzky or Michael Scott?"

"Both." He laughs, and my lips curve into a smile. "What do you say, Sammy? Are you free tonight to have dinner with me?"

I've never been freer in my life.

The question is, should I use that freedom to meet up with Gavin Evans… or is that the kind of idea that ends in disaster?

Chapter Five

I tuck my wrap tighter around my arms and step out of the windy bluster of the street. The lobby of Gadsden—one of the trendiest restaurants in the city—is dark and cozy and absolutely crushed with people.

My hair is fluffed and my cleavage lifted, and boy, do I feel like a fraud and a half. It's been over a decade since I've thought out an outfit or mused over what style of hair and makeup would make me look sexy. My wild children are no doubt ripping Chase's and Mo's and Vinny's wallets and willpower to shreds at the baseball game, and I'm out here...*dating*.

After accepting Gavin's invitation, I ran straight home and re-gussied myself up like some kind of escort for hire.

It feels all wrong, and yet, I know if I don't push past the discomfort now, I may never find my way around it. And as much as my life is in chaos and it's easier to do it all alone, I don't know if I'm prepared to say that in five or ten years. What if I'm left to look back on this time in my life as the turning point of it all? As the moment I gave up on me and let myself fade into oblivion?

Am I prepared to be the woman running out of bars to avoid coming face-to-face with an insanely good-looking doctor, his beautiful date, and an awkward third-wheelership for the rest of my life?

I don't know, but at the same time, I guess not, because here I am.

Nerves sizzle into a tingling feeling at the tips of my fingers as I think about worming my way through all of these people looking for Gavin. It feels daunting and, even, if I'm honest, makes me doubtful.

But a gentle touch at my elbow takes me out of my overanalysis. I spin around to find the culprit and am met with the smiling green-hazel eyes of my date.

"Sammy," Gavin greets tenderly, leaning down to kiss me on the cheek and sparking a zap in my stomach. It's funny. I thought all the butterflies that lived in there were long past dead. "You look absolutely gorgeous."

I blush. It feels good to be noticed.

"They have our table ready, but I thought I'd take the liberty of waiting for you out here. I hope you don't mind."

Mind? Truth is, I could cry I'm so relieved.

"I don't mind at all."

"Great," he replies with a smile. His hand smooths down my back to settle in the small hollow just above my butt, and we're in motion. Side to side and through the crush, this handsome man in a gray suit—who, for some insane reason, wants to go on a date with me—guides us with an ease I didn't know existed before this moment. My step doesn't have to falter or pause, and I don't have to shrink myself to fit through the people around us. He makes a hole for *both* of us, and all I have to do is fill it.

Once we reach our table, Gavin pulls out my chair and then moves to sit in his own once I'm settled. He signals the waiter, and I'm impressed with the level of service when I'm greeted by a man in black slacks and white collared shirt asking for my drink in less than five seconds.

"I'll take a glass of prosecco, and a glass of water also, if you don't mind."

The waiter's face is fond and friendly. "Of course. Is there a specific prosecco you'd like?"

Heat flushes my cheeks. I know this business well enough to know that there must be at least twenty choices of prosecco in their cellar, but I'm so flustered, I didn't even think to ask for the menu.

"She'll take the best you have," Gavin chimes in without prompting. In another circumstance, it could be seen as controlling. The *man* ordering for the *little woman*. But right now, I'm grateful. I lift the corners of my mouth in appreciation to let him know.

Words are far too complex at this time.

Flat out, I'm overwhelmed. I made the decision to meet him here on a whim, and I have no idea what I'm doing. I don't know how to date or flirt or freaking relax, for Pete's sake.

Frankly, after a divorce and momming all the time and moving to a new city, I don't even know who I am anymore.

"You okay, Sammy?" Gavin asks, jolting my attention back to the present in a way that tells me just how out of it I was.

"Yes," I say through a forced smile, sitting up straighter in my chair and picking at the linen tablecloth with frantic fingers. "Of course. I'm sorry, I—"

"Sam," Gavin interrupts, putting his hand on top of mine and calming my fidget. His eyes are warm and his expression soft. "It's okay. I know I sprung this on you last minute, and I still remember what you said yesterday. I promise there's no pressure. Just enjoy a dinner on me, okay? Don't feel like you have to make any decisions or promises other than that."

His words are an instant balm for my anxiety. I don't know what demands I was expecting, but I feel like he just let the hostages go for free.

"Thank you. And I'll try to at least be a little better company for the rest of the night."

"My current company is perfect, okay?" He gently squeezes my hand again. "I can't have you insulting my date like that. I, personally, think she's pretty damn wonderful."

I laugh. "Thanks, Gavin. Really. I think I needed this, even if I didn't think I needed this."

His grin is brilliant, his bright white teeth showing out. "Happy to be of service. Truly. Anytime. I'm glad I called."

I nod. "Me too."

Our waiter returns with both of our drinks and a basket of bread, and I can't help but dive face first into it like a starving animal.

"I'm sorry," I apologize when I look up to see Gavin pushing the bread basket closer to me. "I didn't eat anything today, and I just realized how hungry I am."

"Are you kidding? I think I could watch you eat bread all night."

I nearly snort. "Oh, come on."

"I'm serious," he challenges. "There's something uninhibited about it, and I can appreciate that about someone who's normally very careful."

Taken aback, I search his eyes closely. "You think I'm careful?"

"Oh, Sam. Please don't take that in any way as an insult. I think you're careful because you have to be. You're a single mom, you know?"

I nod, putting down my roll on my bread plate temporarily. "There isn't a ton of room for taking chances."

"I get that. And I'm thrilled you took the chance to come out with me tonight. But I also understand that I'll have to earn another chance after this one."

I lift my eyebrows. "Another chance? After this one?"

How is it possible that he's not balls deep in escaping *this* date? If I were him, I'd be excusing myself to the bathroom and pulling a cliff dive off the roof just to get the hell out of here.

He chuckles. "Listen to me, already planning our second date. I should probably just concentrate on the first, huh?"

I nod slightly, picking up my bread to tear pieces off it again.

It might be harsh, but I truly don't know if I'm ready to do this at all, much less commit to doing it again before our dinner entrees have even arrived.

"I am having a good time, though," I add, my voice quieter than I'm used to. "Just…so you know."

"Good. I'm glad. And you haven't even tried their seafood risotto yet, so I can only earn more points from here."

"So…I…" I put my bread down on the little plate in the corner of my place setting again and dust my hands before attempting to meet Gavin's eyes. "Well, I know it's a little strange for a grown woman, but I don't actually eat seafood."

"Really?"

I wince and shrug, bracing myself for criticism. "Really."

Gavin's smile is disarming. It's the opposite reaction I used to get from my ex-husband Todd. He used to roast me to no end about being a full-grown woman who wouldn't touch an entire category of food, and it wasn't quite as fun as the ones you see celebrities do on Comedy Central.

"Consider your preference noted. What do you like? What are your favorites?"

"My favorites?"

He nods.

"Honestly? I'll eat pretty much anything but seafood."

"Okay, but what would you *choose* to eat if given all the options?"

Me? Choosing dinner for myself without trying to accommodate anyone else's preferences?

"Fancy Chinese food. Or braised beef short ribs. Or a really, *really* good pasta. Oh! Or a juicy steak with extravagant sauces and sides."

Gavin chuckles. "Got it. I don't think we'll be able to hit all of those in one night, though." His mouth lifts into a smirk. "But that means there's potential for a lot of chances. And I'm okay with that."

I open my mouth to tell him how surprised I am that this evening doesn't feel like a disaster at all, when a loud shriek in the kitchen yanks at my attention and that of everyone else in the restaurant. My eyebrows draw together, but I don't have time to be confused for long. Sudden and startling, the sprinkler system kicks on, dousing us and the entire dining room of patrons in a spraying glory of cold water.

"Ah!" I shout, so caught off guard I feel frozen. Gavin recoils at the unexpected drowning too, but he gets his bearings a hell of a lot quicker than I do. Jumping up from his chair in a hurry, he pulls me out of mine and hustles us outside with the herd of other people seeking dry ground like us.

I can feel the water soaking through my black dress—thank God it's the friendliest color and thus the most prominent in my closet—and my nipples starting to perk through the lace of my bra. If I weren't so confused about just about everything in my life, I might have used the opportunity to imagine what Gavin's dark head would look like if he were to play with them.

But I *am* confused. And all the normal female desires inside me feel dulled and disorganized.

Don't get me wrong, Gavin's been charming and handsome, and I can say with one hundred percent certainty, it's not his fault I'm feeling so numb.

No, life did that long before he ever could have.

Three women who I know were previously dressed to the nines scuttle by us on the sidewalk, their mascara running down their faces with an unfortunate intensity. One of them is crying a little, and for as bad as I feel for her, it breaks a dam inside me.

I start to laugh.

Rolling, shoulder-shaking waves that take over my body as I throw my head back and look up to the dark night sky nestled between the huge buildings of Manhattan. Gavin looks on and even starts to nervous chuckle to himself when my laugh turns more manic.

"I swear I'm a walking target for the universe," I declare, throwing my arms up in the air and jostling my head back and forth to shake some of the water out of my now-flat hair. "What else? What else have you got?"

I expect a lightning bolt to strike me from the clear sky or a hole to open up and suck me into the void. But when nothing happens, I'm left staring at the sky with pathetic desperation. At least if I got zapped, it would feel like someone was listening. As it is right now, I feel like I'm trapped in an endless loop of struggling.

"Come on. You've got to be starving," Gavin says gently, ignoring my outburst with an incredible amount of tact. "There's a food truck a couple of blocks up with the most incredible pasta vodka."

"Pasta?" I ask hopefully, and that's all Gavin needs to hear. He wraps an arm around my shoulder and ushers us in the direction of sustenance. I go willingly.

"We can be there in no time." He rubs at my upper arm, and even though it feels a little awkward, I let him. It's not his fault that I've become skittish to all touch like some kind of feral cat. "I'd give you my jacket if it weren't filled with a hundred pounds of water."

I giggle, and it still sounds a little crazy. I swallow hard to try to get myself under control. "I understand."

But my soaked wrap isn't doing much good on this cool spring evening either. I'm wet and shivering and the more I think about the fact that my building isn't that far of a subway ride from here, the more I'm starting to feel pretty dang done for the night. The need to eat and shower and relax for point five seconds before Mo and Vinny and Chase drop the boys off after the game is rapidly becoming my biggest priority.

At this point, I'll even settle for skipping the pasta and gorging on some pizza rolls I know I have in the freezer.

"Do you...would you mind if I take my food to go?" I ask Gavin as we approach the glow of the food truck on the opposite side of the street. "I'm starting to get pretty cold at the moment. I didn't exactly dress for sprinklers." I grimace when I meet his eyes. "I'm sorry—"

"No, no. Don't worry about it at all. We'll order, and then I'll walk you home."

"Actually..." I wince. *Gah.* I'm really something. "I'm not quite comfortable with anyone knowing where I live yet. I... Well, if it's okay, I'd rather say goodbye here."

"Sammy, it's all good." Gavin smiles before leaning down to place a soft kiss to my cheek. It feels nice—truly soothing, even, and my shoulders drop away from my ears for the first time this evening. Gavin's understanding of not only my emotional vacancy but also my outburst and need to get the hell out of here as quickly as possible are really earning him some brownie points. *Maybe he's the kind of guy who's worth taking the chance for.*

"I'll leave you to it," he says. "In fact, I think I'll just head out now, give you some space, and get these wet clothes changed." I feel bad, but he immediately smooths the wrinkle that's forming between my eyes with a gentle touch of his finger. "As weird as this may sound, considering the current state of us, I had a really good time with you. I hope we can do this again soon."

As much as I want to say "Yes, let's do it again soon," every bone inside me feels tired. I just don't know if I have the energy to be doing this right now, and committing seems like a bad idea. I can't even schedule a waxing appointment in advance.

Thankfully, I don't have to say anything. Gavin leans forward to kiss me on the cheek once more and lets me off the hook completely. "Good night, Sammy."

"Good night."

As he turns on his heel and heads on his way, an exasperated breath leaves my lungs, and I sink my head into my hands.

Why can't I find my footing here? Am I messing up?

After one last glance in Gavin's retreating direction, I decide not to even bother with the food truck, my mind settled on the pizza rolls in my freezer, and head for the subway.

I feel like a drowned rat as I walk toward the nearest station, and my arms shiver and my teeth chatter as I step onto the waiting train and find an empty seat across from the doors.

In the name of distracting myself, I pull my phone out of my purse with the full intention of perusing one of the many social media apps I have, just like everyone else does on the subway.

But I only get as far as the locked screen when a missed text message catches my attention.

Figuring it's Mo again with more pictures of the boys at the baseball game, I head straight for my inbox, but my eyebrows draw together and my heart starts pounding like a damn kick drum inside my chest when I see the sender is Dr. Noah Philips.

Oh God, did he see me at the bar earlier tonight?

The mere thought of him witnessing me rushing out like my ass was on fire makes my face heat with embarrassment.

His message came in about an hour ago, most likely when I was in the nervous, anxious midst of my first date in years. Which is confusing as hell because he was still on a date too.

I hover my fingers over the keys as I waver on whether to open it.

Ultimately, though, my curiosity wins out.

Noah: I didn't get a chance to ask you yesterday, but how did it go with Seth's principal?

Relief fills my lungs with air. He didn't see me, *thank goodness.*

And it's super sweet that he's checking in on my son, but I don't have the energy to answer him tonight.

Gavin Evans is a really nice guy, and so is Noah Philips.

The problem is, these days, in the world of Sammy Baker, pretty much all guys finish last.

Chapter

Six

Monday, April 25th

"Why do alligators have legs?" Grant asks, tugging at my hand with his skip as we stroll through Central Park.

"Well, I would imagine it's because they walk on land, buddy. Just like we do."

The day is sun-filled, and even though the spring air is still cool enough to require a jacket, it's more than apparent by the size of the late-morning crowd that everyone in the city is ready to be outside and enjoying warmer weather after the long winter months. I'm still trying to feel completely dried out after Saturday night, and the sun feels like it's the only thing that helps.

Technically speaking, Grant should be in his afternoon kindergarten class right now, but he's off for a scheduled in-service day. La Croisette is closed on Mondays, so Zoe has the day off—deservedly, I must say, after the war zone of sickness she saw on Friday. And Seth is at school.

I'm kind of amazed they didn't make me keep him home for a few days after his "my aunt Brooke writes sex books" outburst on Friday, but I guess the punishment for second graders goofing off isn't exactly sending them to Shawshank.

Plus, his first counseling session with Ms. Sandy Rose is after school today.

"But the water is where alligators lurk, right?" Grant asks.

"Yeah, I guess so." I shrug, silently wishing I'd studied up on alligators prior to getting out for some much-needed air. "Why the sudden interest in alligators?"

"They're *green*," he snaps, like that explains everything. And hell, maybe it does. I don't know. But I don't know much of anything anymore. I mean, are alligators really even green? Or are they more brown?

While I'm still contemplating the color of freaking alligators, Grant is tugging me forward with a renewed sense of energy that borders on forceful. I'm always so amazed how strong such a little person can be at this age—

"Oof," I grunt, bracing myself as I make impact with a heavy body and tangle in the winding vise of something else.

Jeez, what is it with my kids and slamming me into people—

"Sammy?" a voice I *know* asks, and my head snaps up from my wince at Grant.

Gorgeous blue eyes, strong shoulders, dark hair, striking smile…it can only be one guy. And yet, I find myself asking to make sure anyway. "Noah?"

"Hey, guys!" he responds excitedly, reaching down to fist-bump Grant while somehow extricating me from his border collie Dolly's leash at the same time. She's as well-behaved as her boyfriend Benji and has the most adorable pink bow attached to her collar. "It's so nice to run into you. What brings you out in the park today?"

"Walkin," Grant answers matter-of-factly before I can. "Mom said she couldn't be inside our apartment another flipping second."

My eyes bulge, and Noah chuckles. "I hear you on that one, Sammy. Why do you think Dolly and I are out here sucking in the crowded park air?"

Dolly sits like a good girl beside Noah's feet, and all I can do is smile in an awkward way that reminds me of when my mom used to make Brooke and me take family photos at JCPenney when we were kids and the photographer would say something weird like, *Macaroni and WHAT?!* just so we would say cheese.

The thing is, for as comfortable as I normally am around Noah because of his friendship with my sister and Chase and the many encounters that's caused, I'm feeling a little different today.

Maybe it's because of the pretty woman I saw him with Saturday night or the fact that I followed that up by going on a date with Gavin or that I never texted him back after he asked about Seth, but I just don't quite know what to do with myself.

I'm Ricky Bobby in front of the camera, and my hands—and my face and my body—are not my own.

Luckily, Grant can fill any silence like it's his job.

"Noah, did you know I puked five times on Friday?"

Oh, good grief.

"I did not know that," Noah answers with an amused smile. "Are you feeling better?"

"Yep." Grant nods. "I didn't puke on Saturday or Sunday or today. And I hope I never puke again."

"Well, that's good news." Noah meets my eyes. His mouth is still turned up at the corners, visibly entertained by my son's lack of filter. "How is Seth doing?" he asks, and I instantly think about his unanswered text message.

"He's good. Back in school today. No major punishment besides spending a little time with the school counselor," I update before a small grimace finds a home on my lips. "And I'm…uh…I'm sorry I didn't get a chance to text you back over the weekend, but I appreciated you checking in on him."

"Well, he wasn't the only one I wanted to check in on," Noah says, his eyes still locked with mine. "I—"

"You like alligators, Noah?" Grant cuts him off in that way only a five-year-old can. "I love 'em."

Noah doesn't balk or even hesitate to reply. To be honest, his enthusiastic response is somewhat surprising. "Oh yeah! Gators are cool. They're fast too. They move like twenty miles per hour in the water and weigh over a thousand pounds."

Do all men just, like, know things about alligators? I'm so lost.

"Yeah!" Grant agrees eagerly. "They don't live here in New York, though."

"Bummer," Noah replies, shaking his head.

"It *sucks*," Grant corrects, making my eyes grow in size again.

"Grant," I chastise softly.

He rolls his eyes. "Well, it doooes."

Noah's attention shifts to me again, and I'm grossly unprepared for the smile that crests his perfect, kissable lips. "He's got a point, Sammy. The lack of alligators does suck. It's the only real way to put it."

I snort. "I always found the lack of alligators kind of appealing."

Grant scoffs. "You're such a *girl*, Mom."

Noah's smile turns almost mischievous as he mutters in a low whisper, "Now that is something *I* find appealing." And he follows that up with a wink. At me.

Gah. Those winks of his are potent.

"Noah!" a woman says from our side, pulling me up just short from saying something stupid like, "*I think your being a man is pretty cool too.*"

I would have been thankful for the interruption, if she weren't one of the prettiest women I've ever seen. Her nearly perfect fitness-babe body is strikingly obvious in her neon-green bicycle shorts and sports bra and light jacket, and her makeup-free face looks better than mine when I have it slathered on. Even her blond hair is on point, looking healthy and effortlessly bouncy in her ponytail.

And just like the redhead from the bar the other night, she has the expectant face of a woman who came here to meet up with Noah. *He likes the fact that I'm a woman? Yeah, I'm sure he does. And women seem to like him too.*

What's that phrase? *Once bitten, twice shy.* Just exactly how wary are you supposed to be after life takes two bites from your ass?

Probably pretty damn cautious.

My sister is so right. Noah Philips is the catch of the century. And apparently, *every* woman in New York knows it.

The brown Labrador retriever on Blondie Supermodel's leash tugs her straight into the middle of our circle, his tail wagging as he greets Dolly. And I can feel the blood rushing to my cheeks as Noah glances back and forth between us.

"Kendall, this is Sammy and Grant," he eventually introduces. "Sammy, this is Kendall and her good boy, Chanandler Bong."

I'd probably take the time to be entertained by her dog's name if I weren't feeling so…flighty. Right now, everything inside me is shouting, *Run! Get out of here as fast as you can!*

But I don't miss the way Kendall's face jerks to Noah's for a brief second before coming back to meet my eyes. Though, I have no idea what the silent exchange means.

"It's nice to meet you, Sammy," Kendall responds as Chanandler Bong starts to lick Grant's hand, making him giggle. "And I apologize for our abrupt interruption."

Despite her politeness, the urge to flee the scene is too compelling to resist. But since I can't break out into a jog without looking like a total weirdo, my mouth ramps up to full speed instead. "Oh, no worries! You're not interrupting!" I exclaim, my voice all kinds of strange and excitable. "We were…just leaving anyway. Yeah, we were just getting ready to head out! We'll get out of your way, and you can get to…your…well, whatever."

"Sammy—" Noah starts to say something, but I cut him off at the knees.

"No, no." I shake my head and hold up one hand. "We're running late anyway."

"Late for what?" Grant asks, and I silently think, *I love you, but you're a betraying little bastard right now.*

"The thing, honey." I skirt around my lie. "Come on."

Grant digs his heels into the grass. "But you said—"

"Grant. Come on. We have to go."

"But you said we were—"

God bless this adorable, horrible child.

"Sweetie, we have to *go*," I order, grabbing Grant's hand and starting to walk.

I turn to Noah over my shoulder hurriedly, thinking I'll say one last quick goodbye to avoid looking like a complete psychopath, but my toe catches on Dolly's leash and I trip forward. Noah reaches for my hand on a lunge, but the sudden move yanks Dolly's leash taut—right between my legs.

The normally good girl lets out a bark of panic and jerks to a run, jamming the leash straight into my vagina, which, incidentally, really hurts my labia *and* my pride. It's a real two-for-one special the grocery store never talks about.

Both Dolly and I yelp, and everyone else freezes, including Chanandler Bong. It's not like they don't care—even supermodel Kendall's face is a mask of empathy—but this isn't the kind of injury Noah can ask to take a look at, especially in front of his gorgeous lady friend.

I untangle myself in a manic twirl of limbs and lifting of legs, spinning in a complete circle with Grant's hand in mine and absolutely trucking away from the people I've left to gawk.

I swear, the universe is the smitiest of smiters sometimes.

Noah calls out my name one more time, but I manage the cringiest smile in the world and a wave and then set my sights on anywhere but here. My phone pings in my jacket pocket, and I barely even hear it. The embarrassment is too loud.

Grant's mouth moves a mile a minute.

"*Where are we going?*"

"*What are we doing?*"

"*Why are we walking so fast?*"

"*I didn't know old people could move this fast!*"

You name it, he says it, but I'm too wounded to care. My southern lips need an ice bath pronto, and mentally, I need the respite that only the barrier of a locked door can provide.

By the time I manage to get us home, I'm sweating, my beaver is still aching from playing BDSM with a dog leash, and Grant's given up on trying to understand what kind of psychotic break he just witnessed his mother suffer.

Instead, his attention is on watching cartoons while I make his requested lunch of macaroni and cheese, grapes, and broccoli with ranch.

I pour the dry pasta into the now-boiling water and grab the grapes and broccoli out of the fridge. The entire time, I'm still mentally berating myself for the outright ridiculous scene that just played out for all of Central Park to see.

Visuals of Noah's concerned face and the empathy in Blondie's eyes try to filter into my mind, but I shake my head, refusing to experience another replay of the embarrassment.

Instead, I grab my phone off the counter and decide to make my grocery list for the week as I wait for the pasta to cook.

A text notification from earlier sits waiting, and my hand quivers gently as I open and read it.

Gavin: I'll be in New York all next weekend. Dinner Sunday? I'd love to see you again, Sammy. PS: I'll even bring an umbrella just in case.

Chapter
Seven

Sunday, May 1ˢᵗ

Call up Michael J. Fox and get the DeLorean ready because I am at a fancy Italian restaurant, and I still haven't convinced myself it's not because I've gone back in time.

The ambiance reminds me of classic, 1950s Italy with distressed walls and chandeliers and picture frames filled with previous guests and nostalgic memorabilia, and the soft music playing beneath the chatter of the dining room is that of classic crooners like Frank Sinatra and Dean Martin.

And I'm *dating*, and there are *no kids.*

There absolutely has to have been a short circuit in the space-time continuum. Right?

Vincenzo's is located in Lower Manhattan and is a New York staple that's had famous guests like Denzel Washington and Lenny Kravitz dine in the private room at the back. And apparently, the owner is vehemently against reservations, but Gavin Evans, my date, has managed to get one.

And he's gone to all this trouble because I love pasta.

Impressive, I know.

Gavin smiles at me from across the table as he takes a drink of red wine, and I return the gesture, even though, internally, I'm at war with myself.

Shockingly, it's not because of the idea of being on a date. Compared to last time, I'm actually starting to find some sense of peace with it.

It's the mom part of me that's riddled with guilt, wondering why I agreed to this on a *Sunday*.

As one of my only off days, and the only one when the boys are off school too, it's usually a lazy day for the three of us. We've made a habit of going to Central Park in the afternoon and spending the rest of the evening eating takeout and watching a movie together all snuggled up on the couch.

But tonight, because of my choice to go out, they're spending it with Zoe instead of me.

Brooke would probably tell me to cut the shit and stop making myself feel guilty for taking time for myself. *You deserve to be your own person,* I can hear her saying in my head. *Just as long as it's with Noah,* her imaginary voice adds.

Ugh. I just love that even my inner monologue Brooke likes to torture me.

A server in a crisp white collared shirt and black apron tied around his waist stops by our table to drop off our plates of food—veal parmigiana for Gavin and rigatoni Bolognese for me.

"Everything look okay?" he asks, and I smile down at my plate of carbs and cheese.

"Looks great," I compliment, and Gavin chimes in with a similar sentiment.

The server refills our wineglasses and heads off to his next table, leaving Gavin and me to our food and conversation. Well, *sort of* conversation. The only conversation topics that come to mind for me are something funny one of my boys did or said, and since I'm trying not to be that person, my part in the exchange of words has been a little lacking.

"What—?"

"How—?"

We both start to talk at the same time, and a laugh bubbles up from my throat.

"Sorry, you go."

Gavin grins. "I was going to ask you how the boys are doing?"

His question catches me off guard. Damn near disarms me, if I'm being honest. My kids are the last thing I'd expect a handsome, sophisticated, single bachelor like Gavin would want to talk about.

"They're...uh, good. Really good," I comment, keeping the eleven times I used the f-word under my breath just today and the impromptu scissors chase around my apartment with Grant to myself. It's no easy feat being a single mother to two young and rowdy boys. Most days, I wonder how I haven't lost all my hair or, at the very least, turned completely gray.

"Grant is your youngest, right?"

"Yeah, he's five. And Seth is seven."

"And..." He pauses. "Only answer this if you feel comfortable, but...is their dad in the picture?"

"I wish he were, but..." I frown. "No. He has visitation rights, but he can't be bothered to use them."

"No offense, but your ex-husband sounds like a real dick. Maybe it's better he's not around."

"Oh, no offense taken. He's such a dick, his name should be Richard," I agree with a slight laugh as I finish chewing a bite of my pasta. "But for the boys, I wish he knew how to be a father."

Gavin considers me closely, and the weight of our conversation suddenly feels unbearable.

"So...you've never been married? Don't have any kids of your own?" I ask, trying to shift some of the limelight off myself.

"I guess you could say my career took priority for many years." He shrugs cheekily. "Now, if there were to be a woman worthy of my time who happened to have a couple of kids of her own..."

My cheeks pinken. I can't believe there's a man practically offering himself up as a sacrifice to a woman who can barely make it through a meal without having a mental breakdown.

"I have to admit, I envy you a little," I say awkwardly, trying not to make the ginormous thing he just said a bigger deal than I'm prepared to handle. "I gave up my career in marketing to get married and have kids, and that didn't exactly serve me well. Obviously, I don't have any regrets because my boys are my world, but I don't think I took the easiest route."

"You're doing amazing, Sam. Don't sell yourself short." Gavin flashes his handsome-as-hell smile at me, and the only thing that's slightly off with the view on the other side of the table is his choice of meal. Something about veal freaks me out. I just don't like the idea of eating a baby cow. Maybe it's the mom in me. I don't know.

"Would you like a bite of my veal?" he asks, misinterpreting my gaze, and I shake my head. "It's really good," he adds, "I don't mind."

I shake my head again. I suppose I might as well be honest now. I mean, what's the difference at this point in the dating cycle? "The other night when we were talking about food preferences, I forgot to mention that in addition to seafood, I also don't like veal."

"What? Really?"

Guiltily, I nod. "I'm a carnivore with conditions. No babies."

Gavin chuckles at that and eats a bite himself before pausing. "Oh shit. Does it bother you that I'm eating it? I could order something else."

My neck nearly cracks, my mind is melding so hard. I swear, I thought considerate guys like this were a myth before my sister met her husband, and even then, I thought it was a fluke. Not even Hank Baker is this magnanimous with my mother.

"Oh no. Please. You are absolutely free to eat babies all you want."

He chuckles, and I close my eyes tight before opening them again. "Yeah, you know what I mean." I try to explain the strange words that just came out of my mouth. "Cow babies. Or, like, chicken babies or something. I don't suggest you eat human babies, no matter who your date is."

Now would be a good time to stop talking.

"I guess I should make a note of that for our next date," he jokes, and my laugh is completely awkward as I silently wonder why in the hell this guy keeps wanting to go on more dates with me. I am so out of my realm here, it's not even funny. I suck at dinner conversation and flirting and haven't ever been in the same dimension as the word seductive.

I am a dating disaster. And yet, he keeps coming back for more.

Either this guy is a masochist, or he's got a rich bet going that he can make me fall in love with him so he lands the big DeLauer Diamonds account.

And yes, I am referencing How to Lose a Guy in Ten Days *in my everyday life situations. What else is a single woman over forty supposed to do?*

"What?" he questions, searching my eyes for an explanation. "Did I say something wrong?"

"No, not at all. I'm just thinking that you should probably wait for this date to end before you decide if you want another," I tease. "I mean, our first date didn't exactly go swimmingly. What if this one also ends in disaster? Shouldn't you take some kind of precaution to protect yourself?"

"Sammy, you're incredibly beautiful and funny and kind. You're everything I look for in a woman." Gavin gently squeezes my hand from across the table. "Trust me, I don't need this date to be over to know that I want another one."

When he says it like that, I have to wonder if I'd be crazy to turn down another date.

Gavin *is* handsome and successful and charming—he's all the things a woman hopes to see in a potential partner. And he sees the same in me?

I start to open my mouth to commit, to rip off the Band-Aid and put myself out there and go for the gold, but the shrill sound of my phone ringing from inside my purse stops me in my tracks before the first syllable can leave my lips.

"Shoot. Sorry," I apologize, digging for it desperately to shut it off. "I thought I put it on silent."

When my fingers finally make contact, I pull it out and scramble for the volume button, but with Zoe's name flashing on the screen, panic over the noise I'm making quickly switches to an entirely different kind of anxiety altogether.

Zoe never calls me when I'm out unless it's important.

"It's my nanny," I explain in a rush, and I don't wait to see his response before I hit accept.

"Hey, Zoe," I whisper into the receiver, even cupping my hand around my mouth and the bottom of the phone so as not to interrupt the other guests around us. "Everything okay?"

"Uh…well…not exactly," she says, and her voice has an edge that makes my heart stop for what feels like a good five seconds. "We're in an ambulance right now—"

"I'm sorry, *what?*" My voice rises with each word. "Did you say *ambulance?*"

"I'm so sorry, Sammy!" she bellows, and I can hear tears in her voice. "I let Grant and Seth play at the small playground by your place after dinner, and Grant fell off the swing and I'm pretty sure he broke his arm."

"What do you mean, you're pretty sure?"

At this point, I can actually hear Grant crying in the background. I can also hear Seth's nervous chatter as he rambles off a million questions.

"Well…a small part of the bone is…sort of…" she drops her voice to a whisper "…not under the skin."

"*Oh, holy shit!*" I exclaim, hopping up from my chair and tossing my napkin onto the table. "What hospital?"

"St. Luke's," Zoe says, and I quickly end the call with an, "I'm on my way."

"I'm so sorry, but I have to go," I tell Gavin as I grab my purse and throw it over my shoulder.

He's already on his feet. "What's wrong?"

"Grant. He's been in an accident and is being taken to St. Luke's Hospital."

"I'll go with you."

"No, you don't have to—"

"Sammy, I'll go with you," he says and tosses a wad of cash onto the table. "St. Luke's is quite the trek from Lower Manhattan. We can take my car to save time. It's in a garage half a block from here."

His arm is at my lower back, and he's guiding me out of the restaurant before I can even question him. And I don't think twice about it because the only thing on my mind right now is getting to my kid.

"Just stop right here," I practically shout at Gavin when I see the Emergency Room sign for St. Luke's. I'm already getting out of his car before it even comes to a stop.

"I'll find a place to park, and I'll meet you inside," he says, but I barely hear him. The only thing I can think about is that my youngest child is in a hospital without me. He's probably scared and crying and worried, and his mother isn't by his side because she was too busy going on a stupid date.

The emergency room doors slide open as I step up to them, and I run to the desk. "I'm here for Grant Brown. I'm his mother."

"Room Twelve. You can go on back," the nice lady behind the reception desk tells me and opens the doors without another question. I'm sure she's seen enough frazzled moms to know which ones are the real deal.

It takes everything inside me to walk at a semi-normal pace as I rush toward Grant's room.

But when I get there, he's nowhere to be found. The bed isn't even in the room. Just Zoe and Seth sit in two chairs beside a medical cart.

"Where is he?" I ask. Zoe jumps up to wrap me in a big hug.

"They already took him back. He needs surgery." A large part of me wants to scream, but the other rational part of me can hear the edge of tears in Zoe's small voice. "I'm so sorry, Sammy. I didn't mean—"

"It's okay, Zo." I hug her back tightly. "I know it was an accident."

Not even a second later, I pull Seth into a tight hug, even picking him up off the floor to do it. "You okay, buddy?"

"Grant's arm looked gross, Mom! We could see his bone!"

"God, I'm so sorry," Zoe apologizes again. "I asked them if they would wait until his mom got here, but they said they couldn't. Something about infection and nerve damage if they waited any longer."

This is not good. I want to break down in uncontrollable sobs, but I know that's a useless endeavor and the last thing Seth needs to see his mom doing while his little brother is getting ready for surgery.

I have to keep it together and be strong for both of my boys and Zoe.

I scrub a hand down my face and look back at them. My nanny is currently fighting the urge to cry, and Seth's eyes are so wide, I can see the reflection of my face in his pupils.

"What can I do?" Zoe asks, and her voice shakes. "I feel helpless right now, Sammy."

"You've done everything I needed you to do," I tell her and hug her again. "You made sure he got medical attention right away. It's not your fault he got hurt, okay? I know that. And you need to know that too."

She nods, blinking past her tears. But I can tell that she's a mess. And Seth's unusually quiet demeanor makes it obvious he's overwhelmed.

"How about you take Seth back home and grab some dinner on the way?" I tell Zoe, putting a gentle hand on her shoulder. "I'll stay here with Grant." I squat down to talk to Seth. "Buddy, how do you feel about going home with Zoe and eating some pizza?"

"Pizza Hut pizza?"

"Whatever pizza you want. Your choice."

"Heck yes!" he cheers. "I'll order extra so Grant has some when he gets home, too. I'll even get his favorite cookie pizza for dessert. He loves that."

Obviously, this is very wishful thinking on his part, but I don't hesitate to let him believe it will all be that simple.

"I think that's a great idea, buddy."

Zoe looks at me, still unsure, but I offer a soft smile and give her one more hug. "Thank you for making sure Grant got here right away. Now, you and Seth head home, get some dinner, and I'll keep you updated."

"Okay." She nods. "And don't worry about Seth. I'll sleep over tonight."

"You're the best. Thank you."

I give Seth one more hug and kiss on the cheek before they go.

Though, once they're out of the mostly empty room, I plop down in one of the chairs, put my head in my hands, and give myself a moment to be emotional. Tears stream down my cheeks, and I don't try to stop them as I let my guard down.

Fucking hell. My baby is in surgery, and I didn't even get to tell him I love him.

For a mother, this is the equivalent of hell. We're supposed to be there for our kids—*always*. When they get hurt or are upset, it's us, their moms, who are supposed to be there.

But I wasn't. And now, Grant is all alone in that OR with a staff of people he doesn't know, and I feel—

"Sammy."

My head jerks up. Noah is standing at the threshold of the room in baby-blue scrubs and a matching surgery cap over his thick, dark hair. And for some strange reason, his unexpected presence makes me want to cry more.

"Noah?" I swipe at the tears on my cheeks and stand. "W-what are you doing here?"

"I'm Grant's anesthesiologist tonight," he says and closes the distance between us. "When I saw his name on the board, I made sure I was on his case. I'll be in the OR with him the entire time."

Something about his being with my baby gives me a small sense of relief. Maybe it's knowing that the last face Grant will see before they put him to sleep is at least one he knows.

"How is he?"

"He's doing well." Noah places a gentle hand on my shoulder. "I gave him something to calm him down a little, and it worked like a charm. The OR nurses even have his favorite *Paw Patrol* theme song playing through the speakers while they get him ready."

"Did he ask for me?"

"Of course he did, Sammy. And I told him you were on your way."

My bottom lip quivers, and I have to swallow hard against the ball of emotion in my throat. "God, I feel awful."

"It's okay. He's okay."

I'm hugging him before I even know it's what I'm doing. My face is pressed into his chest and soft sobs rack my lungs. "I feel horrible, Noah. I wasn't home when it happened, and I didn't get to see him, didn't get to tell him I love him before they took him back."

"That kid knows you love him," Noah whispers into my hair. "And he knows you were doing everything you could to get here."

"I should've been here."

"Sammy," Noah whispers and hugs me tighter. "You're here. That's all that matters. Kids get hurt. And unfortunately for their loving moms, sometimes it happens at the most inconvenient of times."

"This is very inconvenient, that's for sure." My breath is a half snort, half sob. "If my kids are going to break their arms, they should at least have the courtesy to do it while I'm there, right?"

Noah's smile is soft. "You chose a nanny who loves and cares for your boys.

A nanny who did everything she needed to do," he says and places one gentle finger beneath my chin, guiding my face up to meet his eyes. "And now, I'm going to do what I have to do. I promise. I'll be with him the whole time. Grant will be okay, Sammy." A quiet cry makes my lips quiver. Noah rubs a barely there hint of his finger over them. "When we can't do things ourselves, we have to choose the best people to do them for us. You've done that."

"Thank you." I search his eyes. "I don't know what I'd do without you right now."

"I wouldn't want to be anywhere else."

I don't know what it is about being in Noah's arms or staring up into his eyes, but I feel like a blanket of warmth envelops my body. The solace and relief of his presence are overwhelming and, frankly, unexpected.

It's nearly overpowering.

Noah reaches down to swipe a few rogue tears from my cheeks, and I find myself leaning into the tenderness of his touch.

"Sammy," he whispers, and my heart beats erratically inside my chest.

I search his eyes, and for the briefest of moments, my gaze flits down to his full lips. I'm immediately consumed with inappropriate thoughts of kissing him right now and the comfort it would bring.

I swear, his eyes run the same circuit as mine, going from my gaze to my lips. And his embrace grows tighter around my body to the point that we are as close as two people can be while hugging.

"Sammy," he says my name again, and I can feel my face and his move closer.

And closer.

And *closer*.

"*Sammy!*" I hear my name again, but it's from someone else's mouth, and the tone is altogether different.

Over Noah's shoulder, I see Gavin rushing into the room.

Before I know it, I'm stepping away from Noah, breaking whatever it was that was happening between us, and Gavin is at my side.

"Sorry it took me so long. The parking garage was packed," Gavin apologizes, pulling me into the crook of his arm consolingly.

Noah looks at me and then at Gavin, and I kind of wish I could melt into the floor. I'm not in a relationship with either of them, and yet…there's an incredible amount of underlying tension in the air.

"Hello," Gavin greets, holding out his hand toward Noah while keeping me tucked firmly into his body with the other. "I'm Gavin."

I swear, Noah's eyes stare at Gavin's hand on my hip for a good five seconds before he eventually shakes his hand. "Dr. Philips."

"And I'm Sammy," I say, hoping to break up the rhythm of my pounding heart long enough to prevent an eventual upchuck. Both men have the good grace to at least chuckle.

My son's headed into surgery for a severely broken arm, I'm already tapped out financially, and of the two men in the room with me right now, the one I tried to kiss is not, in fact, my date.

I hear what you're saying universe, and it's a big *fuck you.*

But how about this? Since you decided to break my baby son's arm and all…

Fuck you too.

Chapter Eight

Sitting in the waiting room while your child is in surgery has to be the most excruciating situation for a mother. The clock says I've only been sitting in this same uncomfortable hospital chair for an hour, but it might as well be days.

"You doing okay?"

I look up from where my hands are white-knuckling the scuffed-up wooden armrests of my seat and find Gavin's eyes on me. He's still here, sitting beside me in the waiting room. I didn't ask him to, but for some reason, he stayed.

His forest-hazel eyes search mine, and I clear my throat, trying to push the ball of emotion out of the way so I can speak words.

"Yeah," I lie. "Just hoping everything is going okay in there."

"I'm sure everything is fine," he says with all the confidence in the world. That statement feels a lot easier for someone who isn't the mother of the five-year-old child who is currently in surgery.

He puts his arm around my shoulders and urges me closer to his side…just like he did when he first arrived to Noah and me only inches apart. Instantly, I feel some of the same tension I felt until Noah left to head into the OR.

Which, of course, makes me think about my baby boy all over again.

At least Noah is with him, my mind reminds me. Whether or not we almost kissed does *not* matter, but his being in surgery with Grant *does*.

Avoidance! Party of one!

Good grief, what is wrong with me?

I lean my head back against the wall and let out a deep sigh. My baby, my Grant, is currently sedated and undergoing surgery, and I'm sitting here thinking about things that shouldn't matter at all.

Truth be told, I really dropped the ball as a mom.

I should've been at home with my kids.

I should've been the one to be there when Grant got hurt.

I should've been the one at his side when he arrived in the ambulance.

And I sure as hell should've been the last face he saw before they wheeled his bed back to the ER.

Me. Not his nanny Zoe. But *me*.

It's bad enough that my boys' dad is a fuckup and a no-show. Their mom is supposed to be stable. Reliable. *There.*

"You hungry?" Gavin asks and gently grips my shoulder. "Thirsty? I could go grab us some snacks and drinks from the cafeteria if you want."

I shake my head. The only thing I want to do is see my kid.

And I definitely want to be the mom to him that I should've been today. Not busy with dates at expensive Italian restaurants with handsome businessmen.

"I don't think this is going to work." The words fall from my lips without refinement, but I don't regret them. Instead, I turn in my seat, shaking off the arm around my shoulders, and face Gavin. "I think you're a great guy, Gavin. And I really appreciate how awesome you've been tonight. The fact that you're sitting here in the waiting room with me says a lot. But I don't think I'm ready to be dating right now. My life is busy enough as it is. I don't think I'm ready to complicate it with a relationship."

His expression is oddly neutral. "Sammy, I understand what you're saying, but I think you're wrong."

"What? Why?"

The last thing I expected was to have him fight me on this.

"You're a single mom of two boys with a busy life and tons of responsibility. I think you deserve to have fun. More than anyone, really, you *deserve* to have fun."

"Deserving something and it being a good idea are two entirely different things," I challenge. "Grant is currently in surgery because he broke his arm, and I wasn't there."

"Babe, this is not something you should feel guilty about," he says and reaches out to pat my thigh gently. "Kids get hurt sometimes. It's what they do. You can't stop or prevent that. This was a freak accident and nothing you could've prevented, even if you had been with him. And what about when he's at school or you're at work? You're away from him then too. It's a reality you can't avoid, no matter how hard you think you should try."

"I don't know, Gavin…" I pause and stare down at where his hand is still gently touching my thigh. "I just don't think I'm ready for dating and relationships."

"You deserve to have fun," he repeats his earlier words. "Don't get lost in details like dates and relationships. Just let me keep taking you out. Use me for fun."

Use him for fun? I don't know what to think of that comment.

"Sammy, I really like you," he adds and reaches out to take both of my hands in his. "We don't need to label this. Let's just take it one day at a time. No commitments, okay? Just fun."

I still don't know what to say, but it doesn't matter because I don't get any time to ponder it. The automatic doors that lead to the OR slide open, and an older man with a green surgery cap and navy-blue scrubs comes striding out.

"Sammy Baker?" he questions, meeting my eyes as he closes the distance between us.

I jump up and out of Gavin's embrace. "Yes! That's me."

"I'm Dr. McCormick," he introduces himself, and I stand up to shake his hand. "I just wanted to let you know that Grant did great in surgery."

"Yeah?" Tears prick my eyes. "Everything went okay?"

"I just finished up, and I'm very happy with the outcome." He nods and offers a genuine smile. "It ended up being a relatively easy surgery. It was a clean break, and the area where the bone broke the skin was relatively small. I'm confident everything is going to heal up nicely without any issues or infection."

"Oh my gosh." Relief floods my chest, and I have to swipe my cheeks to remove a few fresh tears. "I can't even begin to tell how relieved I am to hear that."

"I can imagine," he says and offers a friendly pat to my shoulder. "It's never easy when it's your child in the OR."

"I honestly don't think it's something anyone can get used to," I retort with a sniffle and a shake of my head. "Can I see him now?"

"You'll be able to see him once he's all settled in his recovery room. Probably won't be more than thirty minutes or so." Dr. McCormick smiles. "And I'll come by in a little while to give you a more detailed explanation of what we did during surgery and his current plan of care. Sound good?"

I don't know if it's relief or guilt or worry or a combination of all three, but the urge to sob right here in this waiting room is damn near overwhelming.

All I can do is force a smile to my lips and nod. "Yes. Thank you."

As Dr. McCormick heads back through the OR doors, my phone pings in my pocket. I fully expect it to be Brooke, letting me know her ETA, but when I pull it out to check the screen, I find Noah's name front and center.

Noah: Just wanted to tell you that Grant did awesome. Dr. McCormick should come out to update you if he hasn't already. And I'm going to stay with Grant until he's settled in his recovery room and you can come on back.

For some reason, that message urges a few more tears to escape from my lids.

Me: Thank you, Noah. You have no idea how grateful I am that you're with him right now.

Noah: Wouldn't want to be anywhere else.

When I look up from the screen, I see Gavin sitting in the waiting room chair, eyeing me affectionately—like he's right where he wants to be too.

But with Noah and Gavin and Grant in the hospital all swirling in my mind?

Shoot, I'd definitely flee the scene if I could.

Chapter Nine

"Am I a alligator, Mom?" Grant asks, his groggy eyes meeting mine with widened concern. "I don't know how to be a alligator!"

"No, buddy, you're not an alligator." I grab Grant's uncasted hand for comfort. "You're still an adorable boy named Grant," I reassure, but I also look across my son's hospital bed to where Noah stands, unsure if I should be amused or worried.

"Good old anesthesia," Gavin chimes in with a soft chuckle from where he stands with his back against the wall behind me. "It can definitely make you say crazy things. Right, Doc?"

Noah's jaw flexes. "Right."

Awkward silence stretches across the room, and I shift on my feet, wishing I could say something that would unzip the extremely strained air. Just some breathing room in the shirt collar, you know? I have no clue if anyone else is feeling it. But my body? It could implode.

"Need my shoes, Mom. Gotta go," Grant mutters, but his eyes fall closed.

Besides my son's rambling commentary, it's mostly just been silence for the past ten minutes that we've all been standing in here together. I don't like to leave bad reviews for things, but if pressed, I'd give the vibe a zero out of five on Yelp.

Noah moves around the bed to my side where he places a hand on my back and leans in to talk directly to me.

"This is all very normal. Over the next hour or so, you'll probably hear more silly things before he fully comes out of anesthesia. It's nothing to be concerned about. Just think of it as him dreaming out loud." He leans in even farther, startling me with how intimately close he is. "As you and I know, our guy spends some time dreaming about alligators."

Our guy?

Gavin moves in at my other side then, almost aggressively wrapping an arm around my shoulders, even though it means invading Noah's space as well. "You doing okay, babe?"

My spine tingles with the effort to stand all the way straight under the two of them. I feel like I'm in the window seat of a plane, waiting for my turn to get off, hunched like that guy from Notre Dame.

Before I can respond or do some sort of spin move to shake off my man-cessories, my sister busts through the door like a football team running through their banner.

"Oh my God!" Brooke exclaims as she waddles inside with her service dog Benji following dutifully at her side. "I got here as soon as I could!"

Honestly, I don't think I've ever seen her move this fast in my life, and I certainly haven't since my niece or nephew started baking inside her belly.

Her eyes meet mine and then flash to the two men crowding me, and her movements come to an abrupt halt. Honestly, if the soles of her ballet flats would have been made of tire rubber, I swear they would've left track marks across the tile floor.

One pointed eyebrow is raised in my direction as she not-so-discreetly glances between Gavin and Noah. "Grant must be the new American Idol with the size of the crowd he's acquired tonight," she says, but thankfully, she switches her focus to the still half-asleep, partially sedated little boy in the room.

I can't deny my baby looks so tiny in a bed that could fit a grown man. I almost burst into tears when I first stepped into the room at how small and fragile he looked lying there with his little arm fully casted.

"He's still coming out of anesthesia, but he's doing well," Noah comments for my sister's benefit, finally stepping away from me and moving to a spot at the foot of Grant's bed.

Brooke nods as she reaches out to tenderly run her fingers through Grant's hair. "And the surgery? It went okay?"

"His surgeon said he did great," I update her, purposefully avoiding the giant testosterone-filled elephant in the room that I know she's internally losing her shit over right now. "He's confident his arm will heal completely without any complications or infection."

"Thank goodness," she comments and looks over at Noah, whose feet are planted wide while his hands grip the thick beige plastic of the bottom bed railing. "You were in the OR with him?"

"I stayed with him the entire time," he says. "Everything went smoothly."

A nurse peeks her head in from the hall, swinging all four of our heads in her direction. Her cheeks redden as she focuses on Noah. "Sorry to interrupt, Dr. Philips, but they need your assistance in Recovery Room Five."

A moment later, and after a small apology to both Brooke and me, Noah steps out of Grant's recovery room.

Brooke runs one hand through Grant's ruffled hair again, but after giving him a soft kiss to his forehead, she steps away from his bed and directs all her attention on the other adults in the room—*aka me and a man named Gavin whom I haven't told her anything about.* He's unwrapped his arm from my shoulder now that Noah's dick isn't swinging near his anymore, but I'm sure the image is burned in my sister's memory.

"Hi, I'm Sammy's sister, Brooke," she introduces herself. Thankfully, the "*and who the hell are you*" I know she wants to add is silent.

"I'm Gavin." He offers a friendly smile. "It's great to meet you. Though, I wish it were under much different circumstances."

"Definitely." Her words sound harmless, but her eyes are narrowed. "So, how do you two know each other?"

Gavin and I look at each other, almost as if we have to confer on the answer, and I laugh nervously when Brooke's eyes taper even further.

A cell phone starts ringing, and all three of us scramble to double-check if it's ours as Grant stirs a little.

"I'm so sorry." Gavin frowns as he pulls his phone out of his jacket pocket and wiggles it slightly to let us know it's his before checking the screen. "This is work," he says and meets my eyes. "You mind if I take this into the waiting room, Sammy?"

"Take all the time you need."

He offers my sister one last smile, even whispering, "It was really nice to meet you, Brooke," just before he steps out of the room to answer the call.

As soon as the door closes behind him, Brooke doesn't waste any time. She waddles her pregnant ass over to me and grabs both of my shoulders, shaking. "What the bleeping bleep is going on here?" she whisper-yells. She's angry, but she's considerate of Grant.

"What do you mean?"

"*What do I mean?*" Her voice rises as she repeats my question with enough sarcasm to make a good stand-up comedian proud. "If I recall, *you* weren't interested in dating, but tonight, I find you in this hospital room in the middle of a two-man sandwich. From no men to two men? Dang, Sammy. When you make a move, you really make a move."

"Oh my God," I retort on a sigh. "I'm not dating either of them."

She quirks a brow.

"I'm not!" I exclaim. "Noah works here, and yes, while I was out to dinner with Gavin, I wouldn't say we're dating. I've already told him that I'm not ready to be dating right now."

"I love cheese fries!" Grant cries, startling both Brooke and me, but when we look down to find his eyes still closed, my sister goes right back to her interrogation.

"So…" She pauses and searches my eyes. "Tonight, you went on your *first date* in years with Gavin?"

I cringe. "Technically speaking, it was my second date in years."

"What?" she exclaims. "Who else have you dated?"

"Relax. Both dates were with Gavin," I answer and cross my arms over my chest. "And frankly, they weren't even full dates. Both were interrupted half-way through."

"You've gone on two dates with the same guy?" she questions and narrows her eyes at me. "And you haven't told me *anything?* I am seriously livid right now, Sam."

"You're being dramatic."

"How am I dramatic?" She gestures wildly in front of her with both of her hands. "You've been on two dates with a man you've told me *nothing* about, and you're standing there acting like you're not dating. Get real, sis."

"It's just dinner, Brookie," I explain. "Nothing serious is going on."

"So, you're not really dating Gavin, even though you're going on dinner dates with him?" she questions like a real judgmental hag. "And what about Noah?"

"What do you mean, what about Noah?" I retort. "He's here tonight because he works here."

Don't forget about the almost-kiss, my mind taunts like a real b-i-t-c-h. Obviously, I ignore it. That's the last damn thing I'm going to tell my currently riled-up sister about. Lord knows she'd flip her shit.

"Seriously, Sammy?" Brooke questions, but it's not a question at all. It's her version of chastising me. "You can't be that dense," she adds on a scoff, and it's my turn to narrow my eyes at her.

"Excuse me?" My claws are officially out. "How am I dense?"

She searches my skeptical gaze, but eventually, she lets out a big sigh. "Just forget it."

"No, I don't think we should just forget it," I counter and drop my voice to a whisper. "Actually, I think we need to talk about the fact that you keep acting like Noah is the perfect man for me, but he's never asked me out. Not to mention, in the past week alone, I've seen him out on two different occasions with two different—and very pretty, mind you—women. Trust me, Brookie. The man has a lot of options, and I'm not on his radar as being one of them."

"What? When did you see him out?" she questions, but three knocks to Grant's recovery room door stop the conversation on a dime.

"Hello," Dr. McCormick greets as he steps inside the room. "How are we doing in here?"

I discreetly let out a deep exhale, releasing the stress the conversation with my sister just pushed inside my chest, and force a smile on my lips. "He's still a little sleepy but doing pretty well."

Brooke glares at me as the doctor steps up to Grant's bedside, and I narrow my eyes in warning, silently conveying, *Cut it out.*

She flashes Ross Geller's version of the middle finger at me, but thankfully, Dr. McCormick is too busy examining Grant to notice.

"How are you feeling, Grant?" the doctor asks, and I'm happy to see my little boy's eyes open.

"Good," he says, his voice still a little scratchy with sleep.

"Well, you did awesome in your surgery," Dr. McCormick says with a smile. "Do you remember why you had to have surgery?"

Grant nods. "Cuz I broke my arm."

"That's right," the doctor agrees with a nod. "You broke your arm, and you had surgery so that we could fix it."

"Is it fixed?"

"It is, buddy," I say and rub a gentle hand over his cheek.

Dr. McCormick examines the circulation in Grant's fingertips, ensuring that the cast isn't too tight, and Grant just stares down at his red-casted arm with curious eyes.

"You think I'll be able to play the guitar?" Grant blurts out, and the doctor looks over at him with a smile.

Guitar? What is he talking about?

"Yes, of course," Dr. McCormick answers quickly. "Once your arm has some healing time, you'll be able to play your guitar again in no time."

"That's so cool!" Grant fist-pumps the air with his uncasted arm. "I've always wanted to play the guitar! How good do you think I'll be?"

Dr. McCormick bursts into laughter, and his eyes meet mine. "You have quite the spitfire here."

"Tell me about it."

"Well, everything is looking really good, Mom," the doctor announces with confident shoulders. "We're going to keep Grant overnight just to be safe, but for the next few days, I want him to rest and keep his arm elevated."

"Okay." I nod, already mentally making note that I'll need to call Zoe ASAP and make sure she and Seth are settled for the night. The last time I talked to her, they had finished up their pizza dinner and were watching a movie. "And what about his plan of care after this? What can we expect?"

Dr. McCormick dives into the details about Grant's surgery, his recovery time, and the physical therapy he'll need to do. But the entire time, I can feel my sister's eyes boring holes into my skull, and I know it's for reasons that have nothing to do with broken arms and doctor's appointments.

I don't dare make eye contact.

The last thing I'm going to think about right now is men and almost-kisses with men and dating men and having relationships with men. From here on out, my only priority is my kids. Not handsome doctors with adorable dogs named Dolly and too many female acquaintances to count, or businessmen with striking smiles and expensive taste in wine.

Yes. Exactly. My mind is made up.

"Noah!" Grant shouts excitedly, and it makes both Dr. McCormick and me turn toward the door.

"Looks like someone is awake," Noah says with a big smile on his face as he walks toward Grant's bed.

And my son, well, his smile consumes his whole cute face when Noah stops at his bedside to ruffle his hair and say, "You handled your surgery like a champ. Proud of you, bud."

The whole scene makes my heart ache. *I wish so badly my boys had a father who cared.*

And just as Brooke's eyes pointedly meet mine and she tries to silently convey things I don't want to think about, my phone chirps with an incoming message.

Gavin: *I'm still here. Finishing up a work call in the waiting room. Grant still doing okay? Do you guys need anything?*

Are you sure your mind is made up? Because things are starting to feel pretty complicated…

Chapter Ten

Monday, May 9th

At a little after ten in the morning, I hurry Grant through the main doors of the medical building where his orthopedic physician's office is located and head toward the sign in the main lobby to figure out which floor his appointment is on.

Last Wednesday, we had a follow-up appointment with Dr. McCormick, who released Grant into the care of another orthopedic physician. This will be our first time meeting with Dr. Williams, but in typical Sammy fashion, after getting Seth to school and a last-minute "I have to poop" emergency from Grant, we're running a few minutes behind.

Swiftly, I scroll my eyes through the list of physicians, trying to find Dr. Williams, but I only get halfway down the list when Grant shouts for me.

"Mom! Mom!"

When my kids start yelling, I pay attention. In the history of their rearing, I've found a snake in their bedroom, a lit sparkler in the toilet, and a set of scissors embedded in the mattress of one of their beds. When they're quiet, they're dangerous, but when they yell…I go running.

"Mom! Look at this!" Grant exclaims as he uses the weight of his casted arm to propel himself into a circle and just barely misses hitting an older gentleman walking past him.

My eyes practically pop out of my head as I rush forward to grab him by the shoulders and stop his momentum. "Buddy, you know you can't do that."

"Why not?"

"Remember what Dr. McCormick said? Your arm is still healing, and you need to be careful with it." This past week proved that making sure a five-year-old boy rests his arm is far more challenging than one would think—and trust me, I thought it would be challenging. At this point, I'm just thankful he didn't chew off his cast with his own teeth.

"But, Mom. I—"

"Grant." I eye him in a way that says I'm not in the mood for bullshit today. It's a universal maternal look all mothers learn by the time their child is a toddler, and I can personally vouch that it's a crucial skill for survival.

"Ah, shucks," he groans while I gently guide him over to the directory of physicians with me and resume my search for Dr. Williams.

Thankfully, the list is alphabetical, and I find the Ws pretty quickly.

Dr. Waters 304

Dr. Weller 215

Dr. Williams 402

"Okay, buddy, looks like we need to go to—"

"Mom! Noah is here!" Grant yells at the top of his lungs and runs full sprint past me before I can stop him.

In a matter of seconds, he's barreling into a smiling, scrub-wearing Noah and is being lifted up and off the floor and into his arms quicker than I can even register what's happening.

"Hey, little man," Noah greets and sets Grant back to his feet. "How's the arm?"

"Pretty good. Let me show you this cool trick I can—"

Quick as a whip, I close the distance between myself and my wild child and grip both of his shoulders with two strong mom hands.

"Ah, ah," I refute. "I don't think so."

Grant grumbles, and I meet Noah's eyes on a sigh. "He's got all sorts of doctor-unapproved tricks this morning. Not one of them has been a good idea."

"The struggles of having a five-year-old in a cast are real?"

"Oh, no big deal. Something akin to wrangling a great white with my bare hands and then waving my chummed-up arm at its mouth for an hour or so without getting maimed."

For the last week, I've managed to ignore the two man-elephants in the room and the complicated mix of feelings I have about men in general. But Noah's handsome grin and throaty chuckle have the power to transport me back in time. Back to his comforting arms and kissable lips and noticeably jealous attitude toward Gavin.

Otherwise known as the absolute last place I need to be.

Steeling myself against the power of his warm eyes and soft smile, I regain my equilibrium and focus on the priority at hand—Grant's appointment.

"I don't mean to be rude, but we're already running about five minutes late for his follow-up appointment with Dr. Williams. We have to get going before they mark us as a no-show and cancel."

"Actually, that's why I'm here. You're going to be seeing Dr. Howard today," Noah updates, and I tilt my head to the side in confusion.

"No, I'm pretty sure it's Dr. Williams. That's who Dr. McCormick said was available to see him."

"I know," Noah explains. "But I called in a few favors."

"What are you talking about?"

His smile is a little guilty. "I know I might be overstepping here, but I wanted to make sure Grant was seen by the best. And nothing against Dr. Williams, he's great, but Dr. Howard is head of pediatric ortho. He's one of the best in the country. Technically, the world."

I don't even know what to say.

"I hope you're not mad," Noah adds swiftly. "But I couldn't help myself. I wanted to make sure Grant was in the best of hands."

"Wow…I… Noah, thank you." My throat feels thick with unshed tears of gratitude.

The independent part of a woman is something special. It's strong and fearless and determined. It gets things done because it has to.

But even the strongest of people need a system of support, and Noah Philips has made a point in the last couple of weeks to be a part of mine. From helping with Seth to Grant's surgery to texting this last week to check in—and now, this.

Truth be told, lately, Noah has done more for my boys than their own father has done in years. And if that isn't the most wondrous and sad thing at the same time, I don't know what is.

"Dr. Howard is on the fourth floor in Room 406, and lucky for you, Grant's appointment is at *10:20* instead of 10:00. So, you're right on schedule," he continues. "I actually tried to call you earlier, but it went straight to voice mail, so I figured I'd stop over here before my next surgery and make sure you guys were all set."

"This is so appreciated, but you really didn't have to go to all this trouble, Noah," I say while my tiny human bobs and weaves under my grip on his shoulders, knocking me in the shin with his heels more than once. I do my best to ignore the feeling of blood pooling into new bruises under my skin.

"It's not trouble when you want to do it," he responds with a genuine, downright breathtaking smile as he sets his brown leather bag down on the floor to unzip it. "And I also have something very important to give to Grant."

"You have somethin' for me?" Grant asks excitedly, his busy legs actually quieting for a second or two.

"I sure do." Noah reaches into his bag to pull out a stuffed animal. "This, right here, is Sal the Sloth. He also broke his arm and had to get surgery, and I was hoping you'd take care of him for me."

Noah holds out the stuffed animal toward Grant, and it's then that I notice this stuffed animal is special. On the sloth's same exact arm, and in the same color red, is a matching cast just like Grant's.

"We're twins!" Grant grabs Sal, hugging him tightly to his chest. "I'm gonna take the best care of him, Noah! I promise!"

The expression on my son's little face is filled with so much joy that it threatens to bring tears to my eyes. I don't know what it is about being a mom, but it's like your greatest happiness comes from your child's happiness. And it always manages to make your heart feel like it swells to a size your chest can hardly accommodate.

Thank you, I mouth toward Noah, certain if I try to speak right now, the emotion that's clogging my throat will unleash into some kind of weird sob in the middle of the lobby of this medical office building.

God, no wonder all of New York is chasing after Dr. Noah Philips.

That thought has the power to paralyze me in place, but I'm saved by the bell—or Noah's ringing cell—before I can put on scuba gear and take a deep dive into things I really don't want to be thinking about right now. Or ever.

"Sorry." Noah grimaces and holds up one finger as he pulls his cell out of his scrub pocket. "Dr. Philips… Yeah… You can give her 0.25 milligrams of Ativan… Okay…" He glances at his watch. "I'll be there in about twenty minutes." He ends the call with a swift tap of his index finger on the screen and meets my eyes again.

"Looks like duty calls, huh?" I ask and he nods.

"Unfortunately, yes."

"You gotta go, Noah?" Grant asks, and Noah squats down to meet him at eye level.

"Yep. I have to get back to work," he tells him with a soft smile. "But I'm really happy that you're going to be taking care of Sal. I don't think he wanted to spend the next three hours in surgery with me."

"Don't worry," Grant replies with a determined nod of his little head, his arms squeezing the stuffed sloth even tighter. "Sal can hang out with me and Mom. I'm gonna take good care of him."

"See? This is why I knew Sal belonged with you," Noah comments and tugs at the foot of the stuffed sloth. "But you have to promise me one thing."

"What's that?"

"You both need to promise to listen to your mom." Noah flashes a secret smile in my direction. "Can you do that for me?"

"I promise. We'll be good." Not even a second later, Grant steps forward and hugs Noah tightly.

The visual of my son's two small arms wrapping around Noah's broad shoulders with a stuffed animal hanging behind Noah's back makes a twinge of discomfort ping inside my heart.

Todd is the biggest of fucking pricks on the planet Earth, and I finally, unequivocally, feel like I can say that I hate him. I *hate* that his selfishness has left our boys starved for this kind of affection for so long. I *hate* that he's left me alone and confused to navigate all of this myself. And most of all, I hate that I allowed myself to think that I shouldn't hate him.

"Bye, Noah!" Grant exclaims as Noah stands up straight, his small feet already moving toward the elevator. "C'mon, Mom! Me and Sal gotta see the doctor!"

"Looks like you better go too," Noah comments with an amused grin.

"It certainly looks that way," I answer, but then, I can't stop myself from reaching out and lightly gripping his forearm. "Thank you." My gaze is steady as I lock my eyes with his. "For everything. You've been so kind to me and my boys. I honestly don't know if I'll ever be able to repay you."

"No repayment necessary, Sammy." He surprises me by pulling me in for a quick hug. "I do it because I want to do it. I adore your kids… And you."

"Mom! C'mon!" Grant's voice fills my ears. "The elevator is coming!"

"Let me know how Grant's appointment goes, okay?"

All I can do is nod.

"Mom! It's here!"

With a small smile and wave, Noah turns and heads for the exit doors, and I force my feet to move in the opposite direction to where Grant is about to step onto an awaiting elevator.

"Grant, wait for me!" I pick up the pace, jogging to catch up with him, but my determined child just jumps into the elevator without a second thought. Thankfully, I manage to step onto the cart with a few seconds to spare.

The elevator doors slide shut, and I catch one last glimpse of Noah's strong, retreating back.

"Man! You almost didn't make it!" Grant shouts as he lifts his new sloth friend to dance along the metal railing at the back of the elevator.

"Next time, buddy, do not get on an elevator by yourself, okay?"

"Why not?"

"Well, what if the doors closed before I got on? What would you have done?"

"Dunno." He shrugs. "Prolly just pushed all the buttons, I guess."

"Exactly my point." My laugh is exasperated. "Always wait for me. No matter what, okay?"

"Okay, Mom." He steps forward toward the buttons. "What number do I push?"

"Number four."

Grant smashes his index finger into the correct number, and the elevator starts its ascent.

"Mom?"

"Yeah, buddy?"

"Noah's so cool," he says. "You think we can invite him over for a sleepover or somethin'?"

The mere idea of inviting New York's number one bachelor, Dr. Noah Philips, over to my apartment for a sleepover makes me choke on my own saliva.

"You okay, Mom?" Grant asks as several coughs consume my lungs.

"Yeah," I wheeze with a hand to my chest. "I'm fine. Just a little tickle in my throat."

"Oh." He stares at me. "Is it gone?"

"Uh-huh." I nod just as the elevator doors slide open, but in typical five-year-old-boy fashion, Grant sprints into the hallway like a madman. "Grant! Slow down, buddy!"

He barely slows his steps. "What room, Mom?"

"It's 406," I answer just as my phone pings against my hip. "And wait for me outside the door."

"Okay, Mom!"

I pull the phone out of my purse, half expecting it to be Brooke asking what time we're meeting for lunch today, but I'm surprised when it's someone else entirely.

Gavin: Hey, babe. I hope you're having a good day. Let me know how Grant's appointment goes today.

The subway ride from Grant's kindergarten to Midtown is blissfully calm, and I'm happy to be making record time as I finish up the short one-block walk to the restaurant where I'm meeting Brooke for lunch.

As I illegally cross the empty street like all of my fellow New Yorkers, my phone chimes several times in my purse, and I pull it out to find a few missed messages.

Quickly, I scan my inbox.

The first one is from Zoe, letting me know she can handle Grant for a few hours today so I can attend one of Seth's counseling sessions with Ms. Sandy Rose after school.

And the other two are from, well…Noah *and* Gavin. Evidently, I'm the new female version of Kody Brown à la *Sister Wives*.

Noah: I think that's a good and realistic plan of care for Grant. There are two pediatric physical therapists that I'd highly recommend. Let me put in some calls and see who is available and can best accommodate your already busy schedule.

Gavin: Sounds like his appointment went well. I have a business dinner at La Croisette on Thursday. Hope you can make some time to stop by and say hello.

In my defense, both of them asked me to update them on Grant's appointment, and I've already told Gavin I'm not interested in getting serious with anyone. And it's not like Noah and I are involved in a romantic sense. We're just friends.

Friends who sometimes almost kiss…

Honestly, I'm starting to wonder if that's even what was really happening. Annoyed at myself, I shove my phone back into my purse before I reach out to push through the door of the restaurant.

It doesn't take long for me to spot Brooke and Benji, and I don't waste any time, bypassing the hostess with a friendly smile and heading their way.

"Am I actually on time to something?" I ask on a laugh as I plop down into the booth seat across from my sister. Benji is in his normal spot on the floor—underneath our table with only his head peeking out—and I carefully avoid smacking him in the face with my shoes as I adjust in my spot.

After Grant's appointment with Dr. Howard, I dropped him off at afternoon kindergarten and made a mad dash to Midtown to meet Brooke for lunch at one of our favorite lunch spots—Carnegie Diner & Café.

"Technically, you're two minutes late," she updates with a tongue-in-cheek smile. "But I'll count it as on time, given how messed up your life is right now."

"I appreciate that." I grab the menu and start to peruse the options, and that action spurs a laugh from Brooke.

"Oh, get real, Sammy. You and I both know you're going to order the same thing you always get."

She's not wrong. Every time I come here, I end up ordering their BLT chicken sandwich.

"What if today is the one day I decide to live life in the fast lane and order something new?"

Her reaction is an unladylike snort. "Stick with the chicken sandwich, sis. You have enough on your plate with that love triangle you're smack-dab in the middle of."

I purposely ignore her comment and keep my attention on the menu in my hands until our server stops by our booth. Her name tag reads Susan, and her expression is expectant as she asks, "Are you ready to order?"

She punctuates that statement by tapping her right foot in a rhythmic pattern against the tile floor.

Brooke doesn't waste any time ordering—cheeseburger and fries and a chocolate shake—and I give in to my need to keep things simple and go with my usual chicken sandwich and iced tea.

But the moment Susan takes our menus and heads off to put in our order, my sister places both of her elbows on the table and focuses all her attention on me.

"What?"

She searches my eyes, purses her lips, but, eventually, lets out a sigh and asks, "How did Grant's appointment go?"

"It went well," I answer, relieved by the unexpected direction of this conversation. "It's safe to say he's going to be in a cast for a while and will be doing physical therapy for the next several months, but Dr. Howard is happy with his progress."

"Dr. Howard?" she questions with a furrowed brow. "I thought you said his doctor's name was Dr. Williams?"

"Well…it was, but…" I pause and purposely lower my voice as I add, "Noah called in a few favors to make sure Grant was with the head of pediatric or-tho at St. Luke's."

"Noah called in a few favors?" she asks, her eyes lighting up with the kind of curious excitement I pointedly avoid by taking a long drink from my iced tea that our server just dropped off at the table. "So…Noah made sure your son was being seen by the head of pediatric ortho…?"

"Mm-hmm." I nod. Take another drink of my iced tea.

"Wow." Her squinted eyes search mine so hard, I'm wondering if she can ac-tually count my freaking eyelashes. "That was, like, really nice of him."

"It definitely was."

"And what did Gavin think about this?"

It's my turn to narrow my eyes. "What's that supposed to mean?"

"I don't know." She shrugs and takes a long pull of her chocolate milkshake. "I mean, you're dating Gavin, but Noah keeps popping into the picture to do nice things for you and your kids. Surely that might cause some insecurity."

"But I'm *not* dating Gavin. I'm not dating anyone. So, there's nothing to tell."

"Oh, that's right." Her smile reeks of sarcasm. "You've just gone out to din-ner with him—*twice*—and the night Grant broke his arm, he stayed at the hospital for an insanely long time to make sure your son was okay. But yeah, you're not dating. I have no idea why I keep getting that confused."

"*Brooke.*" My sigh is exasperated. "Seriously?"

"What? I'm just trying to understand what's going on in my big sister's life, even though she keeps hiding shit from me."

"I'm not hiding anything from you."

Yeah, okay, so I purposely didn't tell Brooke about Gavin. *Or the almost-kiss with Noah at the hospital.* But I count those as exceptions to our sisterly rule. In her current pregnant state, I'd like to avoid getting her all worked up, and Lord knows, these days, her nosy ass gets pretty dang worked up over being my unauthorized matchmaker. If anything, I didn't tell her those things for the health of my future niece or nephew.

She purses her lips. "The only reason I even know about Gavin is because of Grant's accident. Otherwise, you probably would've waited until you married the guy to tell me about him."

"I'm not marrying anyone, you lunatic," I retort. "And speaking of people who hide shit from other people, why was Seth asking me if I was going to date Noah because he heard his aunt Brooke tell his uncle Chase that Noah and I are lobsters? You wouldn't happen to know anything about that, would you?"

She shakes her head and pointedly uses the time to suck on her stupid milkshake.

"Yeah, that's what I thought," I mutter and pick up my discarded straw wrapper to ball it up and throw it at her head.

She avoids it on a laugh, and I roll my eyes at her as our server drops our lunch plates at our table.

"Can we drop the 'Sammy's love life' convo and talk about something else—anything else—while we enjoy our lunch?"

"Yeah." She pops a fry into her mouth. "After I get one thing off my chest."

I let out a deep exhale, but I also meet her eyes and give her the courtesy of my attention.

"I know you don't think Noah is into you, but you're wrong. He hasn't asked you out because you're too closed off," Brooke states, and I start to open my mouth, but she's quick to hold up her hand in the air, continuing before I can get a word in.

"I get why you're closed off, Sammy. I really do. Anyone in your shoes would be, but that doesn't mean that you don't deserve to have a man in your life. You can be a mom, and you can be in a relationship. You can have both things. And…I know that Noah cares about you. Like, *really* cares about you. A man wouldn't go above and beyond for your kids unless he cared about you too. And I sure as shit wouldn't try to get my big sister to date a man I didn't deem worthy of her and my nephews."

The thing is, I know my sister means well. I know she just wants me to find happiness and be treated like a fucking queen. Her intentions are pure, that's for damn sure.

But she apparently isn't aware that Noah Philips *really* likes to date around. I've seen him out with not one, but two different women in a very short amount of time. He might be an extremely eligible bachelor. But he's also just that—a bachelor who is very much seeking out *all* of his options.

And I'm a single mom with two boys who is still recovering from a shitty divorce. If I would ever even consider being in a relationship with a man, I would need to feel certain I wasn't setting myself up for a repeat of my past.

But that's not a conversation for now. I don't want to break Brooke's heart with reality.

And if I'm honest, I don't want to break mine either.

Chapter
Eleven

Thursday, May 12th

I finish counting the petty cash in the back office and put the money in the safe beneath the desk. We're so busy tonight, Vinny had to send one of the sous chefs out for flour and tomatoes from the store, as we were running out of both, and I always like to do a secondary count on the cash if we have to take money out.

La Croisette is typically busy on a Thursday evening, but tonight, it's on a crushing level.

Every table is filled. The kitchen is working their asses off. And every staff member inside the restaurant is moving on quick feet.

I know I'm needed back in the dining room as promptly as I can manage, but as I stand, a text message stops my progress toward the door.

At one point in my life, I never would have considered touching my phone during a shift. But now, in the era of broken arms and projectile vomit, I can never let a message go unchecked.

Zoe: Grant just told me he's no longer allowed to take baths or showers until his cast is off. I have a feeling I'm being lied to but just want to make sure I'm not missing something…

Me: You probably have that feeling because my son is absolutely full of shit right now.

Zoe: LOL. What a little manipulator! I'm guessing we still have the green light on baths, then?

Me: Yep. Just have to wrap his cast up in plastic to prevent it from getting wet.

She sends a thumbs-up emoji, and I slide my phone back into my blazer pocket and head out of the back office and into the main dining room.

"Mandy, how are we doing with reservations tonight?" I ask one of my favorite hostesses. She's been a part of the La Croisette team for over two years, and her ability to work quickly under pressure while still being professional and courteous to all patrons is unmatched. Needless to say, I'm relieved when I know she's running the front for the night.

"Not too bad. Only running five minutes behind on one party's seating," she answers. "We do have a business dinner reservation arriving in a few minutes for the ten-top in the back that just vacated, but I've already ensured that the bussers are cleaning it up now."

"Who is that reservation for?"

She glances back at her list briefly. "Uh…Mr. Evans."

I just stop myself from slamming a palm into my own face. Wow. I don't know how I forgot that Gavin had a dinner here tonight—I mean, he even texted me about it—but I guess I've been a little busy being a single, working mom trying to juggle all the things.

Not to mention, keeping Grant sticking to doctor's orders and not swinging his casted arm around like it's Thor's hammer is no easy feat. It's a miracle the X-rays they did at his appointment on Monday showed intact hardware and healing bones.

I calm my racing mind long enough to smile at Mandy gratefully. "Any other big reservations I should know about?"

"Nope." She shakes her head. "Everything else is two-, three-, and four-tops that I'll have no trouble accommodating."

"Have I already told you I love you tonight?"

She grins. "You just did."

I start to look for Mo, to check in with her briefly, but when I spot her across the dining room, chatting up a few patrons—ones I recognize as regulars she has a natural chemistry with—I leave her be and start to make my way to the kitchen to see how Vinny and the crew are faring.

"Hey, you." A hand on my shoulder and a whisper near my ear catch me completely off guard. So much so that I startle.

Gavin chuckles and apologizes, "Sorry, babe." Dressed in a smart black suit and tie, he looks undeniably good tonight. His green eyes are bright and happy to see me, and his smile is worth the millions I'm sure he makes.

He pulls me in for a tight hug and presses a gentle kiss to my cheek, and I accept it willingly. He's truly been so good to me from the moment I bumped into him on that busy sidewalk, and for as confused as I feel emotionally, I'm starting to get more comfortable around him physically.

"Sorry, but I couldn't help myself," he whispers sweetly. "It's so good to see you, Sammy." He holds me away with strong hands at my biceps, dropping his voice reverently. "You look beautiful."

I look beautiful? In the middle of my work shift with a busy Thursday-night rush? Has he been huffing glue?

"T-thanks," I stutter over my tongue, still not used to men passing out compliments like candy. About a year into our failed marriage, my ex-husband Todd stopped complimenting me about anything. Instead, he stuck to criticism.

"This might be a little overzealous of me, but do you think you can find some time tonight to join my dinner?"

"Me? Join your business dinner?"

"Yes, *you*. I made sure I secured a table for ten to make room for you just in case." He smiles, and I have to glance down at my feet to calm my now-racing heart. His eyes look particularly green tonight, only flaking golden in the light.

For as lost as I generally feel trying to make small and flirtatious talk when we're on dates, I can't deny that he affects me.

His confidence in himself, in me, in *us*. It's powerful.

But I'm always too nervous to know what to do with it.

Anxiety with someone new has to be normal, though, right? Going on dates, putting yourself out there, sharing parts of yourself, your life, with someone else takes trust and the willingness to be vulnerable. And it doesn't take a board-certified therapist to understand why being vulnerable and trusting someone doesn't come easy for me, especially with someone I still don't know all that much about.

"Wow, that's really sweet of you, Gavin, but I don't want to interrupt—"

"Trust me, you won't be interrupting." He cuts me off. "It'd be nice to spend some time with you. Maybe even grab a drink after your shift?"

"Okay…well…I can't make any promises because, you know—" I pause and glance around the restaurant "—things are a little busy. But I'll try to stop by and say hello for a few minutes."

"You know where I'll be," he says with a sexy smirk. "Come find me when you get a little free time."

I nod, and Gavin presses one more soft kiss to my cheek before walking in the direction of the ten-top table my hostess-with-the-mostest Mandy is currently seating.

I don't waste any time scrambling toward the kitchen and shoving through the swinging doors.

Metal pans clashing, food sizzling as it's tossed into skillets, and orders being called out in succinct waves are all playing in a symphony led by Vinny himself.

He stands behind a stove, his chef jacket firmly in place and his eyes focused on a large piece of steak he's rubbing seasoning into with rough hands.

"You good, Vin?" I call out, and he glances up, meeting my eyes through the stainless-steel shelving between us.

"We're good."

"Need anything from me?"

"Can you check in on the couple at forty-two?" He flashes a knowing grin at me. "Five-star treatment."

Just like Manhattan, our restaurant is a melting pot of people on any given night. But there are two types of patrons we go the extra mile to please— wealthy regulars with big influence and food critics. And it's not because they're more important than the average Joe or because their taste buds are more refined—it's because they're usually judgmental and picky as fuck.

Unfortunately, they also have the sway and social capital to put La Croisette under at any given time.

Playing favorites is part of the game. Everyone wants to be seen here, including celebrities, famous athletes, musicians, and the kind of rich people who vacation on their million-dollar yachts. And because of them and their big mouths, we get to stay in business for other people to enjoy the food too.

"Will do."

Out of the kitchen, I head straight for table forty-two. I observe the other tables on my way, looking for plates in need of busing and drinks approaching empty. Part of my job is to organize the chaos, and the other part is to fill in the gaps in the Wizard's curtain.

As far as the customer is concerned, there should be no need unaccounted for, no time spent waiting. But the waitstaff is human, so I provide a little magic.

I'm halfway across the restaurant when my gaze catches on a two-top and jumps back to a man I've come to recognize easily.

Noah sits by himself, staring down at the menu, and for some insane reason, it's like my heart skips a beat at the sight.

I think I've…missed him.

It's dumb, so freaking dumb, but ever since our almost-kiss the night Grant broke his arm, I don't need an imaginary Brooke to tell me just how great he is anymore. I have it figured out all on my own.

Grant carries around the little sloth Noah got for him like it's his new best friend, taking him to kindergarten and sleeping with him at night and even asking for a separate plate of dinner for the furry friend.

And every time I see it in his backpack or tucked in his arm or at the fourth chair at our table, I think of Noah.

Of how he is with the boys. Of how he is with me.

I shake myself out of my thoughts and focus on the priority at hand—table forty-two. Vin asked me to give them the five-star treatment, and that's exactly what I'm going to do.

"Good evening," I say cordially to the well-dressed man and woman who look about twenty years older than me. "I'm Sammy, the general manager here at La Croisette, and I just wanted to stop by and introduce myself and make sure everything is going well with your meal."

The gentleman smiles up at me after placing his soup spoon back on the plate beneath his lobster bisque. "Everything is splendid."

"Very delicious bisque," the woman adds. "Compliments to the chef."

"I'm so glad to hear that. It's one of Chef Vinny's specialties," I respond with my most professional smile. "He'll be thrilled to hear your praise."

They eat up my ego-fluffing, and I lean forward to whisper conspiratorially. "And if you don't mind, after you finish your dinner, I'm going to have your server bring over a dessert that's not technically on the menu but will undoubtedly finish your meal off perfectly. The only stipulation is that you have to let me surprise you."

The woman beams and rubs two hands together. "Oh, this sounds like fun."

"Just tell me one thing…do you like chocolate?"

She nods with wide, excited eyes. And her dinner mate chuckles. "My wife doesn't just like chocolate, she *loves* it."

"Good." I grin. "Consider your dessert on the house."

Both of them beam, and I don't waste any more time interrupting their meal. "Enjoy your dinner."

But as I walk away from their table, my eyes drift in a very predictable direction again.

Noah is still alone, sipping on amber liquor of some sort. From previous occasions I've shared with him at my sister's behest, I'd imagine it's bourbon.

He hasn't asked you out because you're too closed off. My sister's words at lunch on Monday echo inside my mind. *Noah cares about you.*

Is Brooke right? Is the only reason he hasn't asked me out because I'm not showing signs of being open to it?

Now is your chance to find out, my mind whispers. *Just go over there and talk to him.*

My feet are heading in his direction before my brain even agrees to it. When I make it to his table, his concentration on the condensation on his drink is intense enough to give me time for one last deep breath.

In and out, I try to filter everything but confidence out of my lungs.

"Fancy seeing you here."

Noah looks up with an instantaneous smile. It's like he doesn't even have to see me. He knows the sound of my voice. "Sammy!"

"I didn't realize you were one of our reservations tonight," I respond with an equally big smile. "Please tell me you didn't do all this work to make sure I follow through on the white-wine-soaked-mussels offer. I would have hand-delivered those to your apartment. I probably should have already," I admit sheepishly.

"I've actually had this reservation for a while. I was hoping I'd see you tonight, though. But I wasn't sure if you were going to be too busy to say hello."

Flutters of affection lap at my stomach as Noah's blue eyes hold mine captive.

"I would never not make time to say hi to you, Noah," I confess, forcing myself to hold my position and the eye contact.

"That's a high compliment from someone as busy as you are," Noah remarks tenderly. "I promise to be worth the effort, okay?"

A promise to be worth the effort? If that isn't a sign, I don't know what is.

I have to open myself up to the possibility of more. I have to give myself the freedom to feel love. I have to—

"I'm so sorry I'm late," a hurried voice breaks in, stealing my concentration, my nerve, and the unbelievably comforting hold of Noah's eyes.

The gorgeous redhead from Bailey's is here, completing the party of two on Noah's reservation that he's had for *a long time.* My stomach turns to lead and drops to my feet as Noah jumps up, skirting past me to give her a hug.

"You're not late, Mary. You're right on time," Noah says with a warm smile after pulling back from her embrace. I feel like I'm watching a wreck in slow motion—my own heart getting run over—and yet, I can't seem to look away. "Sit down and take a load off, please."

Mary. Her name is Mary.

She sits down in the seat across from his, and I use that time to try to rub the feeling back into my fingers. *Of course his reservation was for him and* a date.

Not only is Noah an incredibly handsome, charming, eligible bachelor, but he's here, bachelor-ing it up with a gorgeous woman named Mary because that's what fucking bachelors do!

"Oh no! It looks like I'm being waved down!" I outright lie, pushing out my words in a rush, in a voice that's too loud for our proximity. "It was great seeing you, Noah!"

Noah's brow furrows. "Sammy—"

I quickly add, "Enjoy your dinner!" before turning on my heel and heading as far away from him and his beautiful date as my feet can take me.

I peek into the kitchen and tip off my server Martin about the need for re-fills at table fifty, and when I'm back in the dining room, I clear plates from an empty four-top when the bussers are already there. Just to, you know, busy my hands.

But the one thing I don't do is look back toward Noah and Mary.

Tomorrow, I'll get myself put together again. But tonight…I'm allowing myself the messiness of my personal crisis. If avoidance is what I need, avoidance is what I'll get.

Although, I'm surprised at myself—and my stupid feet—when I end up stopping at a table on the other side of the room that's filled with eight businessmen and Gavin Evans.

They're chatting and laughing as they munch on appetizers and wine, and Gavin's relaxed posture makes him look even more handsome than he did before.

His attention moves to me as soon as I come to a stop, a bright and welcoming smile consuming his face. "Sammy!" He climbs to his feet and wraps a strong arm around my waist, claiming me without hesitation in front of all his associates.

"Boys, I'd like to introduce you to someone who's very important to me. Say hello to the absolutely gorgeous Sammy Baker."

All of the men offer friendly waves and nods, and all I can do is lift a hand and offer a sociable smile. My insides feel like they've been whipped in Vinny's spin mixer and salted in every wound.

This kind of attention from Gavin right after finding Noah with another date—it's almost torture.

"Gentlemen, it's nice to meet you," I announce. "I'm also the general manager here at La Croisette, so please let me know if you guys need anything."

"No," Gavin chimes in on a laugh. "You will not be letting her know if you need anything. You lazy bastards will handle it yourselves or else I'll put the kibosh on the deal we're all here to broker."

The table bursts into laughter, and Gavin just smiles down at me.

"You doing okay?" he asks and gently squeezes my hip.

"Mm-hmm," I push out with a smile, trying not to look across the restaurant to Noah and Mary and somehow catching a glimpse anyway.

She laughs at something he's said, and my stomach recoils from the sight.

My sister was wrong about Noah.

Between Noah and Gavin, there's only one man who appears interested in me, and he's not the one with the gorgeous redhead.

He's the one who just told a table full of business associates that I'm someone important to him.

I think it's about time my head and my heart got the difference straight.

Chapter Twelve

Sunday, May 15ᵗʰ

I put the finishing touches on my makeup and make sure my straightener is off before I leave the bathroom.

And then I go back a second time to double-check because fire hazards freak me out.

The apartment is eerily quiet, devoid of the normal hustle and bustle of my two wild boys, and it makes my stomach feel whooshy and nervous. I swear, motherhood changes your factory settings. Everything that was once about yourself becomes about them, and quiet moments alone become few and far between. In between the overstimulation and worry and labor, there are so many moments that only feel right because your kids are there.

And since Grant's accident, alone time and guilt have been in a permanent blender.

The only reason I'm getting ready to meet Gavin for dinner right now? My sister.

Since Grant and Seth are off school tomorrow, they're spending the night at Brooke and Chase's. I honestly have no idea why my very pregnant sister wants to entertain my kids, but ever since we moved to New York, it's like she's been trying to make up for lost time with her nephews.

As I grab my phone and keys and purse and head out the door, I can't stop myself from sending Brooke a quick text to make sure she hasn't changed her mind.

Me: *Are you surviving? Are they behaving? Are you sure you want to keep them for an entire night? I can cancel my plans and come get them. Just say the word.*

Her response is almost instant.

Brooke: *We're all good here. DON'T cancel your plans.*

Not only did I agree to a third dinner date with Gavin, but this time, I even let my sister know my plans. She didn't balk when I told her who I was having dinner with, and she didn't mention Noah once. I'm not sure if her neutrality was genuine or if she was pretending, but either way, it feels like progress. For both of us.

Brooke: *Is it cool that Chase is showing them how to play beer pong? Don't worry, we'll only let them have a few brews.*

I snort as I step out of my building and start the two-block walk to Leyla's, the restaurant where Gavin secured a reservation.

Me: *It's in the name of learning a skill that will become invaluable in college. Who am I to deny them something so important? Plus, they'll be able to teach my future niece or nephew in a few years. Honestly, if you have time, you might as well show them how to play quarters too.*

After I hit send, I can't stop myself from sending her one more message.

Me: *Speaking of my future niece or nephew, I think you should tell your doctor to tell me what the gender is. I swear I'll keep it a secret.*

Brooke is in her eighth month of pregnancy and she's insistent on waiting to find out the gender, but I'm dying with anticipation. I've spent the last seven years eyeballs-deep in superheroes and dinosaurs, and I'm really hoping for the chance to buy pretty dresses and bows.

Brooke: *That's cute. But you're going to find out when I find out, which is whenever he or she makes their big debut. Now, go enjoy a night to yourself.*

Me: Are you sure everything is good? You promise you want to keep them all night? I can come get them anytime…

Brooke: Sammy, stop texting me! We're good. The boys are being little angels.

Me: Angels? My kids? Now I know you're lying. What's really going on over there? Do you need them so you can pretend to be a family in a drug-mule scheme like **We're the Millers***?*

Brooke: SAMMY. Go have some damn fun! Lord knows when harvesting time comes for the little crop I'm growing, Chase and I are going to be calling YOU for help.

With one last sigh of guilt, I push myself to let it go and complete the short trek to the restaurant.

Thankfully, now, the weather is starting to turn just enough that I don't have to shiver my way down the sidewalk anymore.

By the time I reach the swanky place Gavin picked, I can barely get through the door and up to the hostess stand, it's so packed with the dinner crush.

"Can I help you?" the hostess asks right as I spot Gavin at a table directly behind her. He's standing, waving, and smiling at me, so I point toward him.

"I found him. Thank you."

She nods before moving on to the people shoving in the door behind me.

I make my way between the filled tables quickly enough, tucking my light trench coat to my body to avoid skimming it against people as I move. And Gavin is waiting for me with my chair pulled out when I arrive.

"You look stunning," he says, wrapping one strong arm around my waist and pulling me close. I look up into his striking eyes just in time for him to catch my lips with his own in a soft, chaste kiss.

I startle slightly but calm quickly enough. It's unexpected, but not entirely unwelcome. I mean, affection is part of dating. Right?

As he moves on to pull my coat off my shoulders, so do I. I won't make a big deal of this, and I won't shortchange myself the experience of a man showing genuine interest just because there's another one who has burrowed himself inside my brain and who just so happens to be good with my kids.

I clear my throat and smile up at him as he tucks my coat over one of the spare chairs and takes his seat across from me. "You look great too. Honestly, though, I don't think I've ever seen you look bad."

He winks at me. "How about some wine?" He gestures toward the bottle of red on the table.

The mere sight of alcohol is a relief to my slightly frazzled nerves. I'm trying so hard to be confident, but I can't seem to evict the nerves completely. You'd think after a few dates, I would finally be settled in, But a decade, I suppose, is a long time to be out of the game.

"Yes, please."

He pours me a glass, and I don't waste any time taking a hearty sip. It burns a little because of my overzealousness.

"Good?"

"Mm-hmm. Very good." More than half of the bottle is already gone with just our two glasses, and it makes me start to wonder just how late I was running.

"Did I keep you waiting long? I thought I was on time tonight, but I truly don't think I even understand the concept anymore."

"Oh no," he refutes with a magnanimous wave of his hand. "I got here a little early and figured I'd get our table while I waited for you to arrive."

I smile. That makes sense. He probably had a glass or two while he was sitting here by himself. I'm sure with a job as serious as his, he needs to decompress from time to time too.

"Did I mention that you look absolutely beautiful tonight?" He reaches out to place his hand over mine. "Because you really do, Sammy."

"Yes." A giggle jumps from my throat. "But feel free to shower me with as many compliments as you like."

"Well, then I must say how witty you also are." He smiles again, and just like that, we ease into a friendly banter that makes me hopeful.

Hopeful that I'm where I'm supposed to be.

Hopeful that tonight will be a good night.

Hopeful that the dream of someone else—of finding someone to share my life with one day—won't be a shriveled-up memory ten years from now.

Hopeful that I won't find myself longing after the missed shots I should have taken with Noah Philips or Gavin Evans or anyone else.

"Thank you for dinner. Tonight was really fun," I say as Gavin places his hand at the small of my back and guides me out of the restaurant.

When I say it was a good time, I mean it.

Gavin was charming and funny, and the conversation felt easier than it has ever been between us. At least on my end, I finally found some flow. We laughed and flirted and teased each other about the temperatures of our steaks—his rare and mine well-done—and I felt more like myself than I have in a long time.

Instead of worrying over the boys or feeling completely inept at dating or drowning myself in thoughts of relationships with unavailable men, I felt normal.

Like a woman who, even though she's a single mom, can have a personal life too.

"It goes without saying that I enjoyed it too," Gavin comments as he holds open the door for me to walk outside. "Any time spent with you is treasured."

Sometimes, I can't decide if he's tossing lines my way or if he's just really good at delivering compliments, but for tonight's purposes, I'm not going to worry about it.

I laugh instead, patting a hand to his chest in thanks. Unexpectedly, he grips my hips with both hands and pulls me closer to him.

My heart rate spikes uneasily. The pressure of his fingertips is faintly unnerving.

We're on the sidewalk, right in the middle of a crowded public setting, but with the way Gavin stares deep into my eyes, his gaze flitting to my lips, I feel like we're alone.

Tucked there, in a crucial, delicate moment, my mind goes to the one place it shouldn't—*Noah.*

"God, you're beautiful," Gavin says, his voice a throaty whisper, just before pressing his mouth against mine. His lips are firmer than I imagined they'd be, even though his aggression is soft and slow. His hands migrate up my back and over my shoulders and find their way into the locks of my hair, and the kiss turns heated. At least, on his end.

A groan escapes his throat, and his tongue slips past my lips and mingles with mine.

Something about it doesn't feel right at all.

"Spend the night with me," he whispers against my mouth, breaking the kiss just enough that I find the space to scoot back six inches or so. "Come back to my hotel and stay with me."

"I…I don't think—" I start to reject, but he's too busy gliding his hands down my back and gripping my ass to notice my lack of confirmation. He kisses me deeply again, sliding his tongue past my lips and using his hold on my ass to pull my body flush against his.

Why in the hell does rabid attention from a sexy guy like Gavin feel so off? Why can't I just enjoy it?

"So, yes?" he questions, and I can feel his mouth quirk up into a smile against my lips. "You'll spend the night with me."

The presumptive words are finally enough to give me the strength to pull away. Because for as many questions as I have about the whys of how I'm feeling, I don't have to question how I'm feeling at all.

I'm not ready to sleep with Gavin Evans.

I place a hand to his chest and take a step back away from him, putting distance between us. His mouth turns down at the corners while his eyes examine mine, and I know that I need to be honest with myself and him.

"Gavin, I don't know. I just...I don't think I can do that." I'm vaguer than I intend to be, but I imagine it's because of my nerves.

"Would you rather we go back to your place?"

"No." I shake my head. "I don't want to do that either."

His brow pinches in confusion. "What are you saying?"

Tell him the truth.

"I'm saying that I can't spend the night with you," I answer genuinely but gently. "I'm just not ready for that yet."

"Yet? We've been on three dates, Sammy. Not to mention, we talk and text all the time. I really thought we were getting somewhere."

I don't know what to say to him. I can't even explain my emotions to myself, let alone him. The only words that come out are, "I'm sorry."

"Well, hell, Sammy." A shocked laugh jumps from his throat as he runs a hand through his hair. "What are we even doing here, then?"

"What do you mean?" I whisper, starting to tremble a bit. For as nice a man as Gavin is, he's still at least fifty pounds heavier than me and nearly a foot taller. And right now, I'm just feeling really uneasy in his presence.

"I mean exactly what I said. What are we doing here?" he repeats. "I want to be with you, and it feels like you don't want to be with me."

"You're upset with me?" I question, and his response is a frustrated exhale of air.

"Sammy, what am I supposed to think here?" He scoffs. "I've been putting in all this work and effort, and it just feels like you're dragging your feet. Or stringing me along. Or both. I get you being a little uptight, but this, tonight, it feels like you're purposely being a cocktease."

A cocktease? Is that what I've been doing?

None of this is sitting well with me. My stomach hurts and my chest is tight. I don't know if I'm wrong or if he's the one in the wrong at this point. I just know I don't want to do this anymore.

I look out toward the street before meeting his eyes again. His expression is fraught with irritation, and it makes me feel too uncomfortable to keep standing here. "Gavin, I think we should call it a night." Nothing is going to change the course of this conversation right now, no matter what I say or do.

"Yeah. I think I agree," he retorts on a deep sigh before turning and leaving me standing there without a goodbye.

Damn, he really isn't happy with me.

There's a part of me that feels really bad about the whole situation, but there's another part that feels like I'm seeing a different side of him.

A side I'm not so sure I like all that much.

Chapter Thirteen

My legs feel like jelly as I walk the last block to La Croisette, my mind a raging bull of upset.

Gavin's called me at least three times, all of which I've sent straight to voice mail, and now he's switched over to texts.

My phone pings so manically, it feels like my purse might explode if I allow it to continue.

Pausing in front of my workplace's marquee, I slide my phone out of my purse and pause to read the message showing on the screen.

Gavin: Sammy, please call me back. I'm so sorry, and I don't want to leave things like this. You're important to me.

Regret and distrust war inside my chest as I consider the events that just transpired, concluding only that there's no conclusion to be made at all.

I'm not going to know how to feel about any of this unless I give it some time to marinate, and the idea of going home to an empty apartment only makes everything seem worse.

I need some time to decompress first—some time to let the noise of the world wash out the voices in my head.

After placing Gavin's message thread on Do Not Disturb, I tuck my phone back into my purse and start to walk again. I don't know where I'm going, so I focus on the sound of my heels on the concrete until I figure it out.

It's soothing and rhythmic and louder than any of the passing sounds around me.

I pace my heart against it until I feel like I can breathe again, coming to a stop right in front of the little bar where I ran into Noah the first time—Bailey's.

I don't even think about it before opening the door. Chatter fills the softly lit space as I step inside, and the change of pace from the deserted sidewalk makes my ears feel like they want to pop.

I head straight for the long mahogany bar that sits along the right side of the establishment. Only one bartender stands behind the massive structure highlighted by a cornucopia of liquor bottles shining in the overhead lighting, and I find myself hoping it doesn't take forever for him to make it to me.

After the night I've had, I wouldn't blame myself for starting with a shot of hard liquor. And if I didn't know with absolute certainty that three a.m. would become a time of regret as a result, I would do it.

"What's your poison?" the young blond asks when he finally makes his way over to me a few minutes later and tosses one of those cardboard coasters onto the surface of the bar.

"A glass of Chardonnay, please."

His nod is all the confirmation I need as he moves away to fill my order.

Internally, I feel overstimulated and downright overwhelmed at how quickly I've found myself in the center of even more chaos. And regardless of the fact that I'm still wearing my coat, a sudden chill runs down my spine.

Living with my mom and dad postdivorce was traumatic in many—mostly comedic—ways, but life in New York is an entirely different beast. And at forty-one years old, I still feel like a child who's been left alone to start over and find my way.

"A glass of Chardonnay for the pretty lady," the bartender announces magnanimously, setting the glass on the previously placed coaster. "That'll be $11.43. Do you want to open a tab?"

"Thank you." I try my best to replace the current discomfort on my face with a half smile as I dig fifteen dollars from my bag and slide it over to him. "No tab but keep the change for your tip."

"That's appreciated." He grins and turns on his heel to cash out my drink at the register, and I stare down at the ice-cold wine in front of me, more than ready to see if it helps take the edge off. And I've almost swallowed an entire gulp of the liquid when the sound of my name catches me off guard.

"Sammy."

I jerk to look over my shoulder, almost certain I've conjured the man with my imagination.

With a pint of beer in front of him, Noah sits at a table by himself behind and to the left of me, and an exuberant smile is planted on his handsome face. At the sight of him, some small part of me has to wonder exactly how blindly I chose to come here.

Was I hoping he would be here too? Or was it just comfortable because I'd been here before?

Beer in hand, he stands from his chair and moves to sit on the barstool beside mine. "Well, this is a pleasant surprise." The depths of his blue eyes glimmer like stars in the sky. "What are you doing here?"

"Just stopped by for a drink, I guess." I shrug, pointedly avoiding telling him any of the events leading up to that decision. "What about you?"

"Pretty much the same." He runs a hand through his hair and offers a wry grin. "I hope you don't mind, but I've kind of taken it upon myself to join you."

"Of course not," I say, and he reaches out with one hand to tug my barstool a little closer to his. It's the second time tonight I've been relocated by a man, but for some reason, this feels different—safer.

"There." He winks. "That's much better."

My stomach flutters.

"So, you're kid-free for the night?" he asks, and I nod.

"The boys are sleeping over at Brooke's."

"Nice." Noah grins at me over his pint of beer. "You deserve to have some nights to yourself. Probably doesn't make it any easier to leave them, though, huh?"

My whole body sinks an inch into my stool. *Why does it feel so good to finally have someone understand how torn I'm feeling?*

"Mom guilt is a bitch."

Noah grins. "Trust me. Not all moms feel guilty. It just means you're a good one."

"I'm so sorry, Noah!" a voice calls from behind us. "I hope you weren't waiting long!"

We both turn around, and my stomach jolts when I come face-to-face with the pretty redhead who singlehandedly ruined the name Mary for me.

She looks slightly frazzled, but she's still painfully attractive. And my stomach tries to migrate into my shoes at the realization that this is the *third* time I'm seeing them together.

There's no way this is just a fling.

"Don't worry about it, Mary," Noah says through a chuckle, spinning on his barstool to accept her hug as she gives it. "Haven't been here more than ten minutes."

"Thank goodness," she exclaims and kisses him on the cheek.

I feel like an uninvited voyeur, but this time, with the shift Noah made to my stool when he sat down, it feels like there's nowhere for me to run.

"I don't want to interrupt your night, guys," I say, trying to keep my voice casual and taking the last swig of my wine in preparation for dismissal. "And I should probably be on my way anyway."

"Sammy, no. Stay," Noah states quickly and reaches out to gently grip my thigh.

"No, it's okay. I really don't want to interrupt. I—"

"No, seriously, stay," Mary adds with a soft smile directed straight at me. "I'm just dropping keys off to Noah. I'm Mary, by the way." She holds out her hand, and I swallow my pride and take it. I'm too old to play the hostile victim toward a woman who's done me no conscious wrong.

"Sammy," I reciprocate.

"So, *you're* Sammy," Mary states and glances over at Noah like she knows something I don't. "It's really nice to finally meet you."

Finally *meet me? As in, she's been waiting for the opportunity?*

"Mary is my sister's home health nurse," Noah unexpectedly explains, making my gaze jerk violently toward him.

He has a sister? Who requires a home health nurse?

"Honestly, I don't know what I'd do without her," Noah adds with a genuine grin. "Mary has been taking care of my sister Kara for several years now. Most days, she's my saving grace."

"All right. All right. That's enough. Any more compliments and I'll start melting like the wicked witch." Mary waves him off with a laugh and looks at me. "Sammy, if you haven't noticed, Noah is one of the nicest, most charming guys you'll ever meet. Even my husband Jared is in love with him."

Her husband Jared? As in, she's married?

If I weren't sitting down, I'd be on the floor right now. They're going to have to rewrite the end of the Bible if there are any more revelations.

She smirks at me and reaches into her purse to pull out a set of keys. "Speaking of Jared, I need to get home to celebrate the momentous occasion of him cooking dinner for once." She slides the keys across the bar to Noah. "Kara loved our little day-trip to the Central Park Zoo. I got her back to the facility in time for dinner. Your Range Rover is parked in your favorite spot in the garage. And don't worry, I only managed a few dents in it."

Noah rolls his eyes with an amiable chuckle. "Very funny."

"Sammy, it was really great meeting you. I hope I'll get to see more of you in the future," Mary says with a wink and reaches out to grip Noah's shoulder with a friendly pat. "And I'll check in with you tomorrow, boss."

"Thanks, Mary."

And then she's off, heading straight out of the bar after dropping the kind of truth bomb that's going to be hitting me with shock waves until the end of time.

Mary isn't someone Noah is dating. She's a medical caregiver for his sister who I didn't even know existed.

"So…you'll stay and have a drink with me?" Noah asks, and I can't bring myself to answer anything but "*Yes.*"

Chapter

Fourteen

"Is Kara your only sibling?" I ask Noah, casually nudging my questions toward a more and more personal territory.

We've been here at Bailey's for hours, and I've yet to find a subject I'm not interested in.

We've talked about his college days at Columbia and how his roommate's one friend actually had the FBI come looking for him at their dorm one night because of something crazy he had done and how they never saw him again. Kyle something, I think he said his name was.

He also told me how he ran the New York Marathon ten years ago, only to trip embarrassingly on his mostly numb feet after crossing the finish line and need stitches in his knee.

He told me his favorite color is blue and that he's never tried sushi and that anytime the weatherman says something like *the wind blows from the east*, he thinks of Liam Neeson in the Taken movies.

I know more random things about Noah after tonight than I've known in the entire seven months we've been acquainted with each other.

And still, I want to know *more*. I want to go deeper and earlier and into more detail. I want to know his thoughts and feelings and hopes and dreams and the things he would change if he could.

And whenever he's asked, I've managed to find the strength to share the same kinds of things about me. Which, for me, feels nothing short of a miracle.

"Yep. She's seven years younger than me," Noah states as he sets his water back on the bar. He switched from beer about an hour ago in anticipation of being on call tomorrow morning. "When she was born, she was the light of all our lives. A healthy, adorable baby girl, and the little sister this silly little seven-year-old boy didn't think he wanted but fell in love with instantly."

"So…" I pause, unsure if I should ask the question or how I should word it, but somehow, he senses what's on my mind without my saying a word.

"Everything changed when Kara was about four months old. She had several severe seizures that changed the course of her life forever."

Oh my God.

"That's so…tragic."

"It definitely caused a strain on our parents' marriage. They ended up divorcing when Kara was about three years old, and my dad took on the role of her primary caregiver."

"What about your mom?"

"I used to really hate her," he says quietly, shaking his head as he does. "But as I got older, as I grew up, I realized my mom was simply too selfish, too emotionally immature, to handle such a difficult situation."

"I think something like that would be hard on any mother."

"Don't give her too much credit," he contests gently, meeting my eyes with a slight frown creasing the corners of his lips. "She's not like you, Sammy. She's not like anyone you know. After the divorce, she spent most of my youth continually bringing my dad to court over alimony and support, even though he was the one taking care of my sister. Just because I've matured past the point of hating her doesn't mean she deserves kind words."

I'm on the edge of my seat as Noah's already gentle voice breaks around the edges. His life is so much more complicated than I ever dreamed. He's so successful and vibrant and handsome, I figured his upbringing had been perfect. Easy. Devoid of complications.

I guess that's why they have that phrase about what happens when you assume.

"When I was fourteen, I permanently moved in with my dad and helped him with Kara as much as I could." He laughs thoughtfully. "He fought me the whole way. Said he wanted me to be a normal teenager, whatever that means." He shrugs. "I haven't talked to my mom since. I know she's still alive, living somewhere in the city, but that's all I know and that's all I want to know."

"Your dad sounds like a really good father."

"He was," Noah corrects, and I frown. "He passed away a few years ago. Heart attack."

"I'm so sorry."

My dad is a pain in my ass, but just last week, he sent a care package of a couple hundred dollars, beef jerky, and brand-new Cleveland Guardians hats for the boys. He didn't call or text, and he rarely does. But he doesn't have to. He loves me and my kids and finds his ways to show it. I don't know what I'd do if I didn't have him or my mom or Brooke to turn to.

Noah, it seems, is very much on his own.

"Me too." He shrugs. "But I'm thankful I was in the position to take over Kara's care."

Noah's life is the opposite of what I'd pictured in my mind—the carefree bachelor with the entire world at his feet. Instead, he's the sole provider for his disabled sister, while also managing the schedule of being the head of pediatric anesthesiology at St. Luke's.

Looks like Brooke was right about him all along…

"She lives in a full-time care facility, one my dad researched and picked out before he passed, but I hired Mary to give her the individualized attention she deserves. Mary spends forty hours a week with her and takes her out on day-trips all the time. I wish I could do it all myself, but I learned within the first six months that doing it all without help was impossible."

By the way his eyes bore into mine, I have to imagine he's trying to tell me something.

"I guess all of us need help sometimes," I acknowledge rather than dodging. I owe him that much for as open as he's been with me. "Thank you for sharing with me. You didn't have to, and I'm sure it's not easy talking about it all, but I'm really thankful you did." I reach out and place my hand over his. "You're a really good man, Noah. Your sister is lucky to have you as a brother."

He shakes his head. "I'm the lucky one. Kara's what keeps me sane."

"I understand. Sisters are special. I don't know what I'd do without Brooke, but I'm almost positive I wouldn't be doing it in New York. Without her, I never would have been able to manage the move."

"Are you happy here?"

"Yes." My voice is emphatic. "I know with all my heart New York is where I belong. It's where my boys belong. I can't see myself living anywhere else now that we're here."

Noah smiles over at me. "That's good. Because I can't picture New York without you now."

"Don't be ridiculous." I snort and nudge him playfully in the shoulder. "You'd manage without me. And Lord knows the city would certainly manage without my crazy kids."

"It doesn't mean I'd *want to* manage." Noah winks. "It might be selfish, but I'm happy you gave up your Midwest roots to come here."

"It wasn't a hard choice. Ohio isn't the most exciting place to live."

"I'm sure Ohio can be fun."

I eye him skeptically. "Have you ever been to Ohio?"

"Well, no," he answers. "But it can't be that bad."

"Quick question," I say, staring at him with pursed lips. "When you're at the airport and you see the gate for…I don't know…Cleveland, Ohio… Do you think, 'Man, I wish I were going there!' or do you just feel sympathy for the poor souls sitting at that gate?"

His response is pure laughter.

"See!" I exclaim and poke my index finger into his manly bicep.

"But I didn't say anything!" he retorts, his voice still full of hilarity.

"You didn't have to," I counter with a knowing smile. "Your lack of response said it all."

"I plead the Fifth."

"Of course you do!" I laugh. "One day, I'm going to drag you to Hometown, Ohio, with me and let you experience a real Midwest culture shock."

"Is that a threat or a promise?" he questions. "Because I'm hoping it's a promise."

I roll my eyes and take a drink from my *fourth* glass of wine. Since I'm a fair-weather drinker, that's all I need to know about the passing of time. But no matter how long we've been sitting here, it still feels like it's been hardly any time at all.

I'm enjoying myself more tonight, sitting in a simple bar sharing nothing more than conversation, than I have in a long-ass time.

Internally, I cringe. Is it bad that I'm having this much fun with Noah after my night with Gavin ended so horribly? Should I be feeling *this* happy right now?

I don't know. But I am.

I can't believe I almost missed out on it by running away again.

"Can I tell you something that will probably make you laugh?"

Noah looks me over with a curious smile. "I'm all ears."

"I thought Mary was someone you were…romantically involved with."

"Really?" His eyes go wide.

I cringe. "In my defense, I didn't know you had a sister. And Mary is an incredibly beautiful woman. It made sense that you would want to date her."

"Well, we're definitely not dating. Pretty sure Jared would have a problem with it." Noah runs a hand through his hair on a chuckle. "I don't date very often, period."

"Oh. So, you're, like, more of a one-night-stand, casual-hookup kind of guy?"

"One-night stands?" A barking laugh jumps from his lungs. "Uh, no, Sammy. And I'm not into casual hookups either. I'm a little too old for that empty shit. I had a few dates with someone a few months ago that I thought might go somewhere, but…" He shrugs. "It wasn't what I thought it would be."

"Why not?"

"I just didn't have the *feeling*."

"The feeling?"

"Yeah. The all-consuming, heart-racing, stomach-aching, I'm-going-to-throw-up-if-this-doesn't-work-out *feeling*."

I nod. I know the feeling. "It's the same feeling I read about in Brooke's book about Chase that made me know she had to go for it."

He searches my eyes for a long moment that makes all my breath stall in my chest. "What's going on with you and Gavin, Sammy?"

Oh boy. Suddenly, the weight of the world feels like it rests just above where I decide to put this answer.

"We've been on a few dates, and he's a nice person. But I—"

"Last call!" the bartender announces to the half-empty bar, cutting me off midsentence and leaving both my answer and the world hovering somewhere over Manhattan. "Bar is closing in ten minutes!"

"Shit," Noah mutters and glances at his watch. "I can't believe it's already last call."

"What time is it?"

"A little after one."

"It's after *one*?" I laugh. "The last time I stayed up past midnight had to be when Grant was a baby."

He grins. "How about I close out our tab and walk you home?"

"Yes, please," I say with a smile. "This old lady would love to have you walk her home."

Noah tsks. "You're not old, Sammy."

"I'm forty-one, Noah. I'm old."

"Baby, I'm forty-three," he retorts. "If you're old, then I might as well be ancient."

I shrug dramatically. "See, all you really did there is confirm that we're *both* old."

"Grab your coat, Grandma. Grandpa will pay the check."

"How'd you know you wanted to be a doctor? Is that something you always dreamed of, or did it just seem like a practical way to make money?" I ask as I unlock the door to my apartment and step inside. I hold the door for Noah to follow, and he does without hesitation.

It's a little weird that I didn't ask him to come up and he didn't ask either—but it's almost as if neither of us even considered another option.

Noah contemplates my apartment in front of him for a long moment, seemingly studying the layout before meeting my eyes again. "I think abstractly, it was always on my radar. When my sister had the seizures as a baby, everything changed between my parents. My dad sought every bit of information he could from the doctors, and my mom turned in the other direction. She felt betrayed, I think, that they'd messed up her healthy baby and couldn't figure out how to fix it. Her answer was denial. That it was happening, that it wasn't changing, and that doctors were imperfect humans doing their best."

"So, you believed in the doctors, or you didn't?"

Noah smiles. "A little bit of both, I think. I wanted to prove something to myself. Make something concrete out of the information I'd been given. And probably, at the same time, I was hoping I'd somehow be better than them. That I'd have all the answers." He shrugs a little. "Of course, I don't. None of us does. Diagnostics is all educated guesswork." He turns around and leans against my kitchen island. "Anesthesia? That's pretty much science. A calculation of sorts. Hard to screw up if you pay attention."

I roll my eyes and drop my purse on the counter next to him. "I think you're selling yourself a little short. I'm decent at math, but I wouldn't want me at the head of any surgeon's table."

Noah chuckles. "That's just because you haven't been to med school for it. That's where the confidence comes from."

I walk around the counter and grab two glasses from the cabinet, offering one to Noah as I do. He accepts with a jerk of his chin, and I grab a bottle of water from the fridge to pour us each a glass as I contemplate my own life.

"Unlike you, I never knew what I wanted to do," I say, blowing out an exaggerated breath. "I went to school because my parents said I had to and then married Todd because that was the thing women did where I grew up." I take a quick swig before continuing, gesturing to the living room couch. Noah follows dutifully, taking off his shoes and sitting back so he can rest his feet on the edge of the coffee table. "Don't get me wrong. Plenty of women from there went another route or actually married someone they're still happy with, but not me. I was lost." My laugh is dry. "In some ways, I guess I still am."

"But aren't we all a little lost, Sammy?"

"I don't know. Are we? Most of the time, it feels like everyone else is riding on their track and I'm out floating in the wind."

"I think everyone is a little lost. Even the people who seem like they have it all together. They're either faking it, or they've come to terms with the fact that they hardly know anything at all," he says and reaches out with a gentle hand to tuck a strand of hair behind my ear.

Instantly, his touch urges goose bumps to roll up my arms. My nipples are already hard beneath my lace bra, and my eyes can't focus on anything besides his perfect mouth.

"Noah?"

"Yeah?"

"For once. Just once," I whisper, "I'd really like to feel found."

Silence breathes between us like a pulsing wave. My stomach flips on itself, and my chest heaves. I don't know what I mean when I say that I want to be found, but I do know that I mean it to the very depth of my toes.

Noah moves slowly, his feet coming off the coffee table as he sits up straight and removes his suit jacket. He tucks it to the side of the couch behind him, and then he faces me with a burn in his eyes so hot I feel like I'm being licked by the flames.

A vise clamps my throat closed, keeping me unable to say anything, but all I want to say is yes.

Yes to whatever he's thinking, yes to whatever he wants to do. Yes to the possibility of being found, even if it's just for tonight.

Fingers shaking, I pull at the buttons of my blouse, undoing them one at a time from top to bottom, saying all the things I can't actually seem to say. Noah watches avidly until I'm done and then scoots forward to the space directly in front of me.

My heart feels like a thoroughbred in the starting gates, and I know at the very first contact, it's going to kick up into a gallop.

Noah skims my blouse off my shoulder enough to kiss the skin next to my bra strap, and a shiver runs the length of my spine. I'm warm and cold all at once, and the combination of the two seems to have the sensory receptors in my skin on overdrive.

I haven't been touched like this by a man in almost three years. Since Todd, I've been alone, and at the end of our marriage, I hated his guts.

And, well, if I'm totally honest, I haven't even touched myself in that time. I know that sounds crazy, but between my shitty marriage and the stress of starting my life over with two young kids, any drive I had toward sexuality at all dried up until it cracked.

But I'm aroused now, damn near to the point of desperation, and my body aches to have Noah touch me even further.

It feels like a new part of me is awakening, like the sun is shining after a long,

gloomy stretch of night. Like I'm a woman who deserves to feel sexy and experience pleasure. Like I'm worthy of…something.

I moan, and Noah takes the fabric of my shirt all the way down my back.
Nothing but my lace bra remains to cover me, but with as feverish as I feel,
it's still too much.

Noah's touch is soft, delicate even, but unbelievably deliberate. His fingers
skim my skin like it's a sheet of braille with all the answers.

"You're so beautiful, Sam," Noah whispers, his voice steady, strong, and soft
all at once.

My first instinct is one I'm ashamed of. I want to belittle the comment—to
question it—but that would be so unfair to the reverence with which Noah
said it.

I know he means it, even if I don't yet understand why. A little bit more of
this, though, and I might start to believe it.

Brazenly, I take that thought and run with it, taking charge enough to bring
his lips to mine. The kiss is slow at first, exploratory and searching, but with
one soft swipe of my tongue along the seam of his lips, passion explodes.

His hands are in my hair, and I'm leaned over the arm of the couch with the
weight of his strong, warm body on top of me. I can't breathe that well, but
at this point, I don't want to. His hands take the lead to angle my head so his
tongue can get deeper, and I suck in the absolute glory of the taste of him.

It's minty and fresh, and his tongue has the slightest shock of cold from the
water. He manhandles me gently, moving just enough to swing my body up
into his arms without taking his lips off mine.

I have never been touched like this. *Never.*

Noah carries me to my bedroom with ease and shuts the door behind us
with his foot as he lays me on the bed.

I know the boys are gone tonight, but some weird, paranoid part of me still
shimmies off the bed to go lock the knob before coming back.

Noah watches me with a smile and a tilt of one of his perfect eyebrows, but

I shake my head in answer. "Honestly, you don't really want to know what led to that decision."

"I'd love to know," Noah disagrees. "But if you'd rather not tell me, that's okay too."

Yeah, these lips are sealed.

I scurry back to the bed, but not before shedding my skirt first. The urge to cover my body is strong, but Noah's capable hands take my hips and pull me down in front of him before I can even consider executing it.

"God, Sammy. I want you so badly."

His words only urge my desire for him further. There is no confusion. My mind and my body are clear in their need.

"I want you too," I whisper.

With a swift scoot, Noah has the two of us on the bed, atop the covers, and my head in his hands again. Our kiss is deep and slow, and my whole body is starting to shake like a leaf.

Not because I don't want it, but because I *do*. For the first time in ages, I want to feel the high of a climax. I want my eyes to roll back and my toes to curl and for time as I know it to stop momentarily.

And I want it to happen with Noah Philips.

Anxious, I pull at his still-in-place clothes, unbuttoning his shirt as quickly as I can with his mouth on mine. Our bodies are pressed together, and I rip his shirt off his shoulders with greedy fingers when I finally get the buttons free.

Or so I think. The last button still apparently done, I end up ripping the material apart to get it off him completely. He doesn't complain, instead re-marking, "I'm saving this shirt as a shrine to tonight. The night Sammy Baker wanted me so badly she had to rip my clothes off."

I blush through a giggle as he shoves up enough to push his pants down and fish out his wallet from the pocket. I watch unabashedly as he shucks his black boxer briefs in one smooth motion before climbing back on the bed with a condom in his hand.

His dick is on the loose, and it's so flipping big, I'm half surprised not to hear a distant police scanner going off about a man with a deadly weapon in the area.

Noah doesn't falter like I do, being familiar with his own penis, I presume, and jumps right back into the action, rolling me to my back to cover one of my lacy nipples with his mouth. My back arches off the bed, and he uses that opportunity to follow my curves down to my underwear, repeating the action there.

My legs stir and my heart pounds as he peels the thin material down my legs until I'm exposed and bare. I expect to feel self-conscious or nervous, but I'm too far gone for any of that. All I feel is intense, wanton longing.

"Noah. Please."

My soft beg is all he needs to don the condom and sink between the open space of my legs. His hips slot easily between mine, and I have to admit, the feeling is almost startling. Besides being an asshole, my ex was also a larger guy. I never minded it, even found it comforting in a lot of ways. But feeling the strength of Noah's taut muscles is undeniably erotic.

Slow and confident, he sinks inside me with an easiness I don't expect with a cock that large. "Sam," he says simply, his voice rough, as he comes to a stop, fully seated inside me.

I feel full—of him and of life—in a way I haven't *ever* felt. It's all I can do to keep my eyes from falling closed.

He find my cheeks with his thumbs, though, and the gentle stroke of their pads is enough to keep me so in the moment I fear I might never leave it.

His eyes bore into mine, the inky blackness of his pupils softened by the very obvious presence of his soul.

And slowly, so slowly, he begins to move. Steady and firm but gentle at the same time. It pulls at every nerve in me—the ones his strokes touch and the ones they don't alike.

I lick at my lips to try to keep my heart from exploding out of my throat, and Noah leans down to catch a nip of my tongue. It's all so intimate—so genuine—I can hardly believe this is our first time together.

Intensity builds deep inside me, clawing at my every pore to get out. My back arches, my toes curl, my head falls back, and on a cry of ecstasy, I come with a man for the very first time in my life.

Sweet Mary, Mother of Jesus. I just had the best sex of my existence. *And it wasn't with the man I started the night with.*

Chapter Fifteen

Very Early Morning, Monday, May 16th

"Sammy."

"Sammy."

My eyes pop open harshly, eyelids pulling at the dry surface of my corneas, and a gasp sucks all the breath from my lungs.

My mom radar scans the darkness of my bedroom in confusion, trying to find the tiny human who must be in need of something. After all, it's the way I most frequently wake up.

"It's okay," Noah's warm voice comforts instead.

I look to my left to find him sitting on the edge of the mattress, fully dressed. "I have to head into the hospital for an emergency triple bypass."

I scrub a hand down my face. "What time is it?"

"A little after four," he says and reaches out to brush some of my hair out of my eyes. "I didn't want to wake you up, but I also didn't want you to wake up and think I bailed."

It takes my mind a moment to even understand what he's saying, and then it hits me as I glance down at the very naked top half of my body.

My kids aren't home. Which is probably good because Noah and I had sex last night.

"Go back to sleep," he whispers and leans forward to press a soft kiss to my lips. "I'll text you later, okay?"

I nod. Or at least, I think I nod. All my basic functions are still in sleep mode, and with the way my head feels, I'm pretty sure all the wine I had last night isn't helping either.

Fingers gently holding my chin, Noah searches my eyes for a long moment before he presses one more kiss to my lips and stands up.

When I hear the front door of my apartment click shut, I let my head fall back onto my pillows on a sigh. My eyes are already closed again, and my breaths are growing heavier by the second.

I'm far too sleepy to contemplate what last night means, but I'm not too out of it—or naïve—to understand that I'm going to have to figure it all out soon.

Once a turkey is cooked, it won't be good in the fridge forever.

And it's safe to say mine is… roasted.

A cab honks, and I jump back onto the sidewalk as it zooms right in front of me. I'd love to say he's a reckless driver, but I'm the one with my head up my ass this morning.

Noah Philips and I had sex. S-e-x.

My mind has been reeling over that fact ever since I got out of bed at around nine this morning. Noah was long gone by then, but I vaguely remember him waking me up to tell me he had to leave to go into the hospital.

I don't remember what time that was, but I know it was early. I also don't remember falling asleep together after the sex, but I guess that's exactly what we did.

My phone vibrates in my purse as I shuffle through a small group of tourists that are huddled together for a selfie. Figuring it's Brooke asking for my ETA, I snag it from the front pocket and check the screen.

Gavin: I haven't stopped thinking about you.

This is the second text he's sent me this morning. The first one read, *I'm so sorry for the way I spoke to you last night, Sam. Please forgive me. Call me whenever, okay?*

It's safe to say neither message is helping unclog my muddled head.

I know Gavin was frustrated last night. And I don't condone the way he spoke to me, but I guess there's also a part of me that can understand his frustration. From his perspective, he probably felt like I'd been stringing him along for God knows how long and everything was pointing to some kind of conclusion on my part.

That doesn't make any of it right, but in his defense, he probably feels like I've taken him on a wild-goose chase with how back-and-forth and wishy-washy I've been this whole time.

Don't forget that on the same night you declined sex with him, you ended up having sex with Noah.

Guilt nags at the lining of my stomach and burns nausea up into my throat.

How on earth did I get here?

It's like I'm some lying, secretive, two-man-dating woman.

Or at least, that's how I feel as I wave to the doorman at Chase and Brooke's building and head for the elevator at the back. Honestly, it's a modern miracle that my body can walk and tie itself in knots at the same time.

The elevator ride is quick, and Brooke answers my three knocks to her door even quicker. I'm instantly thankful for the distraction that is my sister's smiling face.

"You survived," I tease and reach out to affectionately rub my hand over her rounded belly.

"Not a single casualty." She holds open the door, and two tiny torpedoes hit me at full speed as soon as I enter her apartment. I rub at my sons' fluffy heads as they smile up at me, their mouths moving a mile a minute.

"Mom, I beat Aunt Brooke and Uncle Chase *five* times at Uno last night!" Seth yells his excitement.

"Way to go, dude."

"I won too!" Grant shouts, not wanting to be left out.

"Yeah, but you only won two times, and I won five!"

"But two times is good, Seth!" Grant declares with a swing of his still-casted arm. "Two times is really good!"

"Two times is good, but it's not five times like me!"

"All I'm really hearing here is that Aunt Brooke and Uncle Chase were the big losers of the night." I look over at my sister, who is now leaning against the doorway that leads into the living room.

She bites her lip with a shake of her head before stating, "We did not perform at all."

But you know who did perform last night? Noah.

The rogue, completely inappropriate thought hits me like a Mack truck just drove itself into my sister's living room. My mind gnaws and my stomach clenches, and I find myself looking at Brooke with a face that makes her stand up straight. "Boys!" she says with both an immediacy and a cheeriness I wish I could muster. "Uncle Chase is in our bedroom. Go wrestle him until he screams."

"Ayyye!" Grant shouts like a banshee and takes off at a run, followed closely behind by his older brother.

Poor Chase.

Brooke wastes no time waddling toward me, her back curved like a hundred-year-old tree under the weight of her growing child. Benji walks closely at her side, seemingly unfazed by the crazy kids who just tore by him to head down the hall.

She takes a seat on the couch, patting the spot next to her. "Take a load off."

After a singular deep breath, I plop down beside her. I don't even have a choice at this point. I can't keep this to myself. I *have* to get it off my chest. I'll suffocate if I don't.

"As you know, last night, I went on a date with Gavin." I start at the beginning but keep the extraneous details to a minimum. I have a quota on words I'll be able to get out without crying.

She nods but doesn't say anything. She knows I need the floor, and she's giving it to me.

"It went fine, and I enjoyed his company as I always do, maybe even more so. But when it got to the end of the night, he asked me back to his hotel, and I said no."

She swallows, nodding again.

"He was upset, and, to be honest, I understand. I've been signaling to him that there's a chance by continuing to go out with him. If not for a relationship, at least for sex," I say, whispering the last word just in case little ears have escaped the wrestling match with Chase without my knowing it. "Most people over forty don't need an offer of marriage to…fornicate."

Brooke's eyebrows draw together critically. "What do you mean, upset? Like, he was visibly disappointed but a gentleman?"

"He…well. He asked what the hell we're doing. He said he thought we were *getting somewhere.*"

"No, ma'am," she interrupts with a raise of her hand.

"Brooke. He didn't, like, physically do anything, if that's what you're thinking. He—"

"No way. It doesn't matter. Your body autonomy is yours, and you are allowed to say no, no matter how much you think you've been 'signaling.' Him getting upset about not getting his *cookie* at the end of the meal is bullshit."

She's one hundred percent right. No woman should feel like she owes a man sex or feel guilted or pressured into having it if she doesn't want to.

"I know," I agree. "That's why I held my ground. But I can still understand where he's coming from, okay? I get why he was irritated with me last night, and he's been texting me this morning and apologizing. I'm more upset with myself than I am with him."

"Why, in God's name, *why* would you be upset with yourself in this situation?"

"Because after I told him no, I left and went to a bar."

Her head bobbles up and down like one of those dashboard dolls. "Okay…"

"Bailey's."

Her eyes widen. She obviously knows that Noah is a regular there. I had a feeling she would.

"I ran into Noah, and we ended up talking all night. He told me about his upbringing and his sister and so many things about his life I had no freaking idea about."

"Okay…"

"I drank three and a half glasses of wine, and then he walked me home and we talked some more."

"Three and a half?" Brooke asks on a snort. "That explains the mismatched socks this morning."

I glance down at my feet before dropping my head in my hands. "Jesus."

"Whatever, Sam. Forget about the socks, would you? I'm dying here."

I swallow and take a deep breath. "We talked, and then at some point, everything else just faded away. All I could see was the burn in his eyes, like the two of us were in a tunnel, right there in your old apartment."

"Oh my God," Brooke whispers. "You slept with Noah."

I nod slowly. "And I was probably the one who initiated it…" I cringe and sink my head back into my hands on a groan. "*Gah.* What is the matter with me?"

"Nothing!" Brooke protests and tugs my hands away from my face. "You have the weight of the world on your shoulders, Sammy, and anyone on earth would understand if you made the occasional mistake. But I'm telling you, this *wasn't* one. You made a choice you were allowed to make, and it sounds to me like you had reason to. You weren't committed to either of these guys, and you are allowed to do what you want, do you hear me?"

"Oh, I hear you, all right. You're kind of yelling."

She sucks her lips into her mouth and backs away from my face by a foot. "Sorry."

"I just…I don't know, Brooke. I feel so guilty. Like any second, it'll eat me alive."

"You don't owe anyone *anything*. You don't need to feel guilty."

I scoff. "You know that's like telling someone to relax, right?"

Brooke keeps her mouth shut, but I can see the desire to say something written all over her face.

"Please, whatever it is you're thinking, just say it. Lord knows I am all ears on how to deal with this mess."

"I just… Sammy." She pauses and reaches out to hold one of my hands. "If you forget all the rest of it, there's only one detail that matters."

When she pauses too long, I almost explode. "Yeah? And? What is it?"

Her voice is painstakingly gentle. "You said no to Gavin, but you said yes to Noah. Why is that?"

"I…" I search my mind for the differentiating details of last night or last week or since the moment I started this ill-fated bounce between the two of them. Maybe it's the hangover or the uncertainty of exactly what the future would hold with either of them or the fact that Noah and I didn't establish even an inkling of what sleeping together last night would mean, but I come up completely empty. "I don't know."

"Well, maybe it's time to slow down and think about it."

I frown. "I don't want to willfully hurt someone, but it feels like I am, and I don't know how to stop."

"You aren't doing it willfully, Sammy. But if you want to stop, you've got to look for the answer inside you. There's a part of you that knows what it wants. It's time to call it up for a lifeline."

"Don't find it, just feel it," I say, repeating the advice our mom always gave us as teenage girls as we were learning how to navigate the messy world of dating.

Brooke nods. "Exactly."

I don't have to find the answer. I just have to feel it, deep inside me, in the part that *knows* what Sammy Baker, and Sammy Baker alone, wants.

PART TWO

Noah

Chapter Sixteen

Late Morning, Monday, May 16ᵗʰ

Kendall stretches while her brown Lab, Chanandler Bong, dances beside her with readiness for our run.

Dolly and I, however, have already done our stretching, and after being woken up for an emergency surgery at four this morning, I'm now considering getting a waffle from the Wafels & Dinges truck parked at the entrance of the park instead of engaging in our weekly group exercise.

Truthfully, I'm exhausted. But I'm also amped. It's this weird combination of feeling tired and wired. My body wants to lie down on the closest park bench and take a nap, but my mind wants to replay last night like some kind of highlight reel.

Fuck. Last night with Sammy was... I can't even explain it.

It was a culmination of months and months of feelings on my part. A conclusion, if I'm honest, I never thought we'd actually reach.

When I saw her sitting at the bar at Bailey's, I never imagined I'd end up back at her place. In her bed. Touching her. Kissing her. Exploring her. *Making her come.*

The sex was explosive. Ten years ago, I would've just chalked it up as a night of hot, mind-blowing sex. But I didn't know my head from my asshole back then.

Bottom line, last night meant something to me. And while I wish I could say it meant something to Sammy too, I'm mostly in the dark about her feelings. She always keeps everything so close to the vest, which I can't even blame her for. Her life for the last decade has had some serious ups and downs highlighted by a lot of disappointment—courtesy of a shitty ex-husband and the family he left her to take care of all on her own.

And to add insult to injury, I didn't even get to wake up with her this morning and do something pathetically telling like fawn all over her while I made us breakfast. Instead, I watched Dr. Weller, our lead cardiologist, perform a six-hour triple bypass on a little boy with Kawasaki disease after he came into the emergency department in bad shape.

I couldn't use or check my phone for the entire morning, and now I'm wondering if she was even truly awake when I told her the reason I left so early.

Shiiit. Does she remember? Or does she think I left in the middle of the night like some kind of dick?

I glance at my watch and see it's a little after eleven. *Surely she's awake by now.* Two seconds later, my phone is out of my pocket, and my fingers slide across the keys as I type out a message.

Me: I can't remember a better night than last night, Sam. I'm sorry I had to leave so early this morning to go into work.

I hit send, but I also reread it three times, trying to decide whether it's right. There's only so much you can convey in a text, you know?

I almost send her a second message, but Chanandler Bong's impatient whine grabs my attention. I look over at Kendall to find her still stretching. "Be patient, Chan," she tells her big Lab, scratching the top of his head. "He'll be here soon."

"I'm with Bong." I make a show of dramatically looking at my watch, even though nary a full minute has passed since the last time I looked at it. "Where in the hell is your husband?"

I roll my eyes when Kendall shoots me a glare that suggests I will never, ever know the annoyance she feels.

"Trust me, if I could control his arrival, my life would be a lot different." She leans over to stretch out her hamstrings. "As it is, my only revenge tactic against his constant tardiness is trying to look as hot as possible so he'll at least have to worry about other men hitting on me when he's not here."

I chuckle. Kendall is a blonde bombshell any guy would be hard-pressed not to notice. But she's also intimidating. I don't think half the guys who think about hitting on her even bother with an approach. No doubt her husband Dale knows that.

"Hey, guys!" the man of the hour finally greets, strolling down the path with a coffee cup in hand. "Sorry I'm late."

"Hey, guys? Hey, *guys?*" Kendall questions loudly, making me smother a laugh. She's going to have his balls.

Dale's eyes dance with amusement. "I mean, hello, beautiful, amazing, brilliant love of my life."

"That's what I thought you meant to say." She purses her lips. "And don't forget Noah."

"Right. *And* Noah," he agrees with a chuckle and rubs an affectionate palm over a wagging-tail Chanandler's back.

"I hope that coffee cup is an optical illusion, Dr. Hopkins," I say chidingly. "Because I know you didn't keep us waiting on you while you stopped to caffeinate."

"I got it from the hospital cafeteria…six hours ago. So, you can relax. Some of us didn't have the luxury of sleeping in our own beds for the last twelve hours."

"That's because you chose to work in the ED," Kendall teases. "Chump move."

"Excuse me?" I question with narrowed eyes. "I didn't sleep either because your ass called me in."

"Oh yeah," he answers with a nod. "I almost forgot about that."

"That's convenient because I sure as shit didn't forget about you ruining my night."

"Ruin your night?" Dale scoffs. "I called you at four this morning, Philips. What else were you doing besides sleeping?"

Sleeping with a soft, warm, perfect, very naked Sammy wrapped around my body like ivy, my mind silently corrects him.

"And how bad could it have been?" he questions with a real dickish smile. "It's not like sitting on a little stool and monitoring O2 sats is hard labor."

"The guy who spends most of his night playing stand-up comedian in the nurses station is talking to me about hard labor? Ha." My fake laugh is the definition of mockery. "That's cute."

"Oh, boys, boys, boys." Kendall steps in between us. "Could you save your pissing match for another day? Chanandler and I are ready to run, and by the looks of Dolly, she is too."

Dolly wags her tail, and Chanandler barks his approval.

"All right," I agree and reach down to give Dolly's head a rub. "Let's do it."

Dale tosses his cup in the nearby garbage can. "Start us off, babe."

Kendall takes the lead, jogging in front of our group, and only turns back to look at Dale and me to make a final point we're both entirely familiar with after ten years of friendship. "Plus, both of you know if we're going to get into a dick-measuring match about our jobs, I'd win any day!" she calls over her shoulder, her smile snide enough to match her words.

Since she's a fucking neurosurgeon—the top one in the country, actually— Dale and I don't even bother with a response.

We also don't try to keep up with Kendall and Chanandler's swift pace. It's not long before they've left us in the dust. In no time at all, Dale, Dolly, and I are almost startlingly alone on the path of the park that skirts Columbus Circle.

"How'd that bypass go, by the way?" Dale asks.

"Took nearly six hours," I answer and guide Dolly to my left side to give a guy on a bike a little more space to pass. "His heart was a mess, but Weller managed."

"I knew that surgery was going to be complicated. It's why I called you to come in, even though you were second call."

"Wait…I wasn't the only anesthesiologist on call?"

"Blake Houston was first call."

"You bastard." I purposefully shove him with my free hand.

"Hey," he says with a chuckle as he finds his balance again. "You and I both know Blakey boy would've only caused Weller more stress. He's too new. Too young. He still needs time to get his feet wet before he can handle the big-boy surgeries."

All I can do is sigh and keep jogging.

"Wait…are you pissed at me for calling you in?" Dale asks, a smile firmly intact on his face. I've known this man for years, and unless he has a gunshot victim bleeding out on his ER table, taking anything seriously isn't his forte.

Which is why I don't even dignify him with a response. Instead, I focus on running. *And mentally thinking about what it would've been like if I'd actually gotten to wake up* with *Sammy.*

"All right," Dale announces about a mile into our six-mile run. "What's your deal today, Philips?"

"What are you talking about?"

"You know exactly what I'm talking about," he states. "You never get pissed when I call you in, you're never this fucking silent on our runs, and you currently have quite the look on your face."

I scoff. "I don't have a look."

"Trust me, you have a look." Dale snorts. "Though, I can't decide if it's constipation or something else entirely. You're a difficult man to read."

"Why are all you ER doctors so obsessed with everyone else's bowel function? It's deranged."

"Gut health is at the foundation of everything. It's smart medicine," he retorts, and his grin is cheeky. "So…is that it? Are you constipated, Noah?

Because I got your back, man. I'll prescribe you the good stuff. Have you shitting in no time."

"I don't need your black-market laxatives." I elbow him in the side, and he blesses my ears with a painful grunt.

"Then what's the deal?" he questions, still holding his ribs while keeping up with my pace. When I don't respond, he adds, "Just so you know, the instant we catch up with Kendall, even if it's at the end of all six miles, I'm going to ensure that she rides your ass about this until you break."

Son of bitch.

"I… Fuck, I really don't think I should tell you this."

"Tell me anyway. That'd be so fun. Plus, it'd save you unnecessary torture from my scary wife."

I roll my eyes.

"C'mon, Philips. Tell ole Papa Bear what's got you in a tizzy."

Dale is one of my closest friends, but he's also annoying as fuck. I waver for ten seconds on whether I want to tell him what's on my mind because I know, without a shadow of a doubt, it'll have consequences.

Unfortunately, so will keeping it to myself.

"You know the woman I told you about?"

"The woman you told me about?" he repeats, craning his neck to meet my eyes. When I don't respond, he furrows his brow for a long moment before his mouth forms a perfect circle. "Oh…*the woman.* The *only* woman you talk about. Single mom, walks on water, is the key to your soul's everlasting happiness? Yeah, I think I've heard of her."

"Why do you have to be such an asshole?"

"It's in my DNA. I'm sorry. But, seriously, you've been mooning over her for, what? A year?"

"Not quite."

"It sure as hell feels like it," he comments with a shit-eating grin. "I mean, I can't deny there's a part of me that misses the good old days when Noah Philips was hot on the prowl."

"That was like five years ago." Shortly after my father passed away, I went through a bit of a phase. Lots of bars. Lots of nightclubs. Lots of women. I'm not proud of any of it, but in hindsight, I'm certain it had a lot to do with grief and the stress that came with suddenly being the sole caregiver for my dear sister.

Thankfully, I grew the fuck up.

"Five years ago? That's it?" Dale questions, but it's not a question at all. "Damn. It feels like a lifetime ago."

"You're a shit friend, you know that?"

"I'm a good, very married friend who enjoyed living vicariously through your debauchery."

My debauchery. I grimace. That's definitely a time in my life I have no desire to repeat. Or think about, if I'm honest.

"Plus, you don't have to hear my wife complaining about how you never go for any of the women she wants to set you up with," he inserts and nudges me with his elbow. "Trust me, it's a serious undertaking having to keep Kendall from doing something rash like putting you on Match.com."

Truth be told, the women his wife tries to set me up with are exactly like her. Which, nothing against Kendall, but she's not my type.

"I can't help it that I'm particular," I comment.

"You're not particular, Noah. You literally only have eyes for one fucking woman."

He's not exactly wrong. Sammy is the first woman who has grabbed my attention in a really long time. There's just something about her that…I don't know…ensnares me. Pulls me in. She's beautiful and funny and smart, and she's real and raw and genuine.

She's all the things I look for in a woman, plus a million other things I never imagined were possible.

"So…" Dale pauses to look over at me. "Are you going to tell me what happened with her, or am I supposed to guess?"

"Last night…" I pause my mouth but keep my legs moving, glancing briefly over at Dale.

"Last night…" he repeats, his eyes trying to search mine while simultaneously trying to stay on the jogging path.

"Last night…we slept together."

"What?!" Dale stops running so suddenly, I nearly trip over Dolly as she turns back to look at him. Not even a second later, we've all come to a dead stop, and the lunatic is throwing his hands in the air and shouting, "Hell yes! What a damn relief! I thought I'd be on my deathbed and still hear you longing for her."

"I stand by my words." I point at him hostilely. "You're a shit friend."

"I'm sorry!" he exclaims, and his always cocky face turns down in apology. "I'm sorry. I just… I'm shocked, okay? And I'm also confused."

"Why are *you* confused?"

"Because if you finally got the girl, why the hell do you look like you lost her?"

"I had to leave her in the middle of the night because *you* called me in. She was half asleep when I left, and I haven't talked to her since." I glare at him. "Plus…I know she's been seeing another guy too. I think she'd even been on a date with him before I saw her last night."

"Ooh, intrigue."

I scowl. "Oh yeah, it's the best."

"Relax, bud." He claps one hand on my shoulder. "At least she gave you a shot last night, right?"

"What's your point?"

"My point is that you're in the game. Now it's your job to prove to her that you're the guy she wants to win. You feel me?"

"It's a little heavy on the sports metaphors, but I get the point."

"No other dude stands a chance if Dr. Noah Philips lays it all on the line."

I smile and shake my head before punching him in the shoulder. "Come on. Let's run."

"Good idea, sweetheart. Now that you're done swimming in your feelings, maybe you'll be able to concentrate so we can catch up to my wife."

I scoff. Catch up to his wife? Get real. That's never going to happen.

Dale laughs. "Yeah, I know. In my dreams, right?"

Yep.

And in my dreams? Sammy Baker.

I unlock the door to my apartment and unclip Dolly's leash, and she heads straight over to her dog bed by the window and stretches out.

"I take it you're tired too, huh?" I question through a chuckle. Her answer is to nuzzle her face between her paws and close her eyes.

If my life were that simple, I'd be doing the same. Between the early wake-up and running six miles and internal worrying over not hearing back from Sammy, I'm running on E—truly the definition of dirty, hungry, and tired.

The first two are easily solved with some food and a shower.

And the third is far more complicated when, deep down, I'm waiting to hear back from Sammy.

But she's a single mom with two boys, and her life doesn't come with a lot of free time. If I want to be with her, I need to get used to coming after a few things on her priority list. That includes hearing back from her when I send her a message.

At least, that's what I'm telling myself.

I could be immaturely worried and jump to conclusions that Sammy isn't really the person I think she is and that she's too busy to answer me because she's on the phone with *Gavin* or something. But that wouldn't be fair to the woman I care about.

Not to mention, the last person I want to think about is that douche in the suit.

Sure, I might be biased when it comes to Sammy, and it might sound real fucking petty of me to write a guy off as a prick without even knowing him, but from the first moment I laid eyes on Gavin in the emergency room a few weeks ago, I didn't like him.

There's something disingenuous I can't quite put my finger on about the way he does things.

And I may not know anything else about the dynamics of Sammy and me and how best to make her life easier, but I sure as hell know that's my goal.

I look over at Dolly once more—she's already sound asleep—and decide to do something about being dirty and hungry. Those things are at least entirely under my control.

Down the hall and into the bathroom, I strip out of my clothes and hop into the shower. The warm water feels good against my skin, and I make quick work of cleaning up.

Once I'm out, dried off, and have tossed on a pair of boxer briefs and lounge pants, I head back into the kitchen to make a quick sandwich. Dolly barely opens her eyes to see what I'm doing, and I know she must be tired when she doesn't even bother waking up to beg for half of my food.

As I spread some mayo over a piece of white bread, my phone pings with a notification, and I snag it off the counter with quick hands.

Though, when I see the sender, the twinge I caused in my neck with my over-excitement feels a little less worth it.

It's Chase. Not Sammy. *How anticlimactic.*

Chase: You busy Friday? Want to get the canine lovers together for a bit?

Ever since Dolly found her boyfriend Benji on a fateful day in Central Park, I've been blessed with the friendship of his owners, Brooke and Chase. And because of Dolly and Benji's propensity to get all mopey and shit if they go too long without seeing each other, we've developed a routine of getting them together at least once a week. Sometimes it's more, sometimes they have what Chase loves to call "conjugal visits," but without fail, it's always at least one time per week.

Me: I should be free after four. My surgery schedule is morning-heavy.

I set my phone back down on the counter to toss some cheese and lunch meat on my bread, and when my phone pings again, I mindlessly pick it up and open the message.

Sammy: I'll be honest. I barely remember you leaving this morning. God, I hope I didn't do or say anything crazy...

Holy shit. I bobble the phone between my hands like a ping-pong ball between paddles as exhilaration floods my veins.

And the stupid smile on my face cannot be contained as I forget about my sandwich and type out a message back.

Me: You just said something about how you wanted to see me again, before doing a live rendition of that "So Long, Farewell" song from **The Sound of Music.** *Nothing major.*

Sammy: YOU'RE LYING.

At this point, my smile is downright embarrassing. If Dolly were awake, even she would be making fun of me for it.

Me: I am definitely lying.

Sammy: Very funny. LOL. And just so you know, I had a good time last night too.

Goose bumps cover my skin. Suddenly, text messaging isn't good enough. I have to hear her voice. With one tap to the screen, a trilling ring fills my ears.

Another one follows suit. But by the third ring, Sammy puts me out of my misery and answers.

"Are you seriously calling me right now?" she questions, but her voice drips with amusement. "Like, on the actual phone?"

I chuckle. "You don't like phone calls?"

"It's not so much that I don't like phone calls, but that I didn't know people still called each other. It feels like we're utilizing an ancient form of technology."

"What can I say, Sam? I'm Grandpa Noah. It was either this or a telegram. And personally, I wanted to hear your voice."

"Yeah?" she asks softly, and I know that honesty here is the only way to put the punctuation on my motive.

This isn't a game for me. And Sammy should know it.

"Sammy, I really like you. Hell, since the moment I left your apartment this morning, I've been thinking about you. So, yeah. I wanted to hear your voice."

Silence stretches between us for what feels like an eternity, but for something this important, I'm willing to bend until she breaks.

"I've been thinking about you too." Her voice is still quiet, and I can't decide if it's because she's unsure about my feelings for her or if she's unsure about her feelings for me.

Frankly, neither of those seems like a good option.

Last night wasn't some casual-hookup bullshit for me. It was real. It meant something. And I'm going to prove it to her.

"When can I see you again?" I ask, choosing to show her how serious I am through actions rather than words.

"My life is pretty dang complicated, Noah," she answers on a sigh that borders on a cry. "Honestly, I'm not sure when I'll have an actual night off without the boys again, and—"

"Sammy, I'm not expecting that," I interject gently. "We can do something together *with* the boys."

"*Oh.* Are you sure? I, well… This is kind of embarrassing, but I thought you were talking about a date."

"I was. I *am.* But when the woman you're interested in is the mother to two awesome boys, dates come in all shapes and sizes."

"Noah."

"Aren't you off on Sundays?" I question. "There's a Yankees game this Sunday, and I know I can get four tickets for us from one of the doctors I work with."

"You want to take me and my two heathens to a Yankees game?"

"Of course I do."

"That's…really sweet of you. Possibly a little sadistic, but also very, very sweet."

"Is that a yes, then?"

"Yeah. It's a yes," she says, and I love the way I can hear an actual smile in her voice. "Though, I'm just letting you know that the last time Chase took the boys to a Yankees game, there was a bit of a tussle with one of the mascots that ended in tears."

"Let me guess… Seth initiated it?"

"Of course he did." She guffaws. "He's my instigator."

"Who cried, then? Grant?"

She scoffs. "No. The mascot."

I laugh. "Well, I can promise you we'll handle whatever they throw our way. And we'll even manage to have a good time too."

"I can't wait. But I'm not telling the boys about this until the day of. Otherwise, I'll have to live through one thousand questions about the Yankees game for the whole week. Every minute of every day, they'll be asking me if it's Yankees game day. The struggle of having kids who haven't quite grasped a sense of time is real, Noah."

I chuckle again. "I fully support your decision."

"So… I guess I'll see you Sunday…"

Hell yes, you will. "See you then, Sammy."

When we end the call a few moments later, I may as well be walking on cloud fucking nine. I barely register the fact that Chase texted back to confirm our doggy playdate for Friday evening, and my sandwich is no longer the center of my world.

I'm officially in the game with Sammy Baker.

Sunday can't come soon enough.

Chapter
Seventeen

Tuesday, May 17th

"That went better than expected," Dr. Weller announces, stepping up to the sink beside mine as I finish scrubbing my hands.

"I'm just happy I managed to keep her blood pressure stable for that last hour."

Valve replacements are a difficult surgery as it is, but performing them on a ten-year-old girl who should have a whole life ahead of her is in an entirely different bracket.

I'm used to surgery on kids, but the difficult cases? They never get easier.

"You and me both," he remarks. "It's always a blessing when I've got you at the head of my table."

"Aw, come on, Milton. If you keep saying sweet things like that to me, I might have to buy you lunch."

"Smartass." He chuckles, and I give him a sturdy pat on the back before I head through the OR exit doors.

My stomach grumbles as I make my way down the hall, and one quick glance to my watch explains why. It's nearing noon, and I've been *up and at 'em* since five this morning. Thankfully, this was my last surgery of the day, and all that's left are patient rounds.

"Dr. Philips, do you mind signing off on some orders for me?" Darla, one of my favorite recovery nurses, asks when I make a pit stop at the nurses sta-tion. "The patient in Room Eight needs an extra dose of Zofran to curb his nausea. And the patient in Room Three could use a little fluid boost before I send her to the ICU."

"You got it." I head over to one of the empty computers to make good on her requests.

It only takes a few minutes to put her orders in, and before I know it, I'm three charts deep into the seven I have to review for rounds. I'm pulling up the fourth when my phone vibrates in my pocket, and since modern tech-nology has allowed my phone to double as my hospital pager, I don't waste any time before checking it.

My brow furrows over two missed text messages and a voice mail from an unknown number. Generally speaking, these days, if someone leaves me a voice mail, it's because they actually need to talk to me.

Phone to my ear, I listen intently. "Hi. Noah. It's Ashley. It's…uh…been a while. I, well, I need to see you. Can you call me back? This is my new num-ber, by the way."

I shake my head and pull the phone away from my ear, pushing delete on the message without a second thought. No offense to Ashley, but I have no reason to call her back or meet up with her again. It's been months since I last saw her, and frankly, there's only one woman I want to see. Her name isn't Ashley.

Quickly, I scroll over to my text inbox. The first message is from Mary—*I just realized I missed your FaceTime call this morning. Kara was in really good spirits, and I took her to that little pancake place she loves, and now we're at Bryant Park.*

I type back quickly, a small smile lifting the corner of my lips.

Me: I'm glad she's having a good day. Give her a big hug for me, and I'll check in with you this evening.

The second is a page from the hospital, alerting me to an additional med or-der I need to fill before logging out. I set the phone down and click around from our chart management system to the med portal, and then back into the charts. My phone vibrates loudly on the surface of the desk just as I'm getting to the meat and potatoes of this patient's latest bloodwork, and I grumble to myself.

Jeez. Maybe I'll get through these charts today if—

Annoyance evaporates when I see the caller on the screen, and a big-ass smile takes over my face. *Talk about a pleasant fucking surprise.*

"Hey, Sammy," I greet eagerly.

"Hey there," she says, her affection tentative but present. "So…I… Are you at work?" I have a feeling this phone call is in some way related to her making an effort, and I truly want to do my best to nurture it.

"I am. What's going on?"

"Are you busy?"

"I'm not too busy to talk to Sammy Baker," I say through a smile. "I'm just finishing up going over some charts and about to go to lunch." A flurry of sudden concern makes my brows furrow. "Why? Is everything okay?"

"Yeah, yeah. Everything is good," she answers in a rush. "I'm just leaving my dentist appointment, and it's in that medical building connected to St. Luke's… and I have a few hours before I have to get the boys from school and go to work, and I just thought I'd call you and see if you…I don't know… wanted to get lunch or something?" she asks. But then she quickly adds, "No pressure, though, okay? Like, seriously. No big deal if you can't. I totally understand."

Her adorable ramble makes me feel like a hormonal teenager all over again. *I've got one hell of a crush.*

"I'd love to buy you lunch, and I know just the place."

"You do?"

"Oh yeah. Have you heard of the award-winning, prestigious, incomparable St. Luke's Café?"

She snorts. "You want to buy me a cafeteria lunch?"

"Listen, Sam, you might not know this, but their chicken tenders are a delicacy. They're basically caviar. People come from all over the city just to eat them."

"Stop." Her giggle is fucking music to my ears.

"Oh, I'll prove it to you if you're willing to meet me."

"I can meet you in the cafeteria—I mean, *prestigious café with the caviar chicken tenders*—in about fifteen minutes."

"Can't wait."

"So, this is an on-call room?" Sammy questions as she pops the last bite of her chicken tender into her mouth. "I honestly never thought I'd get to see what a real one looks like."

"A real one?"

"Oh yeah. I'm an expert in the pretend ones. When I was pregnant with Seth, I watched *ER*, *Grey's Anatomy*, *House*, and *General Hospital* like it was my job." She snorts. "As you can imagine, the second pregnancy with a two-year-old already on my hip went a little differently."

"So, how does this one compare?" I ask with a teasing lilt.

With only a bed, small table with two chairs, a tiny kitchenette, and a basic bathroom, I'm almost positive this is lackluster compared to the ones on her shows. In fact, a part of me feels a little bad that this is where I brought her to eat our lunch.

She shrugs. "Well…it *is* bigger than the ones on *Grey's Anatomy*. But they only served the purpose of sex, so that's no surprise."

I wince. I hope she doesn't think I brought her back here with some pseudo-freaky idea of seducing her. For me, this place is about as unsexy as it gets. When I'm sleeping in here, I usually smell like vending machine burritos and have been on shift for twenty-four hours straight.

"In my defense, I only brought you back here because the cafeteria was packed." Packed with people I know—*cough, Dale*—who would never let me enjoy time with her in peace.

When he saw us in line to check out, his expression was already a mixture of "Holy shit" and "Hell yes" and "I'm ready to be a nosy dick and insert myself into your lunch." I knew it would only get worse the longer we sat there, so I made the snap decision to take Sammy somewhere else to eat inside the hospital.

The thing is, if you're not a doctor or a nurse or a someone with a strong stomach who's not averse to bodily fluids and the like while you're enjoying a meal, the options are kind of limited. My on-call room felt like the only viable place.

"I think you got too much food." Sammy glances at me and then pointedly at the two half-eaten takeout containers sitting in front of us before she taps the top of the additional two takeout containers we haven't touched.

"I just wanted to make sure you had options. It takes at least four lunches at the prestigious St. Luke's Café to settle on your favorites."

"Four whole lunches, huh?"

"I mean, I'm willing to put in the legwork of having those lunches with you."

Her laugh is a cute, melodic giggle. "Your tune might change when I tell you that I only give the chicken tenders a six on a scale of one to ten."

"What? Only a six?" I feign shocked eyes before tapping my chin dramatically. "You know, I think our usual chef is on vacation or something. That's probably why they're not up to snuff today."

"Oh, okay," she mutters with a knowing smile and stands up from her chair to toss her takeout container in the trash. She makes a pit stop at the sink to wash her hands, and I can't stop myself from taking her in. Her full hips and strong thighs and the tiny bump of a stomach that's carried and birthed two kids.

Sammy has the body of a woman, and fuck if I don't love everything about it.

"What are you looking at?" she asks, her hip hitched against the counter of the sink now. Her brow is furrowed, and her eyes search mine.

I pause, wavering on my choice of words before eventually getting straight to the point. "You. You're beautiful."

I stare at her in rapt attention, watching as a hint of a blush forms on her cheeks. She glances down at her shoes and digs her bottom teeth into her lip before she brings her gaze back to mine.

"You know, you're kind of beautiful too, Dr. Philips."

I scoff. Sammy points one index finger at me before heading over to the bed and sitting down. "Women basically fawn over you. The cashier in the cafeteria nearly had to wipe drool off her face when you were paying for our lunch, and more than once, I've found myself admiring you from a distance before I even realized it was you."

I shake my head.

"But the thing that makes you really beautiful is the gentle way you care about people. Brooke and me and my kids and your sister and your friends. I've never heard you speak a bad word about anyone, and we live in New York, for Pete's sake. 'Fuck' is practically an adjective."

"Sam." I stand up from my chair to walk over to the bed. I sit down beside her, and Sammy's gaze locks with mine. "I don't give a shit about the assholes. Right now, quite frankly, I don't give a shit about anyone but you."

"Noah. My life is…"

"Sammy, don't overthink it." I reach out with one hand to gently grip her thigh. "Just feel it."

"Just feel it?" Her throat bobs as she swallows hard around her words.

"I care about you." I lift my hand to caress the smooth skin of her face and tuck a piece of her hair behind her ear as I do. "I've been into you since the moment I met you."

"You have?"

I nod and run the pad of my thumb across her full bottom lip.

"But…but…why did you take so long to show me?"

"I don't know… I guess it's because I didn't want to push you into something you weren't ready for," I answer honestly. "I respect you, Sammy, and I felt like you deserved space to find your way. Space to focus on your kids and yourself. Space to find yourself after going through such a hard divorce."

"But you think I'm ready now?"

"I don't know, Sammy. Only you can know that. I guess…I just…I can't keep denying my feelings for you."

She doesn't say anything, but she surprises the hell out of me by leaning forward and pressing her mouth to mine.

A groan escapes my throat when she deepens the kiss, and my taste buds awaken with the feel of her tongue and the taste of the lemonade she drank with lunch.

Somewhere deep inside me, there are drifting thoughts about *whether this is way too fast* and *what this means* and *what she's trying to convey* and *the fact that I don't know if she's still dating other men*, but all of it disappears in a *whoosh* when our sitting position turns horizontal.

I wrap my big hands around the curves of her ass and pull her body tighter against my chest. My cock is already hard at the feel of her soft body against mine, and it only grows harder beneath my scrub pants when she straddles my hips and starts grinding herself against me.

"Fuck," I mutter, and a moan jumps from her delicate throat.

The intense need for her overpowers any rational thought I have inside my head, and before I know it, I'm flipping her onto her back and pressing my hard cock between her still-clothed thighs.

She moans again, and her eyes are heated as they lock with mine.

And *fuck me*, she looks so beautiful like this. Her hair fanned out over the pillow and her breasts heaving up and down with each erratic breath. Her lips are swollen from kissing, and her cheeks are flushed the most gorgeous shade of pink.

She's a modern Aphrodite. The kind of woman men used to spend months and months sculpting in marble. Soft and supple and feminine. Fucking perfect.

"Noah," Sammy pants, and she reaches both of her hands up to tightly grip my face. "For the love of everything, please tell me you have a condom, or else…I don't know what I'll do, but I know it won't be pretty."

I laugh. I can't help it. "I have a condom."

"Thank everything!" she exclaims, and she slides out from underneath me to hop off the bed and start removing her clothes. When she glances back to the bed to find me watching her, she snaps an impatient finger in my direction. "Get moving, Philips."

I smile. But I also do as I'm told and remove my scrubs and boxer briefs and even pull a condom out of my wallet in the process.

Sammy is naked now as she climbs back onto the bed to straddle my hips, and my brain short-circuits for multiple seconds as my eyes take in the beauty that is her.

Her breasts are full and heavy, and her lips are parted as she presses her hands to my chest and grinds herself against my cock. I don't have the condom on yet, and the feel of her warm and wet pussy sliding up and down my length is almost too much to bear.

"Fuck," I mutter and reach out with two strong hands to grip her thighs to pause her movements so I can glide the condom over my already throbbing cock.

She looks down at me with an intensity I can't explain, and all I can do is grip her thighs and slowly slide myself inside her.

When I reach halfway, I pause, and a moan escapes her lips. Her thighs start to shake with need. "More," she begs. "More."

I push myself a little deeper.

And a little deeper.

And then, I push myself to the hilt with one fluid but strong thrust of my hips. I'm deep inside her now, and I don't think I've ever felt anything better in my whole fucking life. Her pussy spasms around me, and her head falls back as she tries to seat herself even deeper.

She feels so good. Insanely good, actually, but as I take in the sight of her, there's something I want to do…something I need to do.

I slide my hands beneath her thighs and hips and lift her up with steady arms.

She starts to protest, but I don't listen. And I certainly don't stop until Sammy's thighs are spread out over my face, her bare, wet, perfect pussy at eye level with me.

"Noah."

"I'm sorry, but this is more for me than it is for you," I say and take one long lick, pressing my tongue firmly against her core. She tastes sweet and tangy, and it's not long before I'm sucking and eating her with the kind of fervor that induces sweet whimpers to spill from her lips.

Her breasts bounce above me, and I reach up to grab them in my big hands. Her body shakes with desire, and I slide my tongue inside her as deep as it will go.

Fuck me. This woman. I could live off her pussy for the rest of my life and die a happy man.

She's so wet and warm, and I suck at her swollen clit when I feel how close her body is to going over the edge.

Her breasts heave against the palms of my hands, and her thighs grip my face tightly as she starts to grind her hips against me.

She wants to come, and lucky for her, that's exactly what I want to happen too. Making Sammy feel good, feel pleasure, is quickly becoming one of my favorite fucking pastimes.

The instant her body tightens up with her release, I suck even harder on her clit, forcing her orgasm to last as long as it possibly can.

I'm still hard and throbbing inside the condom, and the moment I'm sure her orgasm has started to subside, I lift her body back up and set her straight on my cock, thrusting myself back inside her in one steady, fluid motion.

Goddamn.

She's so warm now, she's borderline hot. And I can feel her wetness through the rubber.

"Ride me," I tell her, and her eyes pop open to meet mine. Her lips are still parted, and her breaths are still coming out in erratic pants. "Ride me, Sammy," I repeat. "Show me how bad you want to come on my cock."

She responds by doing exactly that. With her hands pressed to my chest, she moves her hips up and down my length, and it feels so damn good, my eyes are tempted to roll back inside my fucking head.

But I don't let them. No way. This perfect visual of Sammy riding me is something I refuse to miss.

When the urge to fuck her hard, to push myself as deep as I can go, becomes too strong, I flip her onto her back and do exactly that.

"Sammy," I say, but it comes out more like a growl. "You drive me fucking crazy."

"*Yes.*"

It's all she says, but it's the way she says it and the way her hands greedily grip at my ass and the way she spreads her thighs even farther for me and the way her eyes peer deep inside mine that really push me over the edge.

I can no longer be soft or slow. I just have to…claim her with my cock. I have to show her that she's mine.

And that's exactly what I do. I push myself inside her over and over *and over* again. Sammy's back arches and her lips part and incoherent moans spill from her lips, and I'm following her right off the cliff and coming hard enough to blur my vision.

Goddamn. That was…

"Holy shit, Noah. What was that?"

Those are the first words either of us has spoken in I don't know how long. Five? Ten minutes? All I know is that we're currently just lying here on the bed, me on my back and Sammy's body spread out on top of mine. Even my cock is still inside her.

"I don't know," I mutter. "But sign me up for more of it."

She giggles at that. "So…like…*Grey's Anatomy* wasn't lying, huh? Doctors really do have sex in the on-call rooms."

That spurs a laugh to vibrate through my chest. "No. Not exactly."

"Oh, c'mon, Noah," she retorts and leans up on her elbows to meet my eyes. "Don't lie to me. How many times have you had sex in one of these on-call rooms?"

"Honestly?"

She nods.

"Once."

"So, twice now."

"No." I shake my head. "Once, as in once."

"I was your first sex inside an on-call room?"

I nod again. But I also grin when I note the proud smile on her lips. "You like the idea of that, Sam?"

"Maybe." She shrugs, and I playfully squeeze her ass.

"Just so you know, so do I," I tell her and mean every word. "Now, even though I would love to stay here like this with you all damn day, I'm pretty sure we're going to have to get up and get dressed. I don't want to make you late for picking up the boys from school."

She doesn't say anything, but she does offer a soft smile before leaning down to press a kiss to my lips before she hops off the bed and starts gathering her clothes.

I make quick work of the condom and head into the small bathroom to wash my hands.

But when I step back out, I find Sammy sliding on her jeans, and there's a small part of me that feels guilty for letting things move this fast between us. The last thing I want her to think is that this is all about sex for me.

Because it's not.

This is about so much more than that.

"By the way," I state as I slip on my boxer briefs. "I got the Yankees tickets for Sunday."

"Really?" She grins up at me as she does the zipper on her boots. "The boys are going to be so excited."

They're not the only ones who are excited. Though, my reasons are probably a lot different from theirs. I could give a *shit* about the Yankees.

As I toss my scrubs back on, I waver on whether to broach the sex topic or push my luck and see if I can get her to meet me for a coffee or lunch again later this week. But I know better than to corner someone whose life already tends to make them skittish.

No, aside from making my presence undeniably accessible, I'm going to have to wait it out and let Sammy follow her own map to me.

I just hope she's good with directions.

Chapter Eighteen

Friday, May 20ᵗʰ

The Friday evening Central Park crowd is getting busier by the minute as more New Yorkers head out to enjoy an evening stroll with their dogs after work.

Of course, our dogs don't notice. When Benji and Dolly are together, they only have eyes for each other.

Chase throws a tennis ball across the grass, and both Benji and Dolly race toward it with the kind of energy I haven't had since I was an eighteen-year-old college kid.

When they both reach the ball, Benji backs off and lets Dolly take the win. With the ball firmly in her mouth and the wind ruffling the pink bow on her collar, she prances in a circle, wagging her tail toward her German shepherd boyfriend.

"Always the gentleman, for me and every other girl," Brooke comments with a smile. "It's a shame more men aren't like Benji."

"Hey now," Chase chides. "You and I both know I treat you like a damn princess."

Brooke scoffs. "Maybe before. Now…now, you don't even love me."

My eyebrows draw together at this completely unprecedented lovers' quarrel.

Brooke and Chase are about as copesetic as it gets. This is completely out of character for them both.

"Don't love you anymore? Come on, you're kidding me, right?"

Brooke puts a defiant hand on her hip. "I am *not* kidding. A man who loves me wouldn't have refused to get his pregnant fiancée pizza last night."

"It was three in the morning!" he retorts on a laugh, and my shoulders settle back away from my ears. This makes way more sense. "I didn't get you pizza because nothing was open."

Brooke snorts and turns to me. "See? Nothing was open? This is New York, Noah. You tell me. Was there something open or not?"

I smile at the two human lovebirds while the two canine lovebirds run around together in one of the small fenced-in enclosures within Central Park. "Nope. No way. I'm not getting in the middle of this."

"How about I make sure you get your pizza tonight?" Chase offers, and Brooke shakes her head.

"Too late for that. My pizza craving has been replaced by chicken fried rice."

Chase chuckles and meets my eyes. "Interested in grabbing some Chinese with us?"

"I don't know, man," I answer with a knowing smile. "Not sure I can be around all this tension. I don't like when Mom and Dad fight."

"Oh, shut up, Noah," Brooke remarks on a giggle. "We're not fighting. We're just *discussing* how Chase needs to find a way to give in to his pregnant fiancée's every food whim, no matter what time of night it is."

"You know, Brooke, you always used to be so sweet," I tease her with a sarcastic smirk. "Pregnancy has changed you."

"Yeah, well, you try waddling around with a bowling ball between your legs and tell me how that works out for you."

"Remind me… How much longer until you have this baby?"

"Too long," she grumbles, and Chase wraps his arm around her shoulders, tucking her close to his side.

"June twentieth isn't that far away, babe."

"Speak for yourself," Brooke grumbles. "It might as well be a year."

It's more than apparent that Brooke has reached the uncomfortable part of her pregnancy, and honestly, I can't say I blame her. A month probably feels like a long-ass time when your petite frame is being stretched to its limits and the baby's head is descending into the birth canal.

Benji barks, and all three of us look at the opposite end of the fenced-in area to find our two dogs lying beside their tennis ball, both of their faces staring toward us with expectancy.

Brooke huffs out a sigh and rubs a hand over her belly. "Pretty sure he's calling you guys. Not me."

I laugh, but I also don't hesitate to jog across the grass to assist.

I pick up the ball and toss it toward the other side, cognizant to throw it safely away from Brooke, and both dogs are back to the races, sprinting toward the ball with enthusiasm.

Chase wraps his arms around Brooke, hugging her back to his chest, and the smile on her face as he presses a gentle kiss to her cheek is nothing short of sweet. Being a third wheel in our group isn't anything new for me. And honestly, it doesn't really bother me. If anything, it makes me hopeful that one day I'll have what they have with someone.

Someone named Sammy.

I'm man enough to admit that when I think about Sammy and the way she makes me feel, it's not hard for me to imagine a future with her. She's the kind of woman you cherish. The kind of woman that makes you want to settle down.

And if I'm truly honest, it didn't take more than meeting her once for me to know that.

Seven months ago, Brooke and Chase invited me to dinner, and my world changed forever.

I'd been to their apartment to share a meal with them a dozen times or more, but that night, Brooke's sister Sammy was to attend too.

Sammy, late as usual, knocked on the door while both of the hosts were busy, so I went to answer it. Her arms were full of desserts she'd brought from the restaurant, and a magazine with an article about Brooke she wanted to share hung from her mouth because she had nothing else to carry it with. Expecting me to be Brooke, she called me an ore-hay—*a whore in pig Latin*—before looking up, and when the sound of my chuckle brought her startled aqua-green eyes to mine, she captured a part of me I've never gotten back.

With hope, humor, and embarrassment warring in her eyes, right then, she dropped the magazine and uttered a curse so creative it'll live in my brain forever.

"Well, that's fucktacular."

My thought was immediate, and I haven't changed my mind since.

This is the kind of woman you marry.

And a few days ago, the last time I saw her when we had lunch together in my on-call room and it turned into another round of mind-blowing sex, I had the thought again.

The truth is, I have it all the time.

We've managed to stay in touch through text messages and phone calls since then, and I take that as a good sign. Without hesitation, I pull my phone out of my pocket and let her know I'm thinking about her.

Me: Did you survive Grant's field trip today?

I'm pleasantly surprised when she responds a minute later.

Sammy: Remind me never to volunteer to chaperone ever again. If I smack my head or get amnesia or something, this is your most important task.

Me: LOL. It went that well, huh?

Sammy: Let's just say, Grant's teacher looked like she'd aged ten years by the time we got all forty kindergarteners back on the bus. Also, this morning, I made the grave mistake of telling the boys about the Yankees game on Sunday. So, it's been quite the day.

Me: I take it they're excited?

Sammy: Excited is putting it mildly, Noah. Honestly, coming into work this evening was a breath of fresh air because of all the "excitement." Grant is convinced he can find a way to get the entire Yankees team to sign his cast, and Seth pretty much tore up my living room trying to make a poster to bring to the game. I'm pretty sure Zoe is going to be playing Twenty Questions: Yankees Edition all night.

I smile as I type out a response.

Me: What does Seth's poster say?

Sammy: "My name Seth Brown. I luv Yankes basball!" I didn't have the heart (or the patience) to tell him about the spelling errors.

Me: That's fucking adorable. And it sounds like Zoe is about to have quite the night.

Sammy: Honestly, Noah. She could probably use some "sorrows, sorrows" prayers.

An audible laugh jumps from my lungs at the reference to *Queen Charlotte*, the Netflix show we decided to watch at the same time on Wednesday when we were on the phone together and Sammy had put the boys to bed.

"What's so funny?"

I look up to find that Brooke and Chase have now made their way over to me, and Benji and Dolly are taking a water break near the bowls we always bring for them.

I can't be sure, but it feels like Brooke is craning her neck to check the screen of my phone, and I quickly lock it. "Oh, nothing," I say with a shrug and slide my phone back into my pocket.

"It didn't seem like nothing. It seemed like you were having a full-fledged conversation *with someone.*" Brooke eyes me curiously. "Wait a minute…are you, like, texting with a woman?"

I don't really know what to say to that.

For one, the anger in her voice catches me off guard. And two, I have no idea what Sammy has told her sister about us, and I sure as shit am not going to be the one to spill the beans on something I'm not supposed to be spilling.

That's not my call to make.

"Seriously, Noah?" Brooke continues and puts one hand on her hip. "Are you seeing someone?"

"Uh…"

"Relax, Brooke," Chase chimes in on a laugh. "Pretty sure it's Noah's business, babe. Not yours."

"Not my business?" Brooke glares at her fiancé. "I've only been trying to hook him up with my sister for months and months, and the two of them can't seem to get their heads out of their asses long enough to realize they'd be perfect for each other, and he's texting some *woman*. He and Sammy slept together like a week ago, and now…what? Radio silence? They're just going to act like it didn't happen while he texts some *woman*?"

Slept together a week ago? Damn. I guess it's safe to say Sammy has told Brooke a little bit about us. But with the way Brooke keeps saying *woman* like it's a dirty word, I don't think Sammy told her much after that. *She thinks I'm two-timing Sammy like some kind of dirtbag.*

"Uh…Brooke?" Chase's eyes are wide with shock, and within a few seconds, her expression mirrors his.

"Oh no," she mutters and slaps a hand over her mouth. "Did I just say the quiet part out loud?"

Chase snorts. "Pretty much."

Truth be told, Brooke has been trying to set Sammy and me up for a while now. She always thinks she's being sneaky about it, but yeah, it's pretty fucking obvious. Though, this is definitely the first time she's voiced it out loud in front of me.

Brooke looks at me and then back at Chase and then at me again. "Just forget it. I'm pregnant and hormonal, and sometimes I say crazy things."

Chase cracks up, and I have to bite my bottom lip to fight my smile.

"Oh my gosh, you guys! Look at Benji and Dolly!" Brooke exclaims, pointing to where the two dogs are just lying down by the tennis ball again like they always do.

It's clear that she's desperate to change the topic of conversation, and there's a part of me that wants to leave her hanging for a little bit longer. But another part of me is too kind not to throw her a life vest. Especially when she thinks I'm treating her sister like a spring-break-style fling. I don't know if she knows Sammy's plans this weekend, but if she does, this should settle her doomsday imagination.

"Do you guys have plans on Sunday?" I question. "I'm going to the Yankees game, and I was wondering if I could drop Dolly off at your place to hang with Benji for a few hours so she doesn't get bored in the apartment while I'm gone."

"The Yankees game? On *Sunday?*" Brooke whips her head back toward me. "Who are you going with?" Her eyes are now narrowed, and her lips are pursed in straight-up skepticism. "Because I know someone else who is going to the Yankees game on Sunday."

Yep. Safe to say, she knows Sammy's plans.

"Well, they are playing the Mets." I laugh. "I'm sure a lot of New Yorkers are going to be there."

Brooke narrows her eyes. "Why do I get the feeling you're hiding something from me, Noah?"

"I'm not sure," I comment before walking away to take over ball-throwing for Chase. The dogs aren't even busy with the ball right now, but Brooke is a scary interrogator.

Thankfully, after I walk toward the opposite end of the grass, I discreetly glance back toward her and find her busy with something on her phone.

Cross-examination officially over.

Or so I thought.

After I chuck the ball toward Chase, and Benji and Dolly sprint in his direction, my phone vibrates in my pocket.

Sammy: Are you with my sister right now?

I quickly look over my shoulder to see that Brooke is now sitting on a park bench, her attention still on her phone.

Me: Yeah. I met her and Chase at Central Park so Benji and Dolly could play.

Sammy: Did you happen to tell her you're going to the Yankees game on Sunday?

Me: Yeah… I asked if Dolly could hang out at their place during the game because Brooke convinced herself I was texting with another woman when I was texting you. Sorry for bringing someone else in on our business.

Sammy: Pfft. It's not your fault that my sister is a nosy little biotch.

Me: I take it she's interrogating you, too?

Sammy: Yep. Her spidey senses have been activated. And I'm sorry for what's about to happen. Maybe you should consider grabbing Dolly and leaving the park?

At first, I'm confused by her text, but then, not even a minute later, Brooke's voice fills my ears. "Freaking finally!" she shouts at the top of her lungs, even fist-pumping the air as she stares down at her phone.

Safe to say, the news of Noah Philips and Sammy Baker has just been made official.

Fuck yes.

Chapter Nineteen

Sunday, May 22nd

At a little after nine in the morning, I head out of my apartment with Dolly happily walking beside me on her leash. With no work today and no emergency call-ins from work last night, I actually managed to sleep a solid eight hours.

The prancy pep in Dolly's step says she was thankful for the quiet night too.

The ride down our elevator is swift, and we're out on the sidewalk, with the rest of the Sunday morning crowd, in no time at all. New York in the spring is one of my favorite times of year, and this morning's sunny skies and warm breeze don't disappoint.

I stop by the food truck that's parked half a block from my building and grab a coffee for me and a few slices of bacon for Dolly before heading into the park.

Once Dolly's done her business, I plant us at a bench that's off the beaten path. She's already drooling for her bacon, and I smile down at her in amusement when I toss her a bite.

In true Dolly fashion, one bite isn't enough, and I end up feeding her all the bacon before I manage a sip of my coffee. She's persistent when it comes to food, that's for sure, but once she's certain all the meat is gone, she stretches out near my feet and busies herself with observing the crowd while her snout rests between her paws.

I lift my to-go cup to get some much-needed caffeine, but the first sip is interrupted by an incoming text.

Sammy: I have bad news. Seth woke up puking. :(I hate to cancel on the game today, but there's no way we can go now. Ugh. I'm so sorry, Noah. The kids are devastated.

Shit. Disappointment sits heavy in my stomach, but clearly, I understand. Kids get sick sometimes.

Me: No need to apologize, Sam. I'm sorry Seth is sick. Poor guy. Are you and Grant feeling okay?

Sammy: For now, we're both good, but I'm pretty sure we all need to quarantine inside the apartment and keep our germs to ourselves.

Me: Is there anything I can do to help?

Sammy. No, but I definitely appreciate the offer. Now, if you don't mind, I'm going to go clean up Seth's round three of puking while I field Grant's whines about the fact that we have to miss the game.

I almost send her another message, telling her to text or call me if she needs anything, but I know she's way too busy to be on her phone.

Though, it doesn't stop me from wishing I could be the man by her side, helping her right now, rather than the man sitting on this fucking park bench, who isn't doing anything at all.

But what the hell? Maybe I *can* be.

Sammy's face is full of shock as she answers the door in a white T-shirt and a pair of flannel pajama shorts and finds me standing on the other side. She looks stressed and flushed and unfuckingbelievably beautiful.

"Noah? What are you doing here?"

After running around all morning and most of the afternoon, I decided it was time to implement Operation "Be the Man by Sammy's Side," starting with an unannounced, six o'clock visit to bring her and the boys some sustenance.

I lift the bag of soup and bread I grabbed from a market near her building and hold it there. "I figured you wouldn't be thinking about feeding yourself, and selfishly…I wanted to see you. Is it okay that I'm here?"

"Of course it is." Sammy's laugh is half incredulity, half humor. "But are you sure you *want* to be here? Seth's doing a little better, but this bug must be derived from some Stephen King-type of stuff. It's been horrifying."

"I work in a hospital, Sam. Whatever you've seen, I've had my hands in it before." As she takes the bag of food and welcomes me in, I make sure to distinguish on a chuckle, "I've washed them since, though, I assure you."

"I've also washed my hands today. *A lot*, in fact." Sammy smiles, but it quickly turns into a frown. "God, I'm so sorry about canceling on the game. And trust me, the boys weren't happy we had to cancel either. Grant's been mopey all day, and Seth found time to gripe about it in between his rounds of puke and rally."

"We'll find another day to go," I counter as I follow her into the kitchen. "I can easily get tickets for another game so the boys can get their Yankees fill and Seth can make use of that poster he worked so hard on."

"I just…I feel so badly." She sighs and sets the bag of food on the island that now stands between us. "And I can't believe how many times the kids have been sick this year. Do they sell memberships to doctor's offices? Hospitals? Because I'm starting to think I better sign up now if they do." Sammy laughs, but self-deprecation is rife in every peal, and I can't stop myself from rounding the island and pulling her into my arms.

"Hey, it's okay." I hug her long enough for her body to relax against mine.

"I'm a mess, Noah," she whispers against my chest as she wraps her arms around my waist.

"You're not a mess. You're a mom who just spent the last eight hours cleaning up puke."

"Technically, I've been cleaning up puke since four this morning." She snorts. "But who's counting, right?"

I chuckle and press a soft kiss to the top of her head. "Fourteen hours of vomit duty would push anyone over the edge."

"I also made the stupid mistake of opening the hospital bill from Grant's arm." She takes a step away from my embrace to point to the opened envelope on the counter. "I nearly passed out when I saw how much I owe."

"Listen, don't do anything with that bill yet. I'll talk to administration," I offer immediately. "I'm sure I can get them to knock it down."

Frankly, there's a good chance I can get Dr. McCormick to write off Grant's surgery as pro bono. And if I can't, I'll anonymously pay some of it. I know Sammy's doing well for herself at the restaurant, but she's still a single mom on a budget in one of the most expensive cities in the world. I'll do whatever I can to make sure this isn't another thing on her already-full plate.

"Thank you. Seriously. I…I don't know how I'm going to handle all of this, but I will."

"I'll help. Anytime you let me."

"Be careful saying that. I may just overwhelm you."

"Well, that works out perfectly because I'm looking to be whelmed a lot more than I currently am." I flash a wink at her. "I'm sadly underwhelmed, to be honest."

"Oh, *c'mon*, Noah."

"What? I'm a single guy in my forties. My only responsibilities include my job and my dog. And we both know Dolly gives zero hassle. I could use a little more difficulty in my life, you know? It's character building."

Sammy chews at her bottom lip before waving toward the bag of food. "Well, if you're going to stay, the least I can do is heat up the food you brought so you can sit down and eat."

I smile. "I didn't bring it for me. I brought it for you and the boys."

"Yeah, well, Seth is passed out with whatever viral torture we're dealing with right now, and about an hour ago, Grant decided to go lie in bed too. I'm praying he isn't getting sick, but I'll just say, he's not prone to taking naps without beating me over the head with a proverbial club first. Needless to say, I'm going to need some help eating it."

"You could save it for—"

"Noah, don't make me eat alone!"

"What I meant to say was…*of course*," I agree on a chortle. "Pass the soup."

Sammy's laugh is refreshing.

"Seriously, though. Go sit down," I say and step forward to place my hands on her shoulders and turn her body toward the living room. "I'll get everything heated up and bring it out to you. I know you're exhausted."

"Bone-weary would be putting it lightly," Sammy admits guiltily. "But I didn't let you in so you could wait on me while I sit on the couch."

"Ah, but that *is* why I came in. So let me do it."

She stares at me for a long moment, and I respond by pressing a soft kiss to her lips.

"Go sit down. I've got this."

She finally shrugs and heads for the couch while I round the counter and pull out the large container of chicken noodle soup and the bread bag filled with a loaf of sourdough.

I set the oven to preheat so I can warm up the bread and put a pan on the stove for the soup. Sammy's head lolls back on the couch, and instead of talking, I try to move around as quietly as I can. Her exhaustion is written all over her pretty face. Catering to me is the last thing I want her to feel like she needs to do.

"Did you end up taking Dolly to Brooke's today?" she asks, but her voice sounds drowsy as she shifts her body to a more upright position on the couch.

"Nah." I shake my head. "She ended up hanging with me all day. Though, I'm sure she was disappointed about missing out on her Benji fix."

"I'm pretty sure Brooke tried to call me earlier, but I was too deep in the vomit trenches to answer."

"I'm sure she'll understand," I answer softly.

"I bet the little matchmaker was disappointed we didn't make it to the game," she replies again, her voice fading with each word.

I don't reply this time, allowing her the minute I think she needs to give in to the fatigue while I stir the soup on the stove. By the time the oven beeps with a preheat notification, all motion from the living room has ceased to exist.

It only takes one quick glance toward the couch to know that Sammy is out like a light. No longer sitting up, she's horizontal on the sofa, and her eyes are firmly shut.

Looks like she'll be eating this later.

I shut off the oven and the stove, putting the soup in the fridge and the bread in its bag, and tiptoe into the living room. Sammy's breaths make her chest rise and fall in soft and steady waves, and I grab a cream afghan from the basket near the coffee table to cover her up.

Seeing her sleeping so peacefully like this makes my chest feel light and airy, and without hesitation, I post up in the large chair near the television and pull my phone out of my pocket to check in on my sister—sending Mary a text asking, *How was Kara today?*

With Sammy sleeping and the boys in their beds, there's no way I'm just going to leave her apartment. I can hang around for a bit, keep an ear out for the kids, and give her some time to rest.

The screen of my phone lights up with a new message.

Mary: She was a little grumpy this morning but warmed up as the day went on.

A "little grumpy" most likely means that my dear sister was giving Mary a run for her money this morning.

Me: How grumpy are we talking?

Mary: You remember that summer two years ago when she refused to eat breakfast?

Me: Uh-oh.

It was a rough few months, to say the least. Kara, while nonverbal, sometimes tries to gain control in other ways that can serve up some seriously frustrating moments.

Mary: Yeah. LOL. But good news is that she was back to being a little sweetheart before I left this evening. Even finished all her dinner and took a bath. You still planning on stopping by tomorrow?

Me: I'll be there.

The moment I hit send, the creaking sound of wood pulls my attention toward the hallway, and I find a sleepy-eyed Seth shuffling into the living room. His face twists in confusion when he sees me.

"Hey, bud. You feeling better?" I ask him on a whisper, hoping he'll take the hint to follow along so his mom can sleep.

"Yeah." He nods. "I'm hungry."

I jump up from the chair and head over toward him, giving him a small ruffle on the head while purposefully checking his forehead for a fever. When I note that his temperature feels normal and his face is devoid of discomfort or nausea, I walk into the kitchen.

"How about some chicken noodle soup?"

He nods enthusiastically.

"Good. Climb up on that stool," I instruct with a jerk of my chin.

Seth scrambles to the seat at the island and pulls himself up on it. His Spider-Man pajamas remind me of how little he is, despite the seriousness in his eyes. With all the major life changes he's had recently—his parents' divorce and moving to a new city and going to a new school—I imagine he's carrying some weight on his tiny shoulders that he's probably too young to fully understand.

"Noah, why are you here?"

"I heard you were sick and figured I'd check in on you guys and bring some soup."

"We didn't get to go to the game." He frowns. "It sucks."

"I'll make sure we get tickets again soon."

"Yeah?" he asks, hope in his voice. "You promise?"

"I promise," I answer as I preheat the oven again and put the soup on the stove. "So…how's school been? Get sent to the principal's office anymore?" I tease and Seth laughs.

"Nah. We're not doing that much because it's almost the end of the year. We get to play a lot."

"That sounds cool. Like recess, or something else?"

"Recess is the same, but we've been watching a couple of movies, and Ms. Dayton's been letting us do board-game math."

"Board-game math, huh? That sounds like something you came up with."

Seth scoffs. "I wouldn't come up with anything with math."

I grin. "Not your favorite subject, huh?"

"Heck no." He makes a face that could only be described as, *Ew, gross.* "Math sucks."

"Yeah, math does kind of suck," I agree with a knowing smile.

"But you're a doctor," he states with a skeptical raise of his brow. "Aren't you supposed to be good at math?"

"Just because I'm good at it doesn't mean I like it."

He nods like he can relate.

"But if you ever need help with math," I add, "just give me a call. I'm sure we can find a way to make it fun."

"Oh yeah!" he exclaims, but I'm thankful his voice is still quiet. "You can teach me while we play Cafeteria Battleship!"

"Sounds like a plan," I agree, but then I point one index finger at him. "But don't expect Dr. Shepard to join in again. He's still mad you kicked his butt."

Seth cracks up at that, and I procure the now-hot soup from the stove. After setting the bowl in front of him, I drop an ice cube right in the center of the steam. He watches avidly as it melts.

"Whatcha doin' here, Noah?"

I look up to find Grant standing at the edge of the hallway, and Sal, the stuffed sloth I gave him, is tucked firmly under his tiny arm.

"He brought us soup," Seth explains for me, his mouth working around the giant bite of noodles he's currently chewing on. "But be quiet because Mom's sleepin'."

"I *was* bein' quiet, Seth," Grant refutes with a quick glare at his older brother. "You sleepin' over, Noah?"

Sleeping over? Ha. The innocence of kids is certainly something to be admired.

"Nope. Just hanging out for a bit."

"Ah, man," Grant groans and gestures his disappointment with his still-casted arm.

"You hungry?" I ask, purposefully changing the subject. "How about some soup?"

He shakes his head but climbs up on the stool next to Seth all the same. "I want nuggs. So does Sal."

"Nuggs?" I ask with a raise of my brows.

"Chicken nuggets," Seth explains helpfully. "Mom says he might as well be a chicken nugget."

"Shut up, Seth," Grant replies, offended.

"No. You shut up, Grant."

"You're a funky butt lover!"

Funky butt lover? Why does that remind me of something?

"No! You're a funky butt lover!"

"Hold on," I chime in, holding a hand between the two of them. "Where did you two hear that from?"

"It's from a movie," Seth explains.

"Yeah! It's from *Rookie!*" Grant exclaims a little too loudly. "My favorite movie! When I get my cast off, I hope I'm just like Henry and can throw super-fast so I can pitch for the Yankees!"

"It's called *Rookie of the Year*, Grant," Seth corrects on a sigh. "Get it right."

"Shut up, Seth! You—"

"Guys," I cut in, fearful that their escalating voices will wake their exhausted mother. They both eye me closely, and I know that right now, this moment—on the precipice of an insult battle—I will make or break the respect they have for me. "You're both funky butt lovers who like to sniff stinky, funky butts because you're such funky butt lovers."

They both break out in a hysterical laugh, and Grant even waves his casted arm around like one of those windsock dancer guys businesses always use for grand openings.

"Now that we have that settled," I insert with a teasing grin. "Seth, eat your soup before it gets cold. Grant, I'll make you and Sal some nuggs. And in the meantime, let's try to keep it down so Mom can rest. Cool?"

Both boys nod enthusiastically. "Cool!"

For the next hour or so, the boys eat while we quietly shoot the shit. I glance over occasionally to see that Sammy's still sleeping, and then I clean up the kitchen when the boys are done.

At a little after eight, Seth informs me that they're supposed to get ready for bed, and I play supervisor while they brush their teeth. Grant convinces me to read them a bedtime story, and as I turn the last page, both of their eyes are drifting to sleep.

After I get a quick hug from both of them, Seth groggily climbs from Grant's bed and gets in his own, and I shut off the lights, pulling their door halfway closed before I make my way back into the living room.

Sammy is still sound asleep on the couch, and even though I absolutely hate disturbing her, I don't want her to wake up not knowing what happened or where I went or the state of the boys either.

Gently, I rub a hand down her arm, and her eyes flit open. It only takes a second of semiconsciousness for her to shoot up to sitting ramrod straight, panic in her eyes.

"Oh my God. I fell asleep!" Her eyes look around the room maniacally. "What time is it?"

"A little after nine."

"*Nine?*" Her eyes grow even wider. "Noah, I'm so sorry!"

"Hey, everything is okay." I reach out and put a calming hand to her shoulder. "I'm glad you got some rest. Honestly, I was hoping you'd do just that when I came over."

"Have the boys gotten out of bed?"

I nod. "Both of them have been fed. Seth ate two bowls of chicken noodle soup with bread and kept it down like a champ. Pretty sure he's officially on the mend. I cleaned up the kitchen, but I can make you some soup now if you want before I head out."

"No," she says adamantly. "You don't need to do that." She looks around for a minute, trying to get her bearings a little more, through her sleepiness. "Wait... You fed the boys?"

I nod again. "They even brushed their teeth, talked me into a bedtime story, and are now sound asleep in their beds. I hope you don't mind."

"Mind? You feeding my kids and putting them to bed?" Sammy laughs. "Yeah, I think I'll get over it."

I grin at her. "I wish I could say I got Grant to eat some soup, but it was all chicken nuggets for my guy."

She rolls her eyes. "That's expected."

"Hey, at least it's protein," I offer as consolation, and her eyes turn serious as she reaches out to grip my hand with a gentle squeeze.

"Thank you, Noah. Thank you for everything you did tonight."

"Trust me, Sammy. You and your boys are always worth it." I press a gentle kiss to her lips, and even though every cell inside my body wants to deepen the kiss, I rise to my feet. "I'm going to take off now and let you guys get more rest."

"Okay." She rises from the couch to walk me to the door.

But when I turn to face her again to say goodbye, she catches me off guard by covering my lips with hers and wrapping her arms around my shoulders. She's on her tiptoes now, and my arms wrap around her back all on their own.

My God, she feels so fucking good.

She deepens the kiss enough to give me just a taste of her tongue before she pulls away, her eyes dilated and her mouth flushed from the contact.

"When do I get to see you again, Noah?" she asks, and her lips form the cutest little pout. "I feel like this shouldn't count since I slept the whole dang time you were here."

"Whenever you want," I tell her, and she glances down at her bare feet before meeting my eyes again.

"Are you working tomorrow? I might have some free time."

"My day is open."

"Grant will be at school, and Zoe is going to stay home with Seth while I run some errands. I'll call you?"

"And I'll answer." I touch my lips to hers one last time and then grab the knob behind my back to head out the door. If I don't leave now, I'm liable to stay all night. And I don't think those kids are ready to see what I'd like to do with the time.

Back to the life of bachelorhood. *Too bad the instant I'm heading out of her building, I miss the feeling of family.*

Chapter
Twenty

Monday, May 23rd

Kendall does her victory dance after beating Dale and me again, and I swear a tear starts to form in the corner of my dude's eye.

"What's wrong, Dale? Getting tired of your wife always kicking your ass on our runs?"

"She kicks your ass too, Philips."

"Yeah, but I'm secure in my manhood," I tease. "So, it's not as big of a hit to the gonads for me, you know?"

He flips me off, and I laugh as I sink to a nearby bench to catch my breath while Dolly circles the ground in front of me. My phone pings in my pocket, and I pull it out to find a message that makes me smile.

Sammy: I'm here. Where are you?

I turn to look over my shoulder just in time to catch a glimpse of her on the path behind me, and I quickly type out a response.

Me: Keep walking. I see you.

I hop up from the bench, trying to grab her attention, and Dale's nosy ass follows my gaze toward the path Sammy is walking down.

"Well, look who it is," he says, and a giant, shit-eating grin covers his mouth. "Your favorite lady meeting you for a little afternoon delight?"

I don't dignify him with a response, but that doesn't stop him from continuing.

"You planning on introducing me this time? Or are you going to run away before I can say hello?"

"Say hello?" Kendall chimes in. "To whom?"

"Noah's lady love." Dale waggles his brows. "Sammy Sweetheart."

I roll my eyes at the Jersey Shore reference. And Kendall takes it upon herself to grab Chanandler's leash and jog straight over to Sammy. Her never-out-of-energy Lab follows dutifully at her side, apparently fully recovered from the five miles we just ran.

Dolly sits up, her eyes bouncing around as she tries to understand what's happening, and I just stand there in semi-shock as Kendall runs straight up to Sammy and starts talking.

She points to Dale and me, and all I can do is wave an uncertain hand in her direction.

Before I know it, both of the women and the happy-go-lucky Lab are walking toward us. Though, when Sammy meets my eyes, her half smile feels off—like she's nervous.

The instant she's standing in front of me, I lean in and touch my lips to hers. "Hi," I whisper as I pull away. "Looks like you found me."

"I had a little help." Her eyes briefly flit to a smiling Kendall before she reaches down to rub a hand over Dolly's head. "Hey there, sweet girl."

I step back and open my shoulders to the group at large so I can do some introductions. "Sammy, this is Dr. Kendall Hopkins, and this is Kendall's husband."

Dale shakes his head on a laugh while simultaneously telling me to *fuck off* with his eyes. He knows exactly what I'm doing.

"Husband?" Sammy's head bounces back and forth between the couple. "As in, the two of you are married?"

"Unfortunately for Kendall," I add with a smirk. "They are, in fact, married."

Kendall cracks up at that, and Dale just sticks out his hand as he gives Sammy a friendly smile. "Dr. Dale Hopkins. It's a pleasure to finally meet you." He flashes a teasing glance at me as he shakes Sammy's hand. "Honestly, with the way Noah rambles on and on about you, I already feel like we're friends."

I'm not surprised by his commentary, and I'm also not embarrassed about it either. I'm man enough to accept the fact that I'm simping—as the kids say—for this woman.

"It's…uh…really nice to meet you both," Sammy returns with a still slightly nervous smile. "And I'm just Sammy. Sammy Baker. No doctor or anything."

"We're a bunch of cunts, huh?" Kendall questions through a laugh. "You'll have to excuse us, Sammy, but all we know is the hospital. And as you can see, Dale's social skills are seriously lacking."

Sammy laughs, but she also looks at me with a face that says, *Am I supposed to be laughing this much at Dale?*

And I don't hesitate to give her a nod of approval, reaching out to wrap my arm around her shoulders and tucking her close to my side.

"Listen here, wifey, my social skills used to bring all the ladies to the yard back in the day," Dale interjects, and it only makes his wife laugh harder.

"Honey, you and I both know that you were too busy being late to the yard to come back with any ladies," she teases, and I don't hesitate to join in on the fun.

"And to think, his tardiness is still his strongest attribute."

"I'm pretty much late all the time too," Sammy offers. "So, I think I'm going to have to side with Dale on this one."

"I knew I liked you already," he comments.

"Yeah, but you have kids," I tell Sammy, squeezing her shoulder. "That's different. Dale's just a deadbeat."

"A deadbeat who just worked twenty hours straight," Dale disputes, tossing one of his running gel packets at me on a laugh.

Kendall and Dale start to argue and tease among themselves, and I take the opportunity to speak directly to Sam. "Don't mind us. It's kind of our Monday ritual to get together and shit all over Dale while we fit in a run with the dogs."

Sammy smiles. "Poor Dale."

"Nah. He doesn't deserve any sympathy. The man is the biggest jokester on the planet. I can assure you both he and Kendall serve each other shit sandwiches on a daily basis. It's basically their foreplay."

"I take it you know them both from work?"

"Kendall is a neurosurgeon at the hospital. Dale works in the ED. And we've been friends since we were baby doctors in residency," I explain, and Sammy gets the strangest expression on her face. "You okay?"

"Yeah." She nods. Laughs. And her cheeks turn a gorgeous shade of pink as she meets my eyes.

"What's going on here?" I question, an intrigued grin now forming on my lips. "What am I missing?"

"Nothing, I just…" She pauses and shakes her head, but it's more at herself than anything else. "I'm just an idiot, that's all."

I furrow my brow, and she lets out a sigh.

"I…uh…that time Grant and I ran into you here and Kendall showed up…I thought she was someone you were dating."

"Oh shit," I comment on a laugh. "No. Not at all."

"Yeah." She snorts. "I'm seeing that now."

"Wait a minute… First Mary, then Kendall," I state when my mind catches up to speed. "You must've thought I was some kind of serial-dating asshole."

"Drop the asshole part, and you're fairly close." She cringes. "Talk about a lesson in never make assumptions, huh?"

"It's all good. Understandable, even," I answer, and I *almost* ask her about Gavin. To, you know, clear up any assumptions I might've made. But something inside me doesn't want to bring down the mood, so instead, I ask, "How much time do you have before you need to pick up Grant from school?"

"A few hours. Why?"

"Well—" I start to say, but Kendall cuts into our little powwow.

"Hey, guys. We're going to head out." She hooks her thumb over her shoulder and then wraps her arm around Dale's waist. "Chanandler wants to eat, and Dale wants to sleep."

"I'm definitely ready to crawl into bed," Dale adds through a yawn. "But it was great meeting you, Sammy."

"You too," she says and smiles at both Kendall and Dale. "Both of you."

"We'll see you around soon, yeah?" Kendall asks and reaches out to give Sammy's arm a friendly tap.

Sammy nods, and it's not long before Dale and Kendall and Chanandler are gone, leaving Sammy, Dolly, and me to our own devices.

"So…you have a few hours to hang out?" I ask and turn Sammy's body around so her chest is pressed against my chest. I beam down at her while playfully swaying us back and forth.

"I do." She looks up at me with a little smirk. "What do you have in mind?"

"Well, I was planning on visiting Kara today and was wondering if you wanted to come along?"

"You want me to meet your sister?" She's a little uncertain, I can tell, but I don't have any problems reassuring her.

"Actually, I'd *love* for you to meet my sister."

"Yeah?" She searches my eyes, as if she's trying to confirm my words with my truth.

"Definitely, Sam."

"Okay," she says and presses a soft kiss to my lips. "Count me in."

I don't waste any time grabbing Dolly's leash and wrapping my free arm around Sammy's shoulder, guiding us out of Central Park.

"How was Seth feeling this morning?" I ask, placing a hand to her lower back as we cross the street.

"Rejuvenated," she says in a way that makes me laugh.

"I had a feeling he'd be good to go after I saw him scarf down two bowls of soup."

"Honestly, his little ass was so peppy this morning, I probably could've sent him to school." She snorts. "But the rules say he has to be vomit-free for twenty-four hours."

"And that's where Zoe came in."

"Yep." She nods. "Since she recently made the big decision to attend grad school in Texas next year, she's been trying to get as many extra hours as she can to save up money."

"She's moving to Texas?"

"In the fall." She frowns. "I'm happy for her, but selfishly, I'm not-so-happy for me. I have no idea what I'm going to do when she moves on and I have to find someone else."

"It'll all work out," I reply encouragingly. *If it works out how I'm hoping, I'll be around to help a hell of a lot more.*

I guide Sammy and Dolly toward the subway station, and once we're on the tram and heading in the direction of Kara's facility, my phone buzzes in my back pocket with a text message. I release Sammy's hand to pull it out and check the screen.

Unknown: Noah, I've left you two voice mails. Please call me back. I need to see you. This is Ashley, by the way.

I don't waste any time deleting the message and tuck my phone back into my pocket.

"Something important?" Sammy asks, and I shake my head.

"Not at all."

The subway's brakes squeal when it reaches our stop, and I take her hand in mine again, guiding her and Dolly through the doors and up the steps of the station.

"Kara's place is only half a block from here. It's called Shay's," I update, and Sammy nods while Dolly stays close to my side.

Over the years, my dad tried all sorts of different things, from handling Kara's care himself to having a home health nurse live permanently at his house, but nothing made my sister as happy as living at Shay's. Now, with Mary facilitating her care even further, I feel like she's finally living the life she deserves.

"This is it," I announce and lead Sammy into the building. Her eyes are wide as she takes in the massive fountain in the lobby and the crown molding at the tops of the walls.

"Noah, this is really nice," she states on a whisper, glancing up at me with a smile.

"Yeah. My sister loves it here," I comment and squeeze her hand gently.

The check-in process is smooth as always with the security guard Reggie, and as we approach Kara's door, Mary is stepping out into the hallway with a bag of checkers.

"Ooh, Noah!" she greets eagerly, stepping up to pull me into a hug. "Kara's going to be so excited you and Dolly are here. And a new friend! Shoo!" She laughs. "She's still going to be talking about this at dinner." She turns to Sammy directly to remark, "It's nice to see you again, honey."

"Thanks, Mary. It's nice to see you again too." Sammy's nerves are obvious in the shake of her voice and the slouched shape of her spine, but Mary grabs her hand and squeezes.

"Don't worry, doll. Kara is going to love you."

I think so too. Kara can be shy around new people and even wary of them, but I don't doubt for a second that she'll feel just how much Sammy means to me and be right at ease.

Mary leaves us with a smile and a wave, headed back to the employee area, and Sammy and I step inside the room to my sister sitting on her little pink sofa. She's wearing a pretty smocked dress, covered in watermelons—her favorite fruit.

As soon as she sees me, she cries out, "Oooah!"

My smile is big, and my grip on Sammy's hand is tight as I pull her forward with me. "Hey, Kare Bear."

Kara smiles and twists her body with excitement as I approach, pulling me down into a crushing hug that nearly knocks my feet out from under me. Sammy grabs Dolly's leash and steps to the side, and I glance over at her gratefully.

"Oh wow, sis. You really are happy to see me, huh?"

Kara kisses at my cheeks sloppily, and I chuckle at her enthusiasm. It's a good two minutes before I can free myself from her clutches, but Sammy waits patiently the whole time.

I step back and straighten my stretched shirt and take the leash back from Sammy just as Dolly jumps up to put her paws in Kara's lap, licking her cheeks with affection. Kara laughs and laughs and wiggles back and forth on the couch like you might expect a toddler would while being kissed by their favorite pet.

Dolly slides off her lap and comes back over to my side, and I take the opportunity to introduce Sammy. "Kara, sweetie, this is my friend Sammy. I'm really fond of her, and I know you will be too."

Kara watches her closely as Sammy approaches the sofa and asks, "Is it okay if I sit next to you here?"

Kara smiles, and I interject, "I think she'd like that."

When Sammy sits down, Dolly jerks on my hand to go back over to them. I let her. Only this time, she puts her paws on Sammy's lap, accepting a bevy of pets.

"You know, Kara actually named Dolly."

"Really?" Sammy grins at Kara. "It's such a pretty name."

Kara grunts her excitement, yelling "Oah" a couple of times to tell me she wants me to explain further. I'm not surprised. She loves this story.

"The day I brought Dolly home, when she was just a tiny puppy, I stopped to see Kara, and she put on Dolly Parton and danced on top of her coffee table."

"On the table?" Sammy asks with an impressed laugh, making Kara's mouth curve up too.

"Mm-hmm." I nod. "She kept playing the song over and over again until I got the point. Dolly it was."

"You know, my sister loves Dolly Parton too," Sammy tells her enthusiastically, even reaching out to gently hold Kara's hand. "I know she'd love to meet you, Kara. Her dog Benji is actually Dolly's boyfriend, if you can believe that!"

Kara gasps excitedly and turns to me, and I nod. "It's true. Dolly has a boyfriend, and his name is Benji. Theirs is a romance for the ages."

Kara unexpectedly jumps into Sammy's arms, and Sammy just laughs as she hugs Kara tightly.

My heart, on the other hand, feels like it'll climb out of my chest at the sight.

Sammy Baker, ladies and gentlemen.

Sitting here, seeing her interact this genuinely and empathetically with my mostly nonverbal sister, I know one immutable thing—Dolly and Benji aren't the only ones who are going to go down in romance history.

Not if I have anything to say about it.

Chapter
Twenty-One

Thursday, May 26th

"Hey, Philips, you ready to do the damn thing?" Dr. Gareth greets as I walk through the doors of the OR's scrub-in area to prepare myself for the long surgery ahead.

"I think so," I tell him on a chuckle and grab a blue scrub cap to put on my head. "How are you feeling? Did you get a nap in this time, so you don't get sleepy?"

"You're never going to let me live that down, are you?" Gareth asks through a grin, holding up both of his scrubbed arms to avoid contamination.

"The fact that I had to revive you with smelling salts when you passed out your first year of residency? No. Safe to say, I'm never going to get over that."

"See you in there," he says, his middle fingers raised pointedly on both sterile hands, and nudges the main door into the surgery room with his hip.

My phone vibrates in my back pocket as I step up to the sink, and when I see who the sender is, I've never been more thrilled to be a little slow at scrubbing in.

Sammy: Hey, stranger. What are you up to?

Stranger, indeed. I haven't seen her since Monday afternoon when she went with me to visit Kara, and daily texts and nightly phone calls while we watch *Queen Charlotte* are the only things getting me through. Which is, even though I'm about to step into an operation on an eleven-year-old with congenital defects in his limbs, why my response only requires two words.

Me: Missing you.

Sammy: I can't decide if that's the sweetest thing I've ever heard or the cheesiest...

My smile only grows, and a soft chortle slides past my lips.

Me: Probably both. ;) How did Grant's appointment go this morning?

Sammy: Still casted, but Dr. Howard is confident it can come off in two weeks. Then, he'll start physical therapy and probably be sadly disappointed that his arm didn't turn into a superhero appendage that knows how to play guitar and gets him hired by the Yankees.

Me: Still on that Rookie of the Year *kick, huh?*

Sammy: Noah, I've seen that movie so many times I could recite every damn line.

Instantly, I get an idea. Something I think will soften the blow a little for Grant when he finds out he's not about to become an MLB starting pitcher when his cast comes off.

Me: You know what I think we should do?

Sammy: Start a petition to make the words "funky butt lover" illegal?

Me: LOL. I think we should plan a celebration outing to a Yankees game when Grant gets his cast off.

Sammy: The boys would really love that. And it is a bit of a miracle that his cast is still intact. I mean, it stinks like dirty feet, but it's still on there. Surely that's something to celebrate.

Me: We can even bathe him first before we go.

Sammy: Ha! Sounds like a win-win.

I take a quick glance at the calendar app in my phone before sending her another message.

Me: I'll check their schedule and see what home games they have coming up in June.

Sammy: You think Kara would like to come?

Her thoughtfulness toward my sister doesn't go unnoticed.

Me: I think she'd love to come, so long as she's having a good day when the time comes. I'll talk to Mary about it.

"Noah, you ready?" Cameron, one of the OR nurses, peeks her head out of the surgery room to find me standing by the sink.

"Give me two minutes, and I'll be there."

Fingers to the keys, I send one final text to Sammy.

Me: I'm being called into surgery now, but try to have a good day, okay? PS: My first text still rings true, no matter how cheesy you think it is. I miss you.

Sammy: I miss you too, Cheese Ball. And I'll call you after work tonight.

Yeah, it's official. The all-consuming, heart-racing, stomach-aching, I'm-going-to-throw-up-if-this-doesn't-work-out *feeling* is coming in loud and clear this time around.

Three back-to-back surgeries and several inpatient visits should have me dead on my feet, but I guess Sammy Baker puts too much pep in my step for that.

My normal routine would include a quick stop for takeout and calling it an early night, but since Dolly is sleeping over at Brooke and Chase's, I can't stop myself from stopping by La Croisette to see Sammy.

I know she's probably busy. I know I'll probably have all of two minutes to say hello. I know all of this, but it doesn't deter me from heading straight there after I leave the hospital.

With the way I'm missing her, even two minutes is better than none.

The instant I walk through the fancy glass entrance doors of La Croisette, I'm reminded of the fact that it's one of the most popular restaurants in New York. Bodies fill every available space, and the noise in just the lobby is enough to make my ears ring a little, but when I step up to the hostess stand, Nanette smiles like she's not even feeling the pinch. People book reservations several months in advance just to get a spot, and here I am, walking in like I own the freaking place.

Pays to know the right people, I guess.

"Hey, Noah. You want a table?" Nanette asks, making a couple of heads whip in our direction. I do my best to ignore them.

"No, thanks. I'm just looking for Sammy. Have you seen her?"

"Last time I saw her, she was getting a ten-top ready with Mandy, but I have no clue where she is now. Feel free to go look yourself, though."

With a grateful nod, I scan the dining room for Sammy, but the only familiar face I see is Chase's sister Mo, standing toward the kitchen entrance doors chatting with one of the servers.

Without hesitation, my feet are already moving in her direction.

Thankfully, by the time I reach her, the server has headed inside the kitchen doors, and Mo's relocated to the bar area. When her eyes meet mine, her face lights up with a smile.

"Noah," she greets. "To what do I owe the pleasure? You trying to con me into getting you some food to-go?"

Amusement crests my lips as I shake my head. "Actually, I was hoping to see Sammy for a minute."

"*Ohhhhh.*" Mo's excited expression would make her soon-to-be sister-in-law Brooke proud. "I see. You're here for *Sammy* and not my husband's world-renowned food."

I chuckle at that. "Yeah, but if you wanted to put in a to-go order of his chicken parmigiana, I wouldn't stop you."

"Consider it done." She pats my shoulder. "And Sammy is in the back office." She points toward the opposite end of the restaurant, where the restrooms and a few private, employee-only doors sit. "You can head on back there to say hello. I'm sure she won't mind." Her smile is still intact, nearly too large for her face, and her eyes bounce around with the need to know more.

Obviously, I keep my lips shut. But it's not because I don't want to tell anyone about what's going on between Sammy and me. It's because those details aren't mine to tell. Mo may be a close family friend of Sammy's, but she's also her boss. Which obviously means disclosing any info about our budding relationship isn't my call.

"Thanks, Mo," I answer instead and head off in the direction she pointed.

It takes a little skill to carefully make my way through the maze of tables without disturbing La Croisette's patrons, but I manage it without much issue.

I'm not a hundred percent sure where the back office is, but when I hear the sound of Sammy's voice, I realize she's located in the room at the very end of the narrow hallway with the door ajar.

"Now isn't a good time," she says to someone, her voice holding a slight edge that makes me stop just outside the door. Seeing as she's the general manager of a restaurant like La Croisette, I'm sure she finds herself in the middle of plenty of conflicts—both in person and on the phone—and since I wasn't exactly invited tonight, I don't want to interrupt.

The door is cracked open, so I peer inside carefully to see if I need to come back at another time.

Sammy's back is facing me, and a well-dressed man in a slick suit and dark hair is standing right in front of her. Even if I couldn't see his face, I'd recognize the prick anywhere.

"We need to talk," *Gavin* says, producing a grind between my back teeth.

"I don't think we do, Gavin. I don't want to be rude, but the possibility of something between us was over the night we went to Leyla's."

"Sam—"

"If I'm really honest, it was over long before that."

"You just don't remember how good we are together."

Sammy starts to shake her head, but her movements are stopped when he steps forward and closes the distance between them. My chest tightens at the sight, but it damn near explodes when he places his hands on either side of her face and pulls her in for a kiss.

He's. Kissing. Her.

Another man is kissing Sammy while she doesn't want it. Right in fucking front of me.

I've never been this angry in my life.

I'm going to kill this asshole.

Chapter
Twenty-Two

My stomach is filled with lead. And my heart? With rage.

"Gavin, stop," Sammy commands, stepping away and toward where I stand at the door. Her body is rigid, but Inspector Gadget reaches out with his accordion arms anyway, putting his hands on her face like he's going to try to kiss her *again*.

My fight instincts kick in, and I am pushing past the opened door and inside the office without a second thought.

"Are you fucking deaf?" I shout and step between Sammy and the asshole who doesn't understand consent. "She said *stop*. She doesn't want you kissing her."

"Fuck you, Dr. McStuffins. This is none of your business."

"Noah?" Sammy's questions with disbelief. "What are you doing here?"

I know my presence has to be quite the surprise, but the only thing I care about right now is getting this scumbag out of our faces.

"What the fuck is your problem?" I ask Gavin, pulling Sammy behind me with a gentle arm while I step up to the prick. "You get a thrill out of sexual harassment or something?"

"Sexual harassment, my asshole. You've wanted Sammy's pussy since the moment I met you. This is pure jealousy, plain and simple."

My jaw clicks with anger, and my body vibrates with the urge to wrap my hands around his throat and teach him a goddamn lesson about how to treat a woman.

"Noah, don't. He's not worth it," Sammy whispers from behind me, a tremble in her voice that pisses me off even more.

"Sammy, I just wanted you to know how I feel about you," Gavin says, turning from Hyde and back into Jekyll in an instant. "We had something special. We'd still have it if this fucker would get out of the way."

Fuck this asshole. I clench my fists at my sides, my body half convinced that now is the perfect time to knock his teeth out, but Sammy steps up beside me now, gently pushing me back with a hand to my chest.

"Gavin, the only reason I let you come back here was so I could tell you to stop calling me and texting me. And now, I think it's long past time for you to go."

"It's because of him, isn't it?" His laugh drips with disdain. "I should've known you've been fucking this doctor since that night I saw you together in that ER room. You know, when I drove you to the hospital because your fucking kid broke his arm."

Sammy's mouth gapes open, and I step up, ready to lay this piece of shit out like the dog he is, when the door bangs against the wall so hard, I pull Sammy back against my body to shield her.

"*You bastard!*" a blond woman shouts, her chest heaving with erratic breaths she can't control. "I fucking knew I'd find you here!"

Gavin has his hands up in defense, and it's only then that I see the indentation from a missing band on his finger.

This motherfucker.

"So, this is her?" the blonde asks, swinging her fury toward Sammy with a shaky point of her finger. "You're the home-wrecker screwing my husband?"

"Husband?" Sammy's head jerks back in shock. "What?"

I pull her even closer to my body.

"Carrie," Gavin challenges without shame. "Go home. We'll talk when I get there."

"Go home?!" She laughs, but it's harsh and borderline manic. "You're fucking deranged if you think I'm going to keep living with a lying, cheating, shady bastard!"

"But this is not what you think. It's—"

"Oh, shut the hell up, Gavin!" The woman's voice is getting louder by the second. "I know what you've been up to. And all thanks to the private investigator I had to hire to track your sneaky ass down, I know she isn't the only one you've been fucking behind my back!"

Holy *shit*.

"Sammy Baker, you're a bitch! A home-wrecker!" the woman continues shouting at the top of her lungs, turning all of her attention to Sammy once again. "You should be ashamed of yourself. You're a mother of two boys... What kind of example are you giving them by screwing around with someone else's husband?"

"Hold on." I step forward to stop this woman from pushing her anger onto the wrong person. "Leave her out of this."

"Leave her out of this? She's the one who is fucking my husband!"

"Um, *no*," Sammy refutes steadily. "I am not having, and have not had, sex with your husband. We went out to dinner a few times, but I had *no* idea he was married."

Sammy's glare at Gavin could set the world on fire if it hit something flammable. As it is, it permanently sends a dozen nails into Gavin's coffin.

"Carrie, I think we need to go outside and talk," Gavin says, changing tactics, but his wife is too far gone.

"Are you kidding me, Gavin? Go outside? If we go outside, I'm stabbing you right on the sidewalk!"

At this point, there is no doubt in my mind that every person inside La Croisette can hear this conversation, and that suspicion is confirmed when Mo appears mere seconds later.

Gavin's wife, though…well, she is too far gone with anger to do anything but keep yelling at the slimy prick she married.

"You asshole! You're not even telling these women the truth? You're just acting like you don't have a wife and three daughters at home? You are such a piece of shit!"

"Uh…" Mo looks around the office with big eyes. "What am I missing? Is there a Jerry Springer episode being filmed back here?"

Instantly, Sammy moves from me to her boss, apology in her every feature. "Oh my God, Mo. I'm so sorry."

Carrie slides up the sleeves of her sweater. "I'm going to kick your ass, you dickhead! Someone get their phone out and film this. Because I sure as shit want to remember this moment for the rest of my life."

Mo's eyes stretch wide, and at the sight of it, I know we're long past letting this go on. I step up to order, "You two need to take this outside."

"Yeah," Mo agrees. "Either take this outside, or I'm calling the cops to remove you from my restaurant." She looks at the angry woman, dropping her voice in a half whisper. "Though, if you want, I can try to get one of my staff to film your fight outside. I mean, I'm still going to have to call the cops, but yeah, that's the best I can do."

"Mo!" Sammy exclaims.

"What?" Mo just shrugs. "I mean, if I were in her shoes, I'd probably want some video footage of me kicking my husband's ass too."

Completely overwhelmed, Sammy scrubs a hand down her face, and I try my best to silently reassure her with a gentle squeeze of her shoulder while Carrie shoves Gavin out of the office and toward the exit doors of La Croisette.

When I came here to see Sammy tonight, I sure as hell didn't expect to walk into this.

But I'm glad I did.

Because as of today, I finally know for a fact that Gavin Evans is not a fucking problem.

Chapter Twenty-Three

Night has filled the sky, and La Croissette is completely empty of patrons.

The lights are mostly off in the restaurant, and only the glow of one near the kitchen indicates that anyone is even inside.

After all the drama, Sammy went back to work, and I ran home to change out of my scrubs and into a pair of jeans and a white T-shirt.

She said she was fine, and I believed her. But nothing in this world could have stopped me from coming back here, to this bench out front, to wait for her to get off work so I could make sure of it myself.

The glass door swings open, Sammy's sweet face downturned to the keys in her hand as she steps through it, and I climb to my feet.

She looks tired, and her hair is a little messy from a long shift, but damn, she still looks beautiful.

"Hey," I greet softly, doing my best not to startle her. Her gaze nevertheless whips to mine.

"Noah?" she questions, her steps faltering a little. "What are you doing here?"

"Waiting on you."

"What? For how long?"

"Doesn't matter." I can't stop myself from pulling her straight into my arms. "I had to see you again after what went on tonight."

"But Noah, I said I was fi—"

"I know you were fine." I smile. "But personally, I was a little shaken up."

Her body shakes with a small giggle, and I hug her tighter.

"Are you okay?" I whisper into her hair.

"Yeah. I'm okay." She pulls away a little, and my body misses her instantly. "But I *am* sorry, Noah."

"Sorry? Why are you sorry?"

"Because I was at the center of that scene. Because if I'd let myself be open to you, I never would have dated Gavin in the first place. Because…" She shrugs. "I should have known it was you from the start."

"Sammy, come on. None of this is easy. I don't expect you to be anything but yourself—wouldn't want you to be. If it took this long to know… Well, I'm guessing there's a reason. I'm not mad."

"You're not?"

"What kind of asshole would I be if I was angry with you over something that wasn't your fault? Trust me, I'm not that guy. I'll never be that guy."

"God, Noah," she breathes out on a sigh. "I swear to you, I haven't been out with Gavin since that night I ran into you at Bailey's. We had gone to dinner that evening, and he wanted me to go back to his hotel room, and I… didn't want to do that. He got mad at me, and yeah, I haven't seen or spoken to him since."

He got mad at her because she didn't want to sleep with him? If Carrie hasn't already killed him, I will.

I grit my teeth to keep myself from making Sammy feel any worse than she already does. "I appreciate your telling me that, but I'll be honest, Sam. It doesn't matter. I've decided you're mine. And no history with that fucked-up prick is going to change it."

Immediately, she brushes her lips against mine.

I want to slide my hands into her hair and deepen the kiss. I want to lift her up into my arms and wrap her legs around my hips and push her back against the brick wall of the restaurant, but I force myself to have some restraint.

I don't know what it is about Sammy, but any time her mouth comes into contact with my mouth, it drives me fucking wild. I don't think I've ever had this kind of primitive, primal reaction with another woman in my life.

"Is this okay?" she whispers, and I almost want to laugh at how ridiculous of a question that is right now.

Is this okay? This is more than okay.

"Yes," I answer, leaning back to meet her eyes with a steady gaze. "You kissing me is always okay, Sammy."

"Good." She grins, but it has an edge of mischief to it.

"What?" I question. "What's that look for?"

She searches my gaze before leaning forward and whispering into my ear, "After seeing you go all caveman and standing up for me, and then kissing you just now, a lot of dirty things are floating around inside my head. Things I probably shouldn't be thinking."

Well, *fuck.*

Her coy expression and the way her breasts brush against my chest with each unsteady inhale of oxygen pushes me over the edge. Before I even know what I'm doing, I pull her away from the front of the restaurant and off to the side of the building where an empty alley provides a semblance of privacy.

The second we're tucked away from possible prying eyes, I gently press her back against the brick wall and crush my mouth to hers. This time, I don't hold back. This time, I slide my tongue past her lips and deepen the kiss.

Her hands are gripping my shoulders, and a little moan jumps from her throat. I swallow it down greedily and move my hands to her perfect ass, even lifting her up so that she can wrap her legs around my waist, the entire time her back is still pressed against the brick.

The feel of her curves crushed against me and the way her soft lips meld with mine make my head spin.

I want more. So much fucking more.

But the random city sounds of honking taxis and sirens start to filter inside my brain, and I know that I need to stop before I lose control. Before we lose control.

"Shit," I breathe out, resting my forehead against hers. "I want you. But not here. Not like this."

"I know," she says through a sigh. "And I have to get home to the boys."

"Of course." I nod and brush my hand against her cheek. "And I should get home too and get some sleep. I have an early surgery in the morning."

A mixture of sexual frustration and disappointment form a cloud of silence between us.

"Sammy?" I ask, and her eyes explore mine.

"Yeah?"

"I think it's high time I took you out on a real date."

She grins up at me. "And I think I can free up an evening this Sunday. How does that sound?"

"Sounds like Sunday it is, Sam. You, me, and a real date."

I can't fucking wait.

Chapter
Twenty-Four

Sunday, May 29th

"Can I just say that I'm beyond thrilled that you chose this place for our date tonight?" Sammy comments, smiling at me over her chocolate milkshake.

"Yeah?" I respond with a grin. "I was actually a little afraid you'd be disappointed."

"Disappointed? Are you joking?" she exclaims, swinging a dramatic hand over her outfit. "I got to wear jeans and flats, and I'm currently drinking a milkshake without one of my kids saying 'Mom' every five seconds in my ear. This is date heaven, in my opinion."

I could've easily taken her to a fancy restaurant for our first real date night—and I almost did—but the more I thought about Sammy and the busy life she leads, my gut instinct told me she needed something laid-back.

"Have you ever been here before?" I ask.

She shakes her head, pursing her lips around the mouthful of cold ice cream she's just sucked in.

"No. But after tasting their milkshakes, I'm an instant fan," she remarks, wiping her mouth with her napkin. "Anytime you want to bring me here, Noah, just say the word."

Waverly Diner has been a staple on the West Side for as long as I can remember. My dad used to bring Kara and me here every weekend when we were kids, and the vinyl-padded booths, counter seating, milkshakes to die for, and a menu that covers everything from Belgian waffles to triple-decker sandwiches to cheeseburgers hasn't changed a bit.

Grace, our server, steps up to our booth, holding two plates filled with cheeseburgers and fries in her hands, and sets our food down in front of us. "How's everything looking?"

"This cheeseburger is bigger than my head..." Sammy pauses, and a big ole grin covers her pretty mouth. "Which means everything looks perfect."

The server laughs, and I nod in agreement. "I think we're all set. Thank you."

Grace leaves us to the food, and Sammy takes a bite of her cheeseburger. A giant bite.

Her cheeks puff out like a squirrel in the midst of hoarding nuts, and her eyes roll back in her head like she's having an orgasm—and at this point, I have scientific evidence that the faces are a spot-on match.

I decide not to tell her about it—at least, not yet. I'm pretty sure the embarrassment would be too potent for me to fix in the middle of Waverly Diner. But later tonight? When I can prove just how sexy it is? All bets are off.

As she chews, an adorable smile lifts the corners of her lips to just below the corners of her aqua-green eyes. "I still stand by my words, Noah. Anytime you want to bring me here to eat, I'm your girl."

"You're my girl?" I question. "Does that phrase apply to diner-milkshake-cheeseburger situations only? Or could it apply to other situations too?"

"Do you *want* it to apply to other situations?"

"If it's up to me, Sammy, it would apply to *all* situations."

"All situations?" she questions, but her lips showcase amusement. "That's quite a blanket statement there, Noah."

"It is." I nod and reach out to place my hand over hers. "And I stand behind it fully."

"So, like, when I'm a total freaking mess with puking kids, and you have to get out of bed to bring us soup in the middle of the night?"

"You're my girl."

She narrows her eyes, but her lips are still crested into a smile. "And when you come over to hang out, but I'm too exhausted to do anything but sleep?"

"You're my girl."

"And when I decide to rob a bank and take a hostage and bury a body in Central Park?"

"You're my girl. Though, I would maybe suggest you take money from me instead of the bank, and that hostages are too much work since we've already got two little ones in tow, and I would *pray* that the body is that of one Gavin Evans. But even if I couldn't convince you…you're my girl."

"You seem crazy confident about this whole me-being-your-girl thing."

"Because I am."

"Want to know a secret?"

"Definitely."

"I feel pretty confident about you being my guy too."

"Is that right?"

"Shocking, I know," she says with a giggle. "But Sammy Baker finally knows exactly what she wants."

"Shit, Sam."

She kneels on her booth seat and leans over the table toward me. "Come here," she whispers.

Once we're nearly nose-to-nose, Sammy presses her lips to mine. The kiss is soft and sweet and brief, but it's still a million layers deeper than I've ever had with any other woman in my entire life.

With my fingers beneath her chin, I lock my eyes with hers and whisper the words I've long since known but, as of right now, *need* to say. "I love you."

Her eyes search my steady gaze, excitement and affection and tears brewing in a storm of blue-green.

"I love you, Sammy," I tell her explicitly. "I've been in love with you for a while now."

She pauses for the longest moment, so much so that the breath in my chest goes stale from holding it in. But then, finally, the sweet relief of reciprocation frees me from my temporary hell. "Yeah, actually, I know you do. And more than that, I love you too."

I cup her face eagerly, and I kiss her again before raining playful kisses all over her pretty face.

"Okay. Okay." She giggles and teasingly slaps my hands away. "We better stop, or else everyone in this diner is going to lose their appetite."

"Good. Then we'll have the place to ourselves," I counter as she moves to sit back down in her seat.

Sammy squeezes my hand once more, but the sound of warring text notifications fills the air between us before I can persuade her anymore.

She tilts her head to the side in confusion. "Was that my phone or yours?"

"I don't know. Both, I think." I snag my cell out of my pocket, while she pulls hers out of her purse.

Brooke: *I've decided that the boys and Dolly are spending the night. You're not allowed to pick them up until tomorrow. And, you know, if you want to extend your date night into, like, a nightcap, you definitely should... ☺*

"Did my sister seriously start a group chat with us and then cryptically encourage we have sex tonight?"

"Yeah." I lift my eyes from my phone to meet hers on a laugh. "I think she just did."

Sammy's fingers furiously tap across the screen of her phone, and a second later, my phone vibrates with a new message.

Sammy: Actually, do you mind keeping the boys and Dolly for an extra four days? Noah and I have decided to run off to Vegas and get married.

"Oh *no*," I comment, but I'm also laughing my ass off. "I think your sister's head might explode after reading that."

Not even a second later, Brooke confirms the explosion with a resounding shock wave.

Brooke: SAMMY. YOU BETTER BE JOKING RIGHT NOW. I SWEAR TO GOD, I WILL STRANGLE YOU IF YOU RUN OFF TO GET MARRIED BEFORE ME AND WITHOUT ME THERE.

Sammy grins at me over the screen of her phone. I snort.

"You think I should let her off the hook?"

"Yeah." I nod.

"You're such a softy, Noah," she teases, but she also types out another message with a sweet smile on her face that tells me she appreciates it.

Sammy: Relax, sis. I'm just kidding. But we will take you up on your offer to keep the boys and Dolly so we can have sex all night.

I don't wait to discuss whether she's joking or not before making my move. Because as far as I'm concerned, spending the night having sex with the woman of my dreams is no joke at all.

"Check, please!"

"I think we left our to-go boxes in the cab," Sammy says, her lips basically fused to mine for the thirtieth minute in a row.

The entire way home from Waverly's, we've been kissing and touching and doing pretty much every PDA thing you can do while still out in public and not put yourself at risk for coming face-to-face with the NYPD. And now, with my apartment door officially in view, I've got no plans for stopping.

"Fuck the food," I tell her as I blindly guide us off the elevator and down the hallway toward my door.

Sammy giggles around my persistent lips, and *fuck*, I'm barely hanging on by a thread at this point.

I fumble for my keys when we turn the corner of the hallway, the view of my door nonexistent because Sammy's mouth is still attached to mine. She tastes like chocolate milkshake and Sammy and perfection, and I just hope I can get us into my apartment before I start ripping her clothes off.

"Noah."

My eyebrows pull together as I kiss Sammy harder, fancifully fascinated with how she's managed to say my name and keep her tongue in my mouth all at the same time.

But when she disentangles herself from me and turns around to face my apartment door, I realize the magic of Sammy saying my name while we're making out is that she wasn't the one saying it at all.

"Ashley?" I question, confusion turning my voice raspy. I haven't seen or talked to this woman in months. What the hell is she doing at my apartment?

"I've been trying to get ahold of you, but I guess I can see why you've been ignoring me," she responds, and she glances back and forth between me and Sammy.

"Noah?" Sammy asks. "What's going on?"

"Listen, I'm sorry to catch you off guard like this, but I didn't know what else to do. It's really important."

It's only then that my eyes catch sight of the perfect roundness of her stomach, and a mountain of dread covers me so swiftly I can hardly breathe.

"Noah, I'm pregnant," Ashley says. "And we really need to talk."

PART THREE

PART THREE

Chapter
Twenty-Five

Still Sunday, May 29th

Sammy

Time shrieks and the world stands still as words I never considered a possibility churn over and over and over again in my head.

Noah, I'm pregnant. And we really need to talk.

Noah, I'm *pregnant*.

Noah, I'm pregnant.

Another woman is standing in front of Noah's apartment, her rounded belly evidence of the words I can't unhear, and everything that *was* ten seconds ago is gone in a flash.

And Noah doesn't question this woman. He doesn't ask her who she is.

Instead, he says her name.

"Ashley..." He pauses, and his eyes move from me to her, from me to her, until he just stops on me. Silent apology sits behind his irises as his gaze searches mine. His pupils are constricted, his mouth is set into a firm line, and the only thing I can do is avert my attention to the floor.

This is too much.

"I can see that this isn't a great time." The woman's voice shakes like leaves ready to fall from a tree. "And I'm sorry, Noah, I really am, but I *need* to talk to you."

My heart pounds and my palms sweat, and when I find the strength to look up from my shoes, my vision tunnels around the myriad of emotions that are drifting across Noah's handsome face.

Shock, upset, and maybe most potent of all, acknowledgment, war in his beautiful blue eyes as he works to find a way to make this all okay. It's like he's searching for a way to make me feel secure without dismissing her, to make all of this somehow disappear like it doesn't exist.

But Noah is a magical person, evidence of which I've received on a daily basis for the last month, and the best trick he has up his sleeve is his ability to *not* disappear.

He shows up and shows out, and there's no way he won't—or shouldn't—do that with his own child. He is the antithesis of my ex-husband, and he wouldn't be the man I fell in love with if he weren't.

He has to explore this. He has to hear her out. He has to give himself a chance to be a real father, and most importantly, this baby deserves a chance at Noah Philips's brand of unconditional love.

Children need fathers in their lives; I know this to be true more than anyone else, and there is no way in hell I could allow myself to stand in the way of something this critical. No matter how badly it's going to hurt.

"Noah, I'm going to go. Let the two of you talk." They're the first words I can manage, but they're the only ones that make sense.

"Sammy, no. Stay. Just give me a minute."

I shake my head. "Noah, baby, I can't. You have to face this head on, and you're not going to do that with me here. We'll talk later, okay?"

"Sammy—"

I press my lips to his tight and swift, and then I turn on my heel to jog right into a waiting elevator as an older gentleman steps off with two grocery bags in his hand. The doors close on Noah's sad face, and it's all I can do not to scream as the cart begins its descent.

For the first time in forever, I finally, *finally* thought something was going my way. I thought the universe was done smiting me. I thought all the catastrophe had been a poetic lead-up to the trajectory my life needed to get on track.

I thought…I was going to get my happily ever after.

Tears don't just threaten as I pass the fifth floor, the fourth, and then the third. They fall unchecked down my cheeks like little rivers of devastation, and I can hardly catch a breath.

Why does it feel like I ruin everything?

Why does it have to feel like I'm meant to be alone?

Why does it feel like my life is actually ending?

I don't look at the front desk manager or the doorman as I speed walk through the lobby of Noah's building, frantic for the solace of the street. I don't bother with embarrassment; I'm long past that.

I am *shattered.*

My shoulders ache with invisible weight, my stomach threatening to lurch cheeseburger and milkshake all over the perfect marble floor.

Shoving through the door before the doorman even has it all the way open, I run straight for the edge of the sidewalk. I'm confused about where I am—naturally, since this is the first time I've been to Noah's apartment and I spent my time on the way here kissing instead of paying attention—and I can't even make sense of what direction I need to run to go home.

Agitated, I search for a taxi until I find one coming down the other side of the street.

My chest is tight, and the simple task of exchanging carbon dioxide for oxygen feels like I'm trying to compete in an Olympic-level event.

Impatient to flee this scene so I can breathe again, I step off the curb to cross, and a man shouts something from behind me. I don't even pause. If I don't get out of here right now—if I don't catch my breath soon—I'll die.

Chapter
Twenty-Six

Noah

Sammy's eyes harbor the same kind of wreckage that's produced when a commercial airliner takes a nose dive into a crowded neighborhood.

And truth be told, I'm feeling just about the same.

As the doors close on the elevator, her face disappearing with them as they do, a vise tightens on my heart. I wanted her to stay. I *asked* her to stay.

But it was a selfish request while another woman stands at my door. A woman whose abdomen is rounded with life and whose lips uttered the words, *I'm pregnant.*

Of course Sammy chose to go. Who wouldn't in her situation? A woman from my past, the last woman I actually dated for any extended amount of time, is pregnant.

I'm going to have a kid.

My own son or daughter to upend my life and love like crazy. A little innocent soul to protect and nurture.

Forty-three years of hoping and longing for a life of fatherhood, and I'm finally getting it.

It's a gift. But I never imagined it would come at the expense of the love of my life.

And holy fucking shit, I don't want it to.

I can't let it. I know it's chaotic, but fuck. Having a kid with a woman I dated a few months ago or not, I need Sammy Baker—and her boys—in my life. I need them as my family.

They *are* my family. And I'm pretty sure they've been my family for a lot longer than I even realize.

Ashley stands at my door expectantly—she wants to talk, and it's obvious that we *need* to. But I can't talk right now.

"I'm sorry, Ashley, but I have to go after her," I blurt out the words in a rush.

I turn on my heel, not bothering to wait for her response, run to the end of the hall, and push the elevator call button frantically.

"Noah!" Ashley calls after me. "Wait!"

"Stay here and we'll talk, I promise, but please, you have no idea how important this is! I can't just let her leave!" I shout, not even turning around to look back at her, and smashing the call button with my finger several more times.

But the digital display above the elevator's doors is going in the opposite direction I need it to because the damn thing is still on its way down with *her*.

Impatient and worried, I abandon the ease of a ride and run for the stairwell in the corner, taking the steps down two at a time and even jumping four or so at the end of every flight.

My speed is reckless, but so is my need. I have to get to Sammy before she leaves. I have to remind her what she means to me and ask her for the patience to sort through this mess strategically. *To sort through it together.*

I need to know that she has the faith to believe we can make it work, no matter how muddled this gets, because we're worth it.

The *feeling* we give each other is *worth it.*

I burst through the metal door at the bottom of the stairwell so hard that my downstairs neighbor standing in front of the elevator startles, and all the heads in the lobby turn in my direction. I don't care. I scan the entire space for Sammy, only to catch the front door closing behind her.

"Outside, Mr. Philips," the front desk manager Marco calls out to assist, but I'm already running.

Out and through the door, I bump my doorman with the handle and turn back only briefly to apologize.

But his eyes aren't on me. He's looking toward the street with fear. "Watch out!" he yells, and I turn around just in time to see it.

Sammy is stepping off the curb, her head turned to the right and her hand in the air for the cab coming from up the block, all the while not seeing the cab that's nearly already there coming from the other direction.

God, no!

I don't think; I just move, diving toward her on a sprint and shouting her name. I wrap my arms around her waist and push her from behind just as the cab makes impact with my left hip and sends us both into the air.

Pain radiates up my side, and I clutch Sammy tighter, her screams echoing in my head so loudly, I'm absolutely positive I'll hear them forever.

You didn't think you could live without her, but now, who knows if you'll even get the chance to try.

We hit the ground with an uncontrolled, sickening thud, and that's the end of the world as I know it.

Chapter
Twenty-Seven

Tuesday, May 31ˢᵗ

Sammy

"It's been two days. When is she going to wake up? Is she going to wake up? I don't—"

"Brooke, baby, take a breath. Don't get yourself worked up."

"Take a breath, Chase? How am I supposed to take a breath when my sister is—"

"Shh, baby. I know."

I can hear my sister. And her fiancé. I want to go to them. I *need* to go to them. But murky water surrounds me. It mutes the light and feels thick like swampy sludge against my skin. I struggle against it, but my fight is futile, and I drift deeper and deeper beneath the surface, despite my sister's crying.

"I know this is hard, but you have to give her time. Her body and her brain need to rest."

"But for how long? I need to see her eyes. I can't have this baby without her. I need… God, Chase, I need her."

Soft sobs echo around me, and my head swims with a throbbing vibration.

"The impact she took was significant, and honestly, she's lucky her injuries aren't

worse than they are. We have to be patient." A third voice sounds familiar, but I can't seem to place it right now. I can't make sense of anything, really.

"But what about him?"

There's a pause of some sort. It's weighted, but my thoughts are too sloppy to understand why or how.

"As you know…his injuries are a little more severe. Now, we're just watching and waiting."

"Can't you at least put them in a room together? I feel like they need to be in a room together."

"Let me see what I can do."

The voices fade. Time skips a beat and drifts to blackness. I don't even see the water anymore. The world is a concept rather than a reality.

Roaring pain in my side seems like it should make me jump, but I can't feel myself doing anything.

"You shouldn't be here!"

"I need to be here."

"Are you kidding? Look at my sister. Look at him!"

"Brooke, baby, let's step out of the room for a minute, okay?"

Everything fades away, and I fall back into nothingness. It's such a peaceful contrast to how I normally feel. And yet still, it doesn't feel quite right.

Everything is…missing.

Beep-beep-beep drifts into my subconscious, and I fight the pull of fatigue as hard as I can. My brain feels fuzzy, and I can't remember what day of the week it is.

Were the kids supposed to be dressed up as something today? Or wear a special color?

I have the most nagging feeling that I've already forgotten something, and I'm not even awake yet.

Ugh. It's getting harder and harder to make mornings happen, but I'm a mom. I don't have the option. It's time to get up for work. Time to get the boys to school. Time to start the day.

But damn, I'm struggling to open my eyes.

Did I finally try to use that new lash serum I bought off Amazon months ago? Surely I did it wrong if I've lost the function of my eyelids.

It feels like ripping a stuck Band-Aid off a fresh scab, and my vision could easily be described as legally blind, but I've done it—I've forced the hard start and woken up. Everything is muddled and mashed together, and light forms glowing orbs that distort my surroundings.

I blink what feels like one thousand times to clear the warped fog so I can get my ass moving, only to find that I'm not in my bed...or my bedroom, for that matter.

I'm not anywhere that I recognize at all.

Okay, scary.

I take inventory.

Stark white walls reflect unforgiving fluorescent light, and a scratchy white sheet rubs like sandpaper on my body. There's an incessant beeping from somewhere to my right, but when I go to slap it like I do my alarm clock, a painful cord tugs at my arm.

Ow.

Shit. Is that...an IV?

Am I in the hospital?

I move my head to the left, and pain shoots down my side and around, right into the length of my ribs.

Ow, jeez. Okay, maybe it's good that I'm in a hospital. That really fucking hurts.

More carefully this time, I continue my perusal of the room. My heart lodges itself in my throat when I see *him* in a bed a few feet away from mine.

An onslaught of tenderness, of adoration and affection, floods into my veins.

I want to go to him. But I can't find the strength to move a single one of my limbs.

But wait...his eyes are closed, and there's a white bandage stretched across his head.

Is he okay?

My ribs pull again, and I wince.

Are *we* okay?

Footsteps fill my ears, and I slowly turn my head to the right again. A woman walks inside. Her belly is rounded with pregnancy, and it reminds me of my sister, Brooke.

The woman doesn't look at me. She goes straight to his bed and sits down in a chair beside him. But when she looks across the room, her eyes meet mine and she startles.

"Oh! *Oh!* Oh my God!" She hops up from her chair and grabs something, tapping her fingers against it maniacally.

In a few seconds, a voice fills the room.

"Can I help you?"

"Uh...hello? Uh...hi...Uh...I think she's awake," she fumbles to answer. "The woman...the woman beside my...boyfriend is awake. Her eyes are open."

Boyfriend?

"I'll send the nurse in," the voice replies, but all I can think is, *boyfriend?*

How could he be her boyfriend when I'm in love with him? When he's told me he's in love with me?

"Hu—" I try to speak, but my throat is so dry it's like my vocal cords are stuck together. I swallow against the blockage and try again, but all that comes out is a rough, squeaky sound—one that doesn't sound like anything at all.

The woman stares at me with longing in her eyes as she grabs his hand and squeezes. *She's* holding *his* hand. Everything inside my body wants to revolt against the gesture.

With her free hand, she nervously rubs at her rounded belly, and that movement triggers a memory to break the surface of my consciousness...

We laughed and smiled and kissed as we walked toward his apartment. We stumbled down the hallway, anticipation coursing through our veins, hands greedily grabbing at each other's clothes. We couldn't get close enough.

Everything felt like bliss.

Everything felt perfect.

Until we reached his door, and she was there.

"I'm pregnant," she told him.

Agony rips through every part of me as it all comes flooding back, and I let out a scream I didn't know I was capable of. Doctors and nurses and what feels like a million people flood the room at once, and right in the middle of my cries, everything, once again, goes black.

It feels like a metaphor for my life.

Where Sammy Baker goes, disaster and chaos follow.

"Why did you do that? She was waking up!" I hear Brooke shout, her voice escalating from somewhere close to me.

"Brooke," Chase says softly before the third voice I now realize is Noah's doctor friend Kendall replies, "No, it's okay. It was just a mild push of morphine because she was screaming in pain. I promise she's coming around again."

And that I am. I blink a few times to clear my eyes, and a tear falls unexpectedly from the corner. Brooke looks like herself, if not a little weathered, as she rushes to my side and brings a finger to my face to catch the salty liquid. I just barely spot a ball of fur standing behind her, the fur I know belonging to her sweet Benji.

"Oh, Sam," she whispers, her voice breaking on my name. Her head drops to my chest, and a bolt of pain makes me moan.

She reacts instantly, pulling back and shuffling into Chase's waiting arms. But the entire time, her eyes are fixated on me, and fear and worry and concern are a crushing expression on her pretty face.

"What's..." I lick my lips with a dry tongue, trying to make my mouth work. "What's going on?"

Kendall steps forward then, placing a gentle hand to the edge of my bed. She's wearing hospital scrubs, and I have the vague realization that she's not here as a visitor. She's here as a doctor.

She's my doctor? But why would I need a doctor?

"Sammy, do you know where you are?" she asks, and her hands are busy with a small light that she's shining near my eyes.

"The hospital?" I question, my voice croaking from the dryness at the back of my throat.

Another tear falls down Brooke's face. Chase's mouth is pinched into a firm line.

But Kendall nods, her eyes expectant. "That's right. You're at St. Luke's."

"W-why am I here?"

"You and Noah were hit by a cab," Kendall explains. "Do you remember that?"

A cab? We were *hit* by a cab?

I suck my lips into my mouth on a near sob. *No, I don't. I don't remember anything after stepping off the curb.*

All I can do is move my head just slightly in the negative.

"It's okay. I'm not surprised you don't remember. You took quite an impact." Kendall reaches out to gently caress my hand. "And you've suffered a pretty severe concussion."

"How...how... How long?" I try to formulate a question that I can't quite find the words for, but somehow, Kendall manages to answer.

"You've been out for thirty-six hours."

Thirty-six hours?

My tearful eyes jump to Brooke's, and she nods through her own cry.

I look back to Kendall, whose pretty face is clouded with both sympathy and anguish. Because I'm not the only one hurt.

So is her good friend Noah.

I look around the crowd at my bedside to the other side of the room. Noah is still unconscious, and Ashley is still at his side, clutching his hand.

It's only when she looks up to see me staring at her that that changes. She stands quickly and hustles out of the room past us, offering, "I'll just give you some privacy," as she does.

I'm at war with myself—knowing she must be stressed to capacity and freaking hating her at the same time.

I also want to get the hell out of this damn bed and go to him. I want to curl up at his side and stay there until I hear him say my name.

I just can't believe any of this is happening.

"Sammy, honey," Kendall calls. "Look at me, okay? I need to do a quick evaluation on you. I need to make sure, neurologically speaking, that you're not showing any signs of deficits."

She holds up her penlight and shines it in my eyes again, checking something between the two of them and then clicking it off. "Follow my finger."

I do as she asks, tracing its movements, and she goes on to test some reflexes on my arms and legs before covering me back with the sheet and blanket after each. Brooke and Chase look on with worry etching every line and wrinkle of their normally smooth faces.

Kendall does a few more things and asks me a couple of basic questions about myself and the world before thankfully declaring, "Everything is looking good."

"Thank God," Brooke breathes, a whole pregnant belly worth of air whooshing out of her at once.

"We're going to have to evaluate you a few more times before I'm willing to let you go, but I'm really confident that, besides a little concussion-related amnesia from the accident, you don't have any permanent neurological damage."

"What about Noah?" I find myself asking through a scratchy throat. I can't wait any longer.

Kendall glances to Brooke before stepping forward and putting her hand on my knee. "We're just waiting at this point, honey."

I suck my lips into my mouth.

"His injuries were a little worse than yours. His doorman says he took the brunt of the impact. Most of your injuries were caused in the resulting fall after the cab hit you."

She pats me steadily as my nose starts to sting uncontrollably.

"I know it's hard," she whispers. "But I promise we're doing everything we can to take care of him. We just have to give him time."

I nod and turn my cheek, knowing that if I speak, all the anguish inside me will come pouring out in a horrifying array.

Kendall pats me again before leaving the room, and Brooke rushes forward to take her place.

"Where are the boys?" I ask right away, worry for what they must be feeling racing through me.

"They're with Zoe," Brooke answers, grabbing my hand in hers and squeezing it tight. "They're okay, I promise."

"What did you tell them? They must be so worried."

Brooke shakes her head. "We haven't told them much. Just that you needed a couple of days to recover from a little accident you had."

Oh God. My poor kids.

"I want to see them," I demand, to which Chase complies, whipping out his cell from his pocket.

"On it. I'll call Zoe."

"Can you also just check in with my parents?" Brooke asks, and Chase nods, rounding the bed to step out of the room.

"Mom and Dad are here?"

"They're trying," Brooke updates, reaching out to hold my hand. "They've been trying since Sunday, but the airline delayed and then canceled and then canceled again. They finally got on a plane this morning, just when they were about to drive. They should be here soon."

I look at Noah once more, taking in the bandage on his head and the way his eyes remain firmly shut. The only relief I find is that his chest is still moving up and down in steady waves with each breath he takes. My head falls back on the pillow, and I close my eyes. "I can't believe this is happening."

"Oh, Sam." She shakes her head. "I can't believe you almost didn't date a man who's clearly willing to get hit by a cab for you."

"Brooke!" It is the absolute worst thing she could say right now, but for some reason, it unleashes a manic amount of laughter from my lungs.

Call it stress. Call it trauma. I have no idea, but somehow, laughs spill from both of our lungs.

Though, it doesn't take long for my laughs to morph into tears and my tears to morph into sobs.

Noah's pregnant ex-girlfriend showed up at his apartment, and he chose to run after me. And now, he's lying in a hospital bed unconscious.

It's true. Noah Philips is the perfect man. And my life is such a disaster, it's just about killed him.

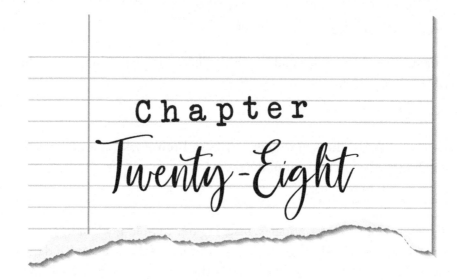

Chapter
Twenty-Eight

Wednesday, June 1st

Sammy

I stare with laser focus at the closed curtain in the middle of the room that shelters the other half as Chase tussles with the boys on the little sofa underneath the TV.

This is the second time they've been to see me since I woke up, and thankfully, this visit has been entirely less emotional than yesterday's. Between the boys', Zoe's, and my own tears, I thought we all might drown.

I'm doing much better, feeling a little strength reentering my limbs, and after six glasses of water, a few short walks in the hallway with a nurse's assistance, and a hospital chicken tender dinner that made me cry for an hour and a half, I can even feel something other than sand in my throat.

And the boys can sense it.

"Mom!" Grant asks on a near shout, wriggling free of Chase's arms just in time to bump into my dad as he walks into the room.

Maybe it's because I'm so hurt, or maybe he's tired from the travel, but Hank just lets him bounce off his body like a bumper car and keeps on moving, my mom trailing behind him.

Of course, Grant is undeterred and continues to me, jumping up to sit on the part of the bed beside my legs.

"Yeah, buddy?" I ask him, reaching out to pat his shoulder.

"Does your bagina hurt?"

What the—?

"Connor from school says girls have a bagina that hurts once a month," he explains without prompting. "Is that why they're keepin' you here?"

Seth stops wrestling Chase to stand up straight and put his two cents into this insane conversation. "It's va-gina, Grant. Jeez."

"Now, now," my mom interjects. "Mommy didn't hurt her vagina, boys. She hurt—"

"Mom," I interrupt, really not wanting to get into the details of my broken ribs, concussion, and torn rotator cuff again. It was upsetting enough the first time. Not to mention, I'd prefer not to speak about my vagina with my entire family in the room.

"Hank, Sue...why don't you and I take the boys to get something to eat? We can give Sammy a little time to rest," Chase offers quickly before turning to address Brooke and give Benji's head a reassuring pat. "And how about you take a load off and elevate your feet for a bit, love? We'll be back in a little while."

I smile gratefully at my soon-to-be brother-in-law, exhaling a huge breath of comfort when the sound of my dad's grumbling fades down the hall—and my mom and the boys disappear right with it.

And a few seconds after that, I let my head fall back on my pillow again, and then slowly, I let it fall to the side—staring again at that damned curtain.

"Sam," Brooke calls on a whisper from my other side, reaching out to touch my hand gently when I don't answer at first.

It feels so wrong, sitting here and having a conversation with my sister about some bullshit topic when I know an unconscious Noah and pregnant Ashley are on the other side. There's a part of me that wants that stupid curtain out of the way, but I know it's a necessity when Grant and Seth are here.

I should be the one at his side. Not her.

"I fucking hate this so much," I whisper to myself, tears stinging my eyes.

"What?" Brooke asks.

"I said *I hate this*," I reiterate, turning to face her and hissing my whisper. "Being this close to him and *her* and just watching and waiting. It's some of the worst hell I've ever been through."

Brooke winces visibly, and my hackles rise. "What? What is it?"

"Well...I kind of requested you be put in the same room," she hedges ever so softly. "I thought... Well, I thought you needed to be together."

"You requested this?!" I snap, the measure of my volume falling away completely. "You requested that your sister be put in a room with her over-lay and the oman-way he ocked-up-nay? Are you azy-cray?"

Brooke's eyes bulge as her gaze jumps to the curtain, and a finger comes to her mouth. "Shh," she suggests, picking up a pad and pen from the telephone table behind her.

She scribbles on the page frantically, and my rage grows with every stroke. Still, I wait to read her message like some kind of fool.

I didn't know any of the backstory! When the hospital called, they just said you'd been hit by a cab and nothing else! I didn't even know Noah was hurt too until we got here because we're not his kin. Then SHE showed up, asking questions about you guys, and they didn't want to tell her anything until she said she was his girlfriend.

I grab the pad and pen from her violently before writing my reply.

Yeah, well, thanks for making this a million times more awkward. We'd just told each other we loved each other, and then BAM. His EX-girlfriend was standing outside his door to tell Noah that she's PREGNANT.

She steals the pen and paper back before I'm even done writing.

You told each other you loved each other?! OMG, Sammy, that's amazing.

"Brooke," I hiss. "Look around yourself right now and tell me again that any part of this is amazing. That woman over there is carrying Noah's baby. His *baby*, Brooke. And let's not forget about the most important detail here. He's still unconscious!"

Truthfully, the only thing that's preventing me from having a full-on breakdown is the fact that Kendall updated us this morning that Noah's MRI and EEG showed normal brain function.

"How the hell is any of this supposed to work out now?" I question, shaking my head as I do. "And every time I look at her, Brooke, I hate her a little more. How terrible is that?"

"At least the curtain is closed today?" Brooke offers, trying to put a stop to my absolute fucking tailspin.

"Oh yeah. The curtain is closed. The curtain is flipping closed because my kids were terrified at the sight of someone they care about unconscious in the bed, Brooke! And I don't need an open curtain to see shit. I can see that woman and Noah's baby and the whole fucking mess every time I close my eyes!"

My voice is a near shout as I lose control of my emotions, but it's only when the curtain rips open to reveal a tearful Ashley standing there that I realize my mistake.

Shit.

"Oh no," Brooke whispers.

"You guys know I can hear you, right?"

I swallow and stare at my sister. "*Brooke.*"

"I really thought she couldn't hear us," she whispers back to me, like, you know, Ashley can't hear us. "I don't know why I thought that, but I definitely thought it."

I nearly snort at the irony of it all. "I was in a coma for two days. What's your excuse?"

Ashley is still staring at us, but I can't seem to address her directly. As fate would have it, though, I don't have to.

Because she says enough for the both of us.

"You have it wrong, by the way."

"Have it wrong?" Brooke asks on a yell. "Do you understand the months I've put in to get these two together, and then you show up out of nowhere all knocked up?! If anyone is wrong here, it's you, missy! Not to mention, Noah is currently un-freaking-conscious at the moment!"

Ashley shakes her head. "I mean you're wrong about the details. I *am* pregnant. But the baby *isn't* Noah's."

"I...uh...what?" I whisper, nearly passing out. Brooke's ability to speak is much more developed.

"What?!" Brooke shouts, and I swear on everything, the glass on the hospital windows shakes. "Who the hell's baby is it, then?!"

Ashley bursts into tears, and without even pausing a beat, Noah groans from behind her.

All three of our heads whip in his direction and find his eyes blinking open. Out of all the time in the world, he's chosen *now* to wake up?

"Sammy," he says through a painful moan, and Ashley runs from the room to get help.

The baby's not his, and the first thing he said is my name.

Maybe hearts really can be sewn back together.

Chapter Twenty-Nine

Noah

Every muscle, every bone, *every cell* inside my body feels like someone has put it in a blender and hit the highest setting. And when I open my eyes, it takes a concerted effort, along with more blinks than my foggy brain can count, to find focus on anything.

First, I see the ceiling.

And then, the bright-white lights above me.

My head throbs as I move my gaze down the wall and spot a whiteboard that has the words **Nurse: Danielle** written out in black marker. *Did I sleep in a patient room last night instead of my on-call room?*

"Is he awake?"

"He's awake!"

"They're getting the doctor!"

"Sammy, I don't think you should be getting out of bed."

"I'm fine."

Familiar voices filter into my ears as my brain tries to put the puzzle pieces together. My own body, inside this hospital bed, an IV in my arm, and a hospital gown on my body.

And bruises. Lots of fucking bruises and abrasions down my arms.

What in the hell is going on?

I try to sit up, but a gentle hand to my chest keeps me in place. "Don't get up yet, Noah."

"Brooke?" I question when I meet her eyes.

But before she can answer, Sammy steps up beside her, dressed in a hospital gown just like me.

"Sammy?"

"Hi, Noah," she whispers, and I swear, a sheen of tears coats her perfect aqua-green eyes. "How are you feeling?"

I don't have time to answer that question, though, because a third woman is now standing at the foot of my bed. A woman who has the power to bring back a waterfall of memories.

Sammy and I were kissing and laughing and trying to make our way into my apartment. The night was perfect. Everything was perfect.

Until I saw her *standing at my door.*

"I'm pregnant," Ashley said. "And we need to talk."

The rest of the memories are fuzzy as they come in.

Sammy walking away. Me going after her.

The sidewalk. The street. The cab.

All I remember after that is sprinting out into the street and the loud sounds of brakes and metal crunching, along with the initial shock of pain that vibrated through my body as I tried to hold on to her with all my might.

Without hesitation, my gaze locks on Sammy again, and I search over her manically, checking for injuries. She looks banged up with bruises like me, but she's standing. That has to be a good sign, right?

"I'm glad to see you're finally awake," Brooke announces with a soft smile.

Finally awake? As in, I've been not *awake for an extended period of time?*

"H-how long have I been out?"

"A few days."

"A few *days?*" I question, and when I spot the ball of fur sitting near Brooke's feet, a million concerns flit through my mind. "Has anyone checked on Dolly? And Kara, oh my God. Has someone talked to Mary? What about the boys, Sammy? Are they okay?"

"Dolly is good. She's been staying at our place," Brooke answers.

And my attention goes straight to Sammy when she replies, "We've talked to Mary, and she's been on standby for updates. Everything is good with Kara. And the boys are with Chase and my parents."

God, she looks beautiful. Even in a fucking hospital gown, she looks beautiful. And the urge to pull her into my arms and never let her go is so strong that I can't deny it.

"No, Noah," Brooke says, and her hand is gently pushing me back again. "You need to stay put. Dr. Hopkins is on her way to see you."

"Here, Brooke, you should sit down," Ashley says as she drags a chair closer to the foot of my bed. Brooke smiles gratefully at her and, with her hand pressed deep into her lower back, waddles over to the chair to sit down.

"You should probably sit down too," Brooke tells Ashley, and Sammy is quick to chime in.

"Yeah, Ashley, you really should get off your feet for a little bit."

"Says the girl who just got out of a coma," Ashley teases her and Sammy laughs. She actually laughs.

The whole scene makes my brain rattle inside my damn head. All three of these women are acting like they're friends. My eyes catch sight of Ashley's rounded belly as she sits down in a chair beside Brooke, and an instant rush of nausea grates at my stomach. *Fucking hell. She's pregnant with my child. My child.*

I start to scrub a hand down my face, but when my fingers bump into some kind of bandage on my forehead and a spark of pain rolls down my spine, I groan. *Shit.*

"Tell him."

I look up to find Brooke staring at Ashley, even nodding encouragingly at her.

"Just tell him," she repeats.

Ashley's gaze flits from Brooke to me to Sammy.

"You should tell him," Sammy whispers, but I can still hear her.

Tell him? As in, tell me?

I move my gaze around the room, looking at each woman and trying to understand what in the hell is happening right now, but the only thing I end up feeling is more confused.

Brooke and Ashley are sitting beside each other—*Brooke is even holding her hand now*—like they're the best of pregnant friends. And Sammy, while still standing at my bedside, isn't the least bit upset that the woman who is pregnant with my child is in this room. This is not at all how I left things, and I have the cab-induced injuries to prove it.

"What's going on?" I ask, and all three women's heads jolt to me.

All three of their mouths open and close like gaping fish, but no words come out.

"What do you need to tell me?" I question again, focusing now on Ashley alone.

At first, she averts her eyes, but then, she meets my steady gaze. "Noah, I'm sorry I didn't tell you sooner, but the—"

"Noah!" Kendall greets as she walks in the door, her gait a near run I just know I'd barely be keeping up with. Ashley shuts up immediately.

Dressed in scrubs with a white lab coat over top, Kendall makes her way over to my bedside, her radiant smile bigger than I've ever seen it before. "I'm so glad to see you're finally awake."

"Yeah." It's all I can say at this point. I mean, the room I've woken up to hasn't exactly made my brain feel any less muddled.

"Everyone's been worried about you," she states as she steps up to my bed-side. She grabs a penlight from her pocket and starts to check my pupils. Even lifts an index finger in front of my face and tells me to follow it with my eyes. "Do you know where you are, Noah?"

"St. Luke's, but apparently I'm a patient this time."

"That's correct. You basically threw yourself in front of a cab," she adds and glances over at Sammy before meeting my eyes again. "The things men do for the women they love."

"Is she okay?" I ask, my attention moving to Sammy.

"Sammy is good. Probably shouldn't have gotten out of bed without a nurse." Kendall grins. "But right now, we're all just going to focus on you, okay?"

I could give two shits about myself, if I'm honest, but I'm kind of powerless at the moment, stuck in this fucking bed.

"Even though you sustained a pretty severe concussion, your MRI and your EEG looked great," Kendall updates. "You have some fractured ribs. A pretty nasty wound on your head that they sutured in the ED. And a small bleed in your spleen, but that was easily fixed in surgery. Truthfully, Noah, I'm shocked your injuries weren't worse than they are."

My fucking spleen was bleeding? Holy shit.

"Is he going to be okay?" Sammy asks, and Kendall smiles over at her.

"His neurological function appears to be intact, and his vitals have been sta-ble since his surgery. So yeah, Sammy, other than being a little banged up, I think he's going to be just fine. Though, I definitely want to do a full evalu-ation of him before I can say with certainty."

I know everything Kendall is saying equates to good news, but all I can do right now is look at Sammy. The last time I saw her, I thought it was going to be the last time I saw her alive and well.

But she's here. In front of me. Living and breathing. *Thank everything.*

I'm not ashamed to admit that I can feel some tears brewing in my eyes.

Kendall squeezes my shoulder compassionately, clearly having noticed my emotional moment. "By the way, Dale's on his way up. He's been asking about you all morning."

"What about—" I start to open my mouth to ask Kendall about Sammy's injuries, but another voice in the room stops me.

"Dale?" The question comes from Ashley, and she's no longer sitting in the chair beside Brooke. Instead, she's on her feet now, and her eyes are insanely wide as if someone just gave her a jump scare.

"Yes, Dale," Kendall answers with a smile. "He's my husband, who is also an ER doctor here. We've all been good friends for many, many years."

"Dale is *your* husband," Ashley repeats, but it's not a question.

There's a part of me that's a little confused by Ashley's confusion about who Dale is. I'm pretty sure when we were dating all those months ago, she met Dale. At least once or twice, *right?*

"You okay?" Brooke questions, and I realize it's directed at Ashley, who is now pacing the tile floor near the windows.

But Ashley doesn't answer, and all the color appears to have drained from her face.

"Ashley?" Sammy asks, concern in her voice. "You okay?"

"Miss, I think you should sit down," Kendall states, her attention no longer focused on me but the pregnant woman who is still erratically pacing near the windows.

Ashley tries to force a smile to her lips, but it's all off. "I'm f-fine." She shakes her head frantically. "I'm fine."

"Oh no." Sammy's voice fills my ears, and I move my gaze back to her. But she's too busy staring at Ashley, and her eyes nearly consume her whole head as she watches the woman intently. "Oh *nooooooo.*"

Oh no? I might've just woken up from a fucking coma, but it sure feels like I'm missing something here...

Chapter Thirty

Noah

"The man of the hour!" Dale exclaims as he walks into the room, his eyes directed at me. He steps up to my bedside, standing right beside Kendall, and places a strong hand to my shoulder. "Glad to see you're awake. How ya feelin'?"

All I can do is shrug. "I think I'm okay."

"Would you mind getting out of my way, Dale? I'm trying to evaluate a patient here." Kendall nudges him with her hip, and he starts to laugh.

"Oh, c'mon, baby, he's awake and talking. I think he's good." Dale winks at me before he starts to survey the rest of the room. "He's even gathered his own fan club," he states, his gaze startling noticeably when he gets to Ashley standing by the windows.

Tell me about. I was surprised to see her, too.

"Were you working when they brought me in?" I ask Dale, trying to make sense of all the things I can't on my own. He surprises me by shaking his head instead of giving me a mouthful of his usual sarcastic commentary.

"Who was working?"

"Scott Shepard," Kendall says. "He's the one who sutured your head."

258 | max monroe

"Well, that's good news," I say, offering a teasing smile toward Dale. "Lord knows Dale is the last person I'd want suturing anything on my body."

Dale doesn't say anything, doesn't even flash a vulgar finger in my direction. Instead, he watches his wife intently as she continues to evaluate me—she's currently focused on the reflexes of my arms and legs while he carefully avoids eye contact with the rest of the room.

It's kind of odd. Honestly, I can't remember the last time I saw Dale being anything but a cutup. But then again, this is my first coma, so what the fuck do I know?

Maybe he's taking it hard?

I try to make eye contact with Sammy, but her eyes are too busy to snag, even in passing. They're hard at work, bouncing between Ashley and Dale. When I look at Brooke, she's doing the same damn thing.

What in the hell is going on?

"What is your deal?" Kendall asks Dale on an annoyed laugh. "If you stand any closer to me, you'll literally be up my ass, hun. Mind giving me some space so I can finish evaluating Noah?"

Dale doesn't respond, but he does try to comply, if poorly.

Kendall sighs and continues her evaluation, her attention now on listening to my heart, lungs, and bowel function with her stethoscope.

And Sammy and Brooke are still playing some weird version of eyeball ping-pong.

Truthfully, my head is starting to fucking hurt from trying to understand what is going on in this room.

There's a part of me that wonders if this is all some kind of hallucination. Like, maybe I've dreamed that I've woken up, but I haven't woken up at all?

"Noah, everything is looking really good," Kendall updates and slides her stethoscope back over her shoulders. "I still want to do a follow-up MRI on your head, as well as a follow-up CT of your abdomen to make sure your spleen is behaving and there's not anything else we missed. But other than that, I think you're well on your way to a full recovery."

"Great news," Dale says, but his voice is quieter than normal. "Now, let's head on out, babe, and let Noah rest."

Kendall looks at him, her expression half bewilderment and half annoyance, evidently feeling as fed up as I am. "Seriously? What is your deal?"

He clears his throat and leans closer to her to whisper, "Nothing, babe. I just think we need to give Noah some space."

While they quietly bicker back and forth, I focus my attention back on Sammy. My head might feel fuzzy as fuck, but I know for a fact that the reason we're both in this damn hospital has everything to do with her walking away from me. I know that when I left the conscious plane, she was not in any way comfortable with the thought of me having a baby with another woman. Hell, neither was I.

But I don't know. *Maybe the accident changed how she felt?*

"Sammy." I lift my hand, reaching for hers, only capable of brushing her fingertips with mine.

She looks down at me, and I search her eyes. "Are you okay?" I ask, and she nods. It's not enough for me. "Seriously, Sammy, I think we need to—"

"Noah," she says, cutting me off before I can finish. "Everything is good."

"But Sammy, I really—"

"Noah, everything is good. Seriously." She steps closer to squeeze my hand. "I promise."

"Sammy, there are things I want to—"

"It's fine," she cuts me off again. "All good in the hood."

What the—?

"Oh, for fuck's sake!" Brooke shouts into the otherwise silent room. "Noah, the baby isn't yours!"

Time pauses. Brakes squeal to a stop inside my head. And in the distance, I'm pretty sure I can hear sirens. Or explosions. Or, I don't know, the end of the fucking world.

"The baby isn't mine?" I question, looking directly at Ashley. "*What?*"

"Sorry, Ashley," Brooke mutters with a frown. "I just…I couldn't take it any longer! Blame it on the hormones."

I look at Sammy and then at Ashley again, and then my eyes make the circuit of the room, realizing that the only person in here who isn't looking at Ashley is Dale.

"C'mon, Ken," he tells his wife and even wraps his arm around her shoulders. "We should give them some privacy."

Kendall shakes him off. "Stop, Dale."

My eyes are back on Ashley, waiting for an answer to the very important fucking question I just asked, but her gaze isn't looking anywhere near me.

No. She's looking straight at Dale.

And the entire room goes silent. Until Kendall asks, "Dale, why is she looking at you?"

Dale's mouth gapes, but then he quickly slams it shut. Ashley now has tears in her eyes.

"Dale?" Kendall questions again, her voice rising in irritation. "Why is she looking at you like that?"

"I'm an idiot," Dale mutters, running a hand through his hair. "Baby, I'm so sorry."

"You're sorry?" Kendall asks. "You're sorry? Why are you sorry?"

"Ken, let's just step outside and talk, okay?"

"No." She shakes her head. "You need to tell me right now. What the fuck is going on?"

"Baby, we really should—"

"Dale!" Kendall steps closer to him, her face mere inches from his as she pokes a finger into his chest. "Tell me I have this all wrong. Tell me you have no involvement with that woman and the child inside her belly."

Dale swallows hard again. "Kendall, I'm so sorry."

"Holy shit," Brooke whispers.

"Are you fucking kidding me?" Ashley isn't pregnant with my baby. She's pregnant with *Dale's* baby. And I probably would have figured it out faster if I weren't coming out of a fucking *coma*.

One of my best friends cheated on his wife with one of my exes, and I got pulled into his bullshit drama. Hell, the woman I love almost fucking died because of *his* drama.

I'm *pissed*.

Kendall's normally confident face is flush with heartbreaking disbelief.

And fuck if that doesn't make me even angrier.

"It didn't mean anything, baby. I'm so sorry," Dale whines, trying to grab his wife's hands, but Kendall pushes him away. If I could move without excruciating pain, I'm pretty sure I'd lay him out.

"Mommy!" Grant's tiny voice breaks through the tension in the room, and Seth's voice follows shortly after that. "Mom, we got ice cream from downstairs!"

Both Grant and Seth run up to Sammy, and Chase—along with two people I believe are Brooke and Sammy's parents—isn't too far behind them.

"I think it's time for us to go!" Brooke exclaims and stands to her feet, moving quicker than I thought was possible with how pregnant she is.

"But—" Chase starts to say, but Brooke is quick to cut him off.

"Time to go, Chase. We need to check on Dolly, remember?" Her eyes are like laser beams as they lock with his. "*Remember?*"

"Uh...okay?" He's fucking clueless, which, at this point, is probably a good thing.

"You get the boys. I'll get my parents. Everyone, let's go!"

Not even ten seconds later, Brooke has managed to clear out the room, leaving me, Sammy, Kendall, Dale, and Ashley.

But then, after Kendall storms out and Dale chases after her, only Sammy, Ashley, and I remain.

If this isn't shit getting real, then I don't know what to call it.

Chapter
Thirty-One

Sammy

"I'm so sorry," Ashley says, and tears are now streaming down her face. "I didn't mean for any of this to happen. I didn't mean to drag you two into this. I feel so guilty for everything that's happened."

There's a part of me that feels bad for her, but there's another part of me that is angry over the whole thing. I mean, Noah and I ended up in the hospital, and for the past few days, I wasn't sure what was going to happen to him, all because of the way she went about this.

"I just don't understand," Noah states, and his mouth is set into a firm line. "Why did you show up at my apartment, then?"

"I didn't know what else to do." Ashley swallows hard against the emotion that's still streaming down her face. "Dale was ignoring my calls and text messages, and I was hoping you would be able to help me talk to him." She grimaces. "I didn't even realize until Sammy got so upset and left that she thought the baby was yours."

Noah's laugh is completely devoid of humor as I reach out to squeeze his hand with my own.

"I messed up, I know." More tears spill down her cheeks. "I'm so sorry."

"How in the fuck did you even get involved with Dale?" Noah asks, his anger evident in the hardness of his beautiful jaw. "He's married, Ashley. And I'm pretty sure you knew that."

"I know!" she cries. "Trust me, I know! And I wish I could take it back, but I can't."

"When did this happen?" All I can do is stand there and listen as he interrogates her.

"About a month after we broke up," she explains without making eye contact. "I saw him out one night at a bar. He was by himself. I was by myself. And we just…I don't know…we got to talking, and one thing led to another, and he ended up back at my place."

"Fucking hell," Noah mutters and looks over at me for a brief moment before looking at her again. "Was that the only time?"

She shakes her head. "We stayed…in touch…for about two months after that."

"Two *months?* Jesus!" he snaps, and a small sob escapes her throat.

"I know, Noah," she says quietly, a whimper highlighting her voice. "I'm not proud of any of it. And I shouldn't have let it happen. I know that."

"You both shouldn't have let it happen," Noah interjects. "Both you and Dale are in the wrong here." When he says his good friend's name, I can hear his disappointment.

It certainly takes two to do the cheating-tango, but I know he must be heartbroken that his friend was willing to be a party to it.

"I'm so sorry," Ashley apologizes again. "To both of you. For everything. I shouldn't have showed up to your apartment like that, Noah."

"Why did you tell them he was your boyfriend?" I ask the one question that's been rolling around inside my head.

"It was the only way they'd let me stay in the room with him. With you both," she explains. "I know it wasn't the right thing to do, but I just felt so guilty about everything. I mean, you both were in comas. Because of me. I felt like I needed to be here. With you guys. I couldn't just leave you to deal with the mess I made."

Goodness. She's blaming herself for our accident. It makes my heart break.

"Ashley, I really don't think you need to shoulder the guilt of the accident and what happened after," I insert without hesitation. "I know that wasn't your intention when you showed up at Noah's apartment that night, and I can only imagine how scared and alone you've been feeling since finding out about the baby."

"No," she comments, shaking her head. "I swear, all I wanted to do was talk to you, Noah. I just wanted you to help me get in touch with Dale. That was it. I didn't mean for any of this to happen."

The room goes quiet. Both Noah and I are unsure of what to say. I don't know what Noah is thinking right now, but I mostly just feel sad for Ashley. Her life has been flipped on its head with her pregnancy, and she's currently facing it all on her own.

And the father of her child just ran out of the room...after his wife.

"I just hope, one day, you'll both be able to forgive me," Ashley says, her voice quiet. "I don't expect that right now, but...one day."

"Ashley, I—" Noah starts to say something, but she cuts him off with a raise of her hand.

"No, Noah. You really don't need to say anything," she says. "Honestly, I think it's more than time for me to go. I don't want to be in the middle of you two any more than I already have. And I'm just happy you're both okay."

Before I know it, she's stepping forward and wrapping me up in a hug. "I'm so sorry, Sammy," she whispers into my ear. A moment later, she does the same to Noah.

And then, she's gone, leaving Noah and me alone in the room.

He's still lying in the bed, and I'm at the foot of it. Suddenly, all I can think about is feeling the heat of Noah's body with my own. I climb into the bed without delay, tucking myself into the crook of his arm with supreme care.

"Sammy," he whispers my name, and I lock my gaze with his.

The past few days have been a fucking whirlwind. But even despite the moments when I thought that Noah was about to be the father to another woman's child, I never stopped loving him. I never stopped worrying about him. I never stopped wanting him.

He's my person. My guy. The only man I want to be with. Frankly, I don't think I've ever been more certain of someone in my whole life than I am of him.

Than I am of us, together.

And truthfully, if we can manage to come out on top of this insane situation that included a pregnant ex-girlfriend and an accident and comas, then it sure as hell seems like we can handle anything.

"Noah?"

"Yeah?"

"Remember that time you told me you were looking to be a little more whelmed in your life?"

He laughs a big belly chuckle that shakes my body along with his own and then groans audibly with a hand to his abdomen. "Shit, Sammy. Don't make me laugh."

"I'm sorry," I apologize through a smile.

He adjusts the blankets over both of us and pulls me tighter to his chest, kissing the top of my forehead as he does.

"I love you, Sammy."

"I love you too." I look up and meet his eyes, and without hesitation, I tenderly press my lips to his. "By the way, thanks for saving me from that cab," I whisper against his lips. "I know it might be kind of soon for this, but it was pretty sexy how you just threw your body in front of mine like that."

Soft chuckles vibrate his chest. "Well, I'm glad I could manage to be sexy while I was absolutely terrified I was going to lose you." His eyes turn serious as they search mine. "But mostly, I'm just so fucking happy that you're okay."

"I'm happy you're okay too," I tell him and mean every fucking word of it. "And from here on out, I think we should try to have a little less excitement in our lives."

"Grandma Sammy and Grandpa Noah?" he asks, his lips curving up into a big smile.

"Exactly. Till death do us part. But this time, only the old-age, natural-causes kind."

Chapter Thirty-Two

Friday, June 3rd

Sammy

I slide away my barely eaten tray of today's glorious breakfast—courtesy of St. Luke's café—and Noah looks over at me with humor dancing in his eyes.

"Not hungry?" he asks, reaching out to squeeze my thigh while simultaneously tossing a piece of cantaloupe into his mouth.

Today is the first day that both Noah and I have been up and moving freely in our hospital room. And ever since yesterday's lunch, we've made a habit of eating together on one of our beds with both of our bedside tables perched in front of us like we're two little old people munching on TV dinners in a nursing home.

It's pretty fucking adorable, but yeah, I'm ready to get the h-e-l-l out of here.

"Oh, I'm hungry," I comment on a snort. "But I'm ready for real food."

"Hold up. Are you dissing St. Luke's Café?"

"Yes," I answer without guilt or shame. "I am most definitely dissing your prestigious hospital cafeteria. And don't even try to tell me the usual chef is on vacation."

Noah chuckles, still eating his fruit cup, and I stand, pushing my bedside table out of my way as I do. "I can't wait for them to release us."

And from what we've been told by the nurses and doctors we've seen, today is the day for discharge. *Thank everything for that.*

"From your lips to God's ears, Sam. I'm ready to get out of here too."

"What?" I question with faux surprise on my face. "You're not going to miss getting all your meals served by your favorite café?"

He laughs, but before he can respond to that, three knocks sound against our door.

"Okay, Dr. Philips, hop into the wheelchair," Ally, our dayshift nurse, announces as she steps into the room. "You need to take a ride with me to CT."

"What?" Noah looks over at her with a furrowed brow. "Why?"

"Because I want one final CT scan of your head and your abdomen before I discharge you," Kendall states as she steps up beside Ally. A small smile makes an appearance on her face, but it doesn't reach her eyes.

I don't know what's happened between her and Dale, but Kendall isn't the kind of woman who shows weakness. She's strong, fiercely independent, and from what Noah told me after he spoke with her yesterday afternoon when I had walked down to the cafeteria with the boys, she's keeping everything close to the cuff.

What happened between her and Dale? It's still a mystery.

What's going on with Ashley and the baby and Dale's involvement in that? Also a mystery.

"But we got follow-up scans yesterday morning." Slow but steady, Noah rises to his feet, but he doesn't make a move toward the doorway where Ally stands with the wheelchair. He quirks an eyebrow at Kendall. "Don't you think you're going a little overboard, Dr. Hopkins?"

"Yeah, well, I want one more set of scans." Kendall puts one hand to her hip. "So, if you want to get discharged, I highly suggest you follow doctor's orders."

Noah sighs. Before he heads over to Ally, he stops at my bed—where I'm currently packing some of my belongings that Brooke brought for me into one of the hospital's plastic bags—and presses a kiss to my lips. "Don't leave without me."

"I'll try not to, but I'm not sure I can make any promises."

"Sammy." He reaches out to discreetly pinch my ass through the pair of pajama pants I'm currently sporting.

"What?" I retort on a squeal. "We've already established I'm starving. I'll do my best to wait for you."

"Your ass better still be here when I get back."

"Fine. Fine." I pretend to be put out by his request, even though the very last thing I'm going to do is leave this hospital without him. "I'll be here, Grandpa. Have fun getting your picture taken."

"Oh yeah, I'm going to have a blast," he mutters as he eases his ass down into the wheelchair. "You know, Ally, I could easily walk there."

"No, you can't," Kendall refutes with a knowing smile. "Hospital policy."

Noah sighs and offers a wave goodbye as Ally wheels him out of our room, and I can't deny that I laugh a little at his expense. If there's one thing my guy isn't used to, it's being on the receiving end of medical care in the hospital.

"How are you feeling, Sammy?" Kendall asks, stepping over to where I'm sitting on the edge of my hospital bed now.

"I'm feeling pretty good." I shrug as she moves forward to evaluate my pupils with the little light thingie in her pocket.

"And the headaches?"

"Haven't had one since yesterday morning."

"That's good," she comments and proceeds to gently scan her fingers over the multiple bruises on my arms. "Don't be surprised if you do get some minor headaches over the next few days after you go home. Along with some soreness as you start to use your muscles more with movement. But it shouldn't be anything you can't manage with some over-the-counter Tylenol. Anything worse than that, and I want you to give me a call, okay?"

"Okay."

Kendall proceeds to listen to my heart and lungs and belly with her stethoscope before making me stand and do a few exercises that she says test neurological function and reflexes.

And the entire time she's doing it, I can't stop thinking about what happened in this very hospital room—about what she must be going through right now. About how fucking strong of a woman you have to be to put on a brave face and come into work even though you just found out that your husband had an affair and got another woman pregnant.

"Well, Sammy," Kendall announces with a barely there smile. "I think it's safe to say I can sign off on your discharge paperwork today."

"How are you?" I blurt involuntarily, my thoughts winning the tug-of-war with my ability to know better, and she jerks her head back in surprise. Instantly, I try to soften the blow. "Look, I know we don't know each other all that well, but I want you to know that you have a friend in me. And I want you to know that I'm so sorry."

"I…" She pauses and glances out toward the window. "I…" Her mouth turns down at the corners, and she swallows hard against it before bringing her gaze to mine again. "I appreciate that. Thank you."

On the outside, Kendall looks like a beautiful supermodel-doctor-woman who has it all together. But behind her eyes, there's a deep sadness. Behind her eyes, she's a woman who is barely hanging on by a thread. A woman who is trying to keep it all together.

A woman who thought she had everything and lost it all in one fell swoop.

And goodness, can I relate to that so much. I've certainly been there.

"I can't," she says, and her voice is so quiet compared to the woman I first met all those weeks ago in Central Park. "I know it's soon and I need to give things time, but I don't think I can ever forgive him for this."

I'm surprised by her candor, but I'm also grateful she is willing to open up to someone.

"Kendall, I think your feelings are valid, no matter what they are." I reach out to gently squeeze her hand. "I also know with certainty that you didn't deserve this."

Her bottom lip trembles ever so slightly, but she pushes past the emotional discomfort with a nod of her head. "I didn't, did I?"

"No, you didn't." I shake my head.

"And you know what?"

"What?"

"Ashley didn't deserve this either," she adds, and her normally full lips look so small as they form a tight line. "Apparently, she had been trying to get in touch with Dale for weeks and weeks. And he knew it. And he ignored her. Tried to act like she didn't exist. Obviously, I don't condone sleeping with another woman's husband, but I definitely don't condone a man not taking responsibility for his actions."

I'm shocked by her words. Ashley didn't reveal all that to Noah and me, but now it's making even more sense as to why she ended up at Noah's door.

"I don't even know what to say, Kendall."

"Tell me about it." She snorts and swipes a hand over her cheeks, where one lone tear snuck out of her eyelids. "Anyway, I better head to my next patient. Tell Noah I'm keeping an eye out for his scans, and if everything still looks good, I'll get you both discharged ASAP."

"He'll be glad to hear that."

She walks over to the sink to wash her hands before drying them with a paper towel and tossing it in the trash. But before she leaves the room, she pauses at the threshold of the door. "Sammy?"

"Yeah?"

"He's one of the good ones," she says. "And he's always been that way. Ever since I've known him."

She means Noah, and I couldn't agree more.

He *is* one of the good ones. He's the best man I've ever known.

And I hope I get to keep him forever.

chapter
Thirty-Three

Saturday, June 4th

Noah

Shooting pain in my abdomen forces my eyes open on a groan. And the groan urges an additional sting in my ribs to occur. *Son of a bitch.*

"You okay?"

I look to my left to find Sammy beside me. In my bed. And a hint of concern in her eyes.

"Yeah, I'm good, hun," I mutter and scrub a hand down my face, but when I do that, I accidentally poke my fingers into the sutured wound on my head. When I groan again, Sammy's mouth quirks up into a knowing smile.

"Let me guess, you also forgot that you got hit by a cab and are still healing?"

I laugh, but it's more of a silent whoosh of air than anything else. "Something like that."

After we were discharged from the hospital yesterday afternoon, Brooke demanded that the boys and Dolly stayed with her and Chase for an extra night, and Sammy and I ended up back at my place, trying to heal and checking in with our friends and family every chance we got. I guess a near-death experience will do that to you.

Mary didn't tell Kara what happened, and honestly, I'm glad. She's so attached to me, she wouldn't have taken the news well. And with Kara, that means neglecting even her most basic of needs.

When I'm healed up a little more, I'll explain it to her the best I can.

Once the pain settles, I realize that Sammy is sitting up in bed and holding a pillow to her ribs. "Are you okay?"

"I mean, I just feel like a seventy-five-year-old woman who fell down the stairs, but I'm good." Her eyes are wide, but her lips are still smiling. "The soreness the nurses told me about is real."

"Did you take anything?" I question, forcing myself to sit up in the bed and rest my shoulders against my headboard.

"Noah, you and I both know that what I'm feeling isn't going to be resolved by Tylenol. It's just going to need some time."

"Yeah, but you also have actual pain medication that would take the edge off."

"As do you, but I don't see you taking any."

"Touché." I smirk. "We're quite the stubborn pair, you and I."

"Nearly hopeless," she adds with a teasing smile. "Though, good news is that I've already DoorDashed us breakfast."

"Let me guess, St. Luke's Café?"

"Very funny." She giggles and reaches out to tenderly brush her hand over my cheek. "We're getting a full breakfast experience from Waverly's Diner. I even got a little wild and ordered us both chocolate milkshakes."

"Sounds very nutritious."

"We deserve it." She grins. "I mean, if there are two people who deserve to drink chocolate milkshakes for breakfast, it's us."

"On that, we can agree."

Sammy smiles over at me, and there's just something about her, something about waking up to her, something about us together in my bed that feels right in a way that I never want to feel wrong again.

"Let's move in together."

"W-what?"

"Let's move in together," I repeat confidently. Sammy and I are meant to be together—this I know for sure.

She searches my eyes. "You want to live together?"

"You, me, the boys, and Dolly," I expand. "I want to be a family, Sammy, with you."

"Where is all of this coming from?" she asks. "You don't feel like this is a little rushed?"

"No, actually, I don't." I shake my head. "I love you. I want to be with you. I want to mix and mingle our lives together. And I sure as shit don't want to spend another morning waking up without you beside me. You're the only woman who has ever given me the *feeling*. Waiting any longer would merely be a waste."

"The all-consuming, heart-racing, stomach-aching, I'm-going-to-throw-up-if-this-doesn't-work-out *feeling*?" she asks, repeating my exact words from what feels like forever ago.

"Yes. *That* feeling." I smile and reach out to take one of her hands into mine, caressing her fingers with my thumb. "You're the woman I want to spend my life with, and I want to start now."

"I don't want to waste any more time either," she whispers, and a fresh sheen of tears makes her eyes shine. "I want to keep you forever."

"Yeah?"

"Yeah, Noah." She nods, and a few tears slip from her lids.

I reach out to swipe the emotion from her face and then carefully close the distance between us so I can press my mouth to hers. My ribs and abdomen sting like a son of a bitch from the movement, but I don't give a fuck.

"I love you," I whisper against her lips, and she returns the sentiment by deepening the kiss.

It only takes another minute or so of us riling each other up to realize that we're in no condition to take things much further than a kiss.

Eventually, we both end it on a combination of laughter and groans and grimaces and smiles.

"Noah, I never would've thought I would say that I literally can't have sex with you right now, but yeah, I can't."

"Fuck, don't make me laugh." I grasp my stomach as chuckles jump from my lungs.

"I'm sorry!" she exclaims, but then it's her turn to whimper in pain as she holds the pillow to her ribs. "Ah, shit. That hurts."

By the time we manage to stop laughing and grimacing in pain, Sammy smiles over at me. "So, I can assume we'll take a rain check on the sex, yeah?"

"Yeah," I tell her. "But on the moving in together part? Hell no. We're going to start figuring that shit out right away."

"You know… Brooke mentioned that there's a three-bedroom apartment that just went on the market in her building…"

"She told me about that too," I answer, and a mischievous smile makes itself known on my face.

"What? What's that look for?"

"I might've put in an offer."

"When in the hell did you do that?" Her eyes nearly bulge out of her head.

"Yesterday."

"While we were in the hospital?"

I nod.

"So, what, I was just a forgone conclusion?"

"Actually, when it comes to you, *I* was the forgone conclusion," I answer. "And lucky for me, not only did you agree to move in with me, but the seller also accepted my offer."

Her answering smile is breathtaking, and the kiss she places on my lips is powerful enough for me to forget about the discomfort for a good five minutes.

Sammy and me, together forever. That's my plan, and I'm sticking to it.

EPILOGUE

Part One

Wednesday, June 22nd

Sammy

I carry the basket of folded laundry into the hall and stop at the boys' room to put their clothes away. Though, the instant I step inside, my heel makes contact with a damn Lego, and it takes everything in me not to curse up a storm.

Holy fucking shit! I mentally scream as my eyes bounce down to see if my foot is still intact, hobbling on one foot as I do. *Son of a motherloving sucking holy hell!*

"Whatcha doin', Mom?" Grant asks, completely oblivious to my agony.

I force a deep inhale of oxygen into my lungs, and once the pain eases enough for me to speak without dropping f-bombs, I announce through still slightly gritted teeth, "Boys, I told you to clean up your toys."

"We did," Seth comments like he can't see the pile of Legos they've managed to leave by the door. You know, the ones that nearly turned my foot into a bloody stump.

I eye him knowingly, a look that says, "You best clean up your shit." And he has the good sense not to make any additional commentary.

Grant, on the other hand, is still completely clueless, swinging a plastic sword around with his newly uncasted arm as he jumps on his bed.

"Grant, what did I tell you about jumping on the bed?"

"You said we shouldn't do it."

"Yeah... So why are you doing it?"

He shrugs. "Because it's fun?"

"Listen, mister, you better get your little butt off that bed and help your brother clean up, or else I'm going to call Zoe and tell her you guys can't go to the zoo today. Do you and Sal want to end up back in casts so soon?"

"Ah, man," he whines, but he also listens. *Thank goodness.*

Once their clothes are put away and I'm certain they're following through on their cleanup orders, I head out of their room and carry the laundry basket into the room Noah and I set up for Kara to occasionally sleep over.

Hers, of course, is much cleaner than my two heathens, and I only have to put on her freshly washed sheets before leaving her room.

By the time I reach our bedroom, I find Dolly spread out on our bed, enjoying a little siesta. Our girl has her own dog bed, mind you, but once I splurged on a fluffy Egyptian cotton comforter and sheets, she's decided that her naps belong on our bed.

I can't blame her. The coziness is real.

"You're a lazy girl, Dolly. But I get it. It's not easy chasing after those two wild boys all day long." I rub a gentle hand down her back, and she responds by wagging her tail for a few seconds.

"Mom! Noah's on the phone!" Seth screams down the hallway, and I give Dolly one last scratch behind the ears before heading into the hallway.

I locate my now-discarded-on-the-counter phone and find both of my sons sitting on the barstools in the kitchen.

"Mom, I'm hungry," Grant announces as I lift my cell to my ear.

"Hey," I greet into the receiver before telling my smallest child, "Zoe is going to take you to lunch, but you can have a banana, if you want."

"But, Mom! I wanted cookies."

"*Grant.*"

"Fine," he mutters and grabs a banana off the counter. "You're so diff-a-calt."

"Sounds like a busy day over there," Noah's amused voice says in my ear while I suck in my lips to keep myself from laughing at Grant's cute take on the pronunciation of the word difficult.

"Oh, you know, just some laundry and cleaning up and nearly amputated my foot with a Lego. Nothing too wild."

He laughs at that. "Those Legos are going to be the death of our feet."

"Tell me about it." I snort. "How's work going?"

"Not bad. Just finished up with my final surgery and only have patient rounds left," he answers. "You think you have some time to grab a late lunch with me?"

"Dolly and I are supposed to meet Kendall and Chanandler at the park for a walk, but other than that, I'm free until work. Zoe's taking the boys to the zoo and said she could keep them busy until around five or so."

Now that Noah and I have gotten all settled in our new place, Kendall and I are creating a bit of a routine. At least once a week, we've promised to meet in the park with the dogs, and for the past two Sundays, she's been joining Brooke and me for lunch at our favorite diner.

Honestly, she's starting to become a pretty close friend of mine.

And Dale, well, that motherfucker isn't in the picture. Last I heard, he's trying to take responsibility for the precious baby in Ashley's belly, but other than the fact that Kendall filed for divorce, that's all I know. Even Noah has pretty much cut ties with him.

The cheating was bad enough, but the way he's handled the aftermath? Noah's been unable to move past it.

"You want to eat together in my on-call room?" Noah asks, but his voice takes on an edge of unspoken promise.

I sure do like the sound of that...

"I think I can squeeze you in, Dr. Philips."

"Well, thank fuck for that." His voice has this sexy rasp to it that urges a secret smile to my lips. "Text me when you're on your way here."

"I'll even pick up sandwiches at that deli I like so much."

"Good idea." He laughs at that, but then his voice drops to a whisper. "Lord knows you're going to be starving after I'm done with you."

"And what about you?"

"Oh, don't you worry about me. I'm going to eat. A lot."

Oh boy.

"Yeah, okay, I'm getting off the phone now."

Noah's chuckle fills my ears again. "Love you, Sam. See you soon."

"Love you too." *You horny, sexy bastard.*

Just as I'm hanging up the call, Zoe is unlocking our front door and stepping inside.

"Zoe!" Grant exclaims, and both he and Seth practically barrel into her on a sprint.

She hugs them both tightly. "You guys ready to hit the zoo?"

"Heck yes! I want to see the alligators!" Grant cheers.

"But we gotta stop at the polar bears first, Grant!" Seth exclaims.

And just before my two boys can start their usual round of bickering, Zoe is quick to chime in, "Do you guys mind if we stop and see the monkeys first?" she asks. "I heard we'll get to see them eat lunch if we go there first."

"Really?" Grant asks, and Seth is already giving in to my nanny's request.

"Oh yeah, let's see the monkeys first!"

"Man, I'm going to miss you when you're off to Texas in a month," I tell her, and she looks up at me with a sad smile.

"And I'm going to miss you guys like crazy too."

"Just know, you're always welcome back here. Anytime," I state and step over to wrap her up in a tight hug while the boys put on their shoes. "Even if you just want to come hang out in the city for a week or two during breaks or summer, we'll always have a place for you."

"I'm probably going to take you up on that," she says, and I release her from my embrace with a smile.

"You better."

It doesn't take long before Zoe ushers both Seth and Grant out the door, their little asses far too excited to get to the zoo to dillydally, and I start to get ready to head to the park with Dolly.

But I only manage to get her leash in my hands before my phone starts ringing from my purse.

Incoming call Brooke sits front and center on the screen.

"Hey, sis," I greet, but all I get back is a good ten seconds of moaning. But, like, not the good kind of moaning. It's mixed with panting breaths. "Brooke? Are you okay?"

"I...*ah*... Contractions! L-l-l-labor!" she eventually pushes out. "Ch-chase isn't h-home."

Shit!

"Sit tight. I'm coming over right now!" I end the call and am instantly thankful I didn't start the process of getting Dolly hyped to go to the park. She's still snoozing on our bed.

Quick as my feet can take me, I rush out of our apartment, only pausing to lock the door behind me, and sprint down the hall to Brooke and Chase's. I don't even bother knocking. Instead, I use my emergency key to get inside.

Instantly, my eyes are graced with the view of Benji pacing around Brooke while she grips the kitchen counter, breathing through what I'm assuming is a contraction.

"You okay?"

"Do I look okay?" she cries through gritted teeth. "I'm pretty sure my water broke, and these contractions feel like a real motherlover!"

Definitely in labor.

I step up to exert a little counterpressure on her lower back. "Did you call your doctor?"

"They told me to come right away, but Chase ran to the office and isn't answering his stupid phone!"

"That's strange," I comment because it is. If there's one person who is at Brooke's beck and call, it's her fiancé. "Maybe it's not going through?"

She huffs out a sigh when the contraction subsides and snags her phone off the counter. Instantly, her fingers tap against the screen, and she puts the receiver to her ear. "Chase! I'm in labor! What? What pizza? This isn't the time for jokes! I'm in la—" When another contraction begins, she drops her phone to the counter again and only focuses on breathing through it.

Quickly, I pick up her cell and try to take over the call while still giving her lower back some counterpressure. "Chase?"

"Ma'am, do you want to order a pizza or not?"

Huh? "Who is this?"

"This is Darryl from Pizza Hut. Who is this?"

Oh, for the love of everything.

Instantly, I hang up the phone and start to scan her contacts for her actual fiancé.

"Is he coming?" Brooke asks.

"Brooke, honey, you weren't calling Chase. You were calling Pizza Hut," I tell her, but she's beyond caring at this point. The pain of her contractions is her only focus. "Let's head to the hospital," I add as I try to guide her to a standing position. "And I'll work on getting Chase on the phone."

She doesn't respond, but she also doesn't protest.

Once I grab her hospital bag from the baby's nursery, I put Benji's service dog vest on and usher all of us out of her apartment and onto the elevator.

Benji follows dutifully, and Brooke curses up a storm as we make our way out of the building. And once we're in a cab, I manage to get Chase on the phone and tell him to meet us at St. Luke's.

I also text Kendall and Noah and Zoe and our parents, updating everyone that Brooke is in labor and we're headed to the hospital now.

Because, *holy moly*, my baby sister is about to have a baby of her own.

"Mom! Mom! Did Grandma and Grandpa get here yet?" Seth shouts the moment he spots me in the waiting room of the maternity ward. Both he and Grant leave Noah's side to sprint over to me.

"Not yet, buddy," I say, kneeling down to hug them both. "They just got on a flight, though, so they should be here in a few hours."

"Can we see the baby?" Seth exclaims.

"Yeah! I want to see the baby! Do we have a boy cousin or a girl cousin?" Grant asks, bouncing on his little feet.

I smile over at Noah as he closes the distance between us. He's still dressed in his scrubs and has been keeping the boys busy for the past few hours while I stayed in the room with Brooke and Chase.

The moment Noah reaches me, he pulls me in for a tight hug. "Mom and baby healthy and happy?" he asks, and I lean back to meet his eyes.

"Mom and baby are healthy and happy."

"But is the baby a girl or a boy?" Grant asks again, stomping his little foot in annoyance.

Both Noah and I laugh.

"How about I take you guys to see Aunt Brooke now, and you'll get to find out?"

"Yes!" Grant cheers, and Seth fist-pumps the air.

Noah wraps his arm around my shoulders as I lead them toward Brooke's room. Though, it's no surprise that the boys can hardly contain themselves when we reach her door.

"Now, hold on," I say, and while I'm gripping Seth's shoulders to stop him from bursting in, Noah is doing the same to Grant. "We all need to be calm when we go in there. We don't want to startle the baby, okay?"

"Okay, Mom." Both of the boys nod.

Once I open the door, they both skip inside and head straight for Brooke's bed, where she is now sitting up with her little bundle of joy in her arms. She looks exhausted from labor and pushing for two hours, but she also looks beautiful. And happy. So insanely happy.

Mo and Vinny are standing beside Chase, and both of the men grab Seth and Grant, lifting them into their respective arms and helping them get a better view of the baby.

"Is it a girl or a boy, Aunt Brooke?" Grant asks my sister, and she smiles up at him.

"You guys, I'd like you to meet your baby *girl* cousin, Emmy Rose."

"She's so cute!" Seth exclaims.

"She is really cute!" Grant agrees.

Emmy startles a little at their loud voices, but other than that, she just peers at the room filled with so many people who love and adore her through her little newborn eyes.

"You know, if she can already handle our wild Seth and Grant without tears," Mo comments with an amused smile, "then I think she's going to fit right in."

"Definitely," Noah agrees, tucking me closer to his side. "Congratulations, you guys. She's beautiful."

"Beautiful and perfect," I add, smiling over at my sister.

Noah presses a soft kiss to my forehead, and I have to swallow hard against the emotion that wants to spill down my face.

What a day. What a perfect day, inside this happy and awesome life of mine.

Part Two

A year later…

August

Sammy

Dolly Parton-inspired pink tulle runs in ribbons around the floral bouquets sitting in a jug of water in a corner of the room, and my sister smiles into the mirror in front of her as our mom tucks her veil into the top of her hair.

My sister's fairy tale is finally complete, because today, she marries Chase Dawson. The man of her dreams, one of the best guys in the world, and her real-life Romeo.

Benji sits at her side, a bow tie and a top hat making him absolutely dapper, and Mo drinks from a small glass of red wine with a tissue nearly permanently attached to her eyes as she watches Brooke.

I can't blame her. I'm emotional too.

My sister looks downright gorgeous in a silk gown that skims her figure, soft but elegant makeup, and bountifully curled hair. Her body has been curved by motherhood, but I swear the weight suits her even better than her thin figure of before. But the most beautiful part of her altogether is the never-ending smile on her happy face as she gets ready to say "I do" to her literal book boyfriend.

Mo and I are her only bridesmaids, and because of that—or maybe because

Brooke is a cool customer about everything other than me and Noah Philips—she let us choose our own dresses.

Mo went for a more structured blush-colored number, and I chose a lavender gown with a satin bodice and feather details at the bottom.

It'd be too much for any other wedding, but for Brooke's, it's just the kind of Dolly Parton-inspired exaggeration she's looking for.

Brooke smiles at my mom as she whispers something in her ear, and Mo runs to the restroom to touch up her lipstick one last time, setting her nearly gone wine on the table outside the door.

Emmy Rose sleeps soundly in her pack n' play near the small sofa on the other side of the room.

And while I'm not being watched, I sneak my phone out of my bag and answer the text I got earlier from the guy who makes *my* world light up.

Noah: I don't know if I'm supposed to admit this about the men's club, but we have no idea what we're doing over here. The wedding better start soon, or we might end up in the local mud run or a pub. How's it going in the land of the ladies? Have you told her yet?

I glance up at Brooke to make sure she's still occupied before typing faster and more furiously than I've ever typed before.

Me: Have I told my sister that you and I eloped two months ago and have been keeping it a secret this whole time? Considering the only words I've come up with are "Hey, so since you're getting married today, you should probably know I went behind your back and did the one thing that you'd lose your mind over." Um, no. I think I'll save it for another time.

Noah: Sammy, baby, you should tell her. I know you think she's going to be upset, but all she's ever wanted is for us to be together and you to be happy. You don't think she'll be thrilled that I sealed the deal and put a ring on it?

Me: Thrilled that I forgot to invite her? Yeah, no. I think it'll probably end in my murder.

The sound of Seth's voice yelling, "What's up, biotches?" brings my head up from my phone in a flash, and my texts with my *husband* are long forgotten.

There's an incredible amount of danger that comes with having my kids in this room, even now that they're a little older. My first glance goes to the baby, but she's still fast asleep.

"Seth. Language, please," my mom chides, and normally, I'd be right there with her. But in a bridal suite scenario, I've got way bigger priorities for my "Nos" than a little bit of colorful language.

"What?" he questions with a smirk, his aura in his little tux radiating Mr. Cool Dude to the max. "I didn't say, like, the actual word."

"Biotches," Grant chants, dancing behind him in a small black suit of his own that makes his six-year-old stature look almost grown. As Seth joins in on the dancing, they fly around the room like a couple of dogs with the zoomies.

Brooke's eyes cut to me, and I jump up from my seat to corral them both before they can get close to the color white. If my kids do something to my sister's very expensive gown, I will hyperventilate. It's moments like these when I miss Zoe's help the most.

"What are you doing in here, boys?" I ask, trying to gauge just how long I'm going to be playing NFL-level defense in a feathered dress. "I thought you were hanging out with Vinny and Noah."

Seth smiles and straightens his tie, and then Grant waggles his eyebrows, explaining, "We have the wedding gift from Uncle Chase. He said to give it to Aunt Brookie along with a big kiss."

"Aw, boys. That's so sweet," Brooke whispers then, welcoming them both toward her and opening her arms in expectation of a hug.

I grab my phone to take a picture of the momentous moment, but everything pretty much goes to shit when Grant bumps into the table at Brooke's side and knocks Mo's glass of red wine to the floor in a spray of glory that makes my blood run cold.

"Oh my God!" Brooke screams as I rush forward to the crime scene to pull Grant away and inspect her dress. She steps to the side on a horrified jog, and I follow, inspecting every inch of the silk until I'm sure it's still spotless. Benji crowds her, waiting for disaster.

"It's okay. It's okay, Brooke. Your dress is good. Nothing on it, I swear," I practically shout, hoping to catch her with the facts before her blood pressure tanks to the basement.

"Sammy," Brooke whispers. "Please get these little angels away from me. Right now!"

Mo, just returning from the bathroom, reads the scene immediately and steps in to help. "Come on, boys. Let's go see if we can steal a couple of appetizers from the kitchen."

Since her and Vinny's restaurant is doing the catering, she's allowed to say things like that.

"I'll come with," my mom offers, knowing that Brooke's anxiety is always higher when more people are around. "That way, I can find someone to clean up the wine."

Sue Baker is the sweetest. *And she'll probably hate me just as much as Brooke will when she finds out I ran off and got married without telling any of them.*

Finally alone, I stare at my beautiful sister and fan at my face as the tears hit my eyes. She's so stunning, I can hardly stand it.

"Sissy Sam," she whispers, grabbing at her nose as tears start to sting her face as well. "Don't you dare make me cry right now! I'm five minutes away from walking down the aisle!"

"I know, I know. I'm sorry!"

She turns to check herself in the mirror, carefully avoiding the spill. "Ah, well, it's okay. I guess I can understand why you're doing it. I'm definitely going to cry when I finally get to see you and Noah say I do."

"Hah," I force out, hoping it sounds at least kind of like a laugh instead of the sound of a cry.

"I'm serious. You're so next! I'm going to make sure you get my bouquet in the toss if I have to sew it to your hand ahead of time."

Oh my God. She's going to kill me.

I can only hope the endorphins from pledging her vows to the love of her life are enough to stop her.

"Happy people just don't kill people." Right? At least, that's what Elle Woods said.

Noah

My *wife*—I still can't believe she agreed to marry me—is the most beautiful woman I've ever seen as she walks down Brooke and Chase's wedding aisle to take her place on the stage across from me.

She surveys those around her, undoubtedly uncomfortable that all the attention is on her, and I do my best to follow her gaze so I might have an idea what she's thinking about.

She searches the crowd for the boys first, finding them in the front row with her mom, Sue, before moving on to a proud and eager Chase Dawson, super groom, and then her eyes come to me, which results in the kind of smile that gets me out of bed in the morning.

I don't let go of our eye contact until I absolutely have to, holding her stare through the end of her journey, her stepping up onto the stage, and Chase and Brooke's daughter Emmy's wagon processional down the aisle, and then finally give up her eyes when the wedding march starts.

Brooke stands proudly in the center of her dad, Hank, and a distinguished gentleman version of her superhero service dog Benji. There's a smile, I swear, on all three of their faces as the crescendo of piano music starts and they make the slow walk toward us.

My good girl Dolly shuffles at my feet at the sight of her boyfriend, but everyone else's eyes find Brooke and hold.

There's something captivating about brides in general, but Brooke, today, is in a whole other league. She looks gorgeous and happy and relaxed and so incredibly eager to be next to Chase Dawson, it's not even funny.

A couple of times during the march, I actually wonder if she's going to kick up into a run.

Chase's mom sniffles a soft cry, and his dad wraps an arm around her shoulders. They're so happy, they're sad. It's one of the most amazing circles of emotion.

Still, seeing them and the Bakers together helps me believe in the longevity of love.

My parents didn't have it, but Sammy and I will. And so will Brooke and Chase.

When it's right, it's obvious—even if it takes some of us a while to figure it out. I smile at Sammy, and she must feel my eyes on her because her gaze jerks from Brooke to me, and she smiles back.

Brooke stops at the end of the aisle, and Hank offers her hand to Chase, who takes it eagerly.

"Who gives this woman today?" the officiant asks.

"Her mother and I do," Hank replies, a slight break in his normally macho voice.

Chase and Brooke join hands, their expressions absolutely giddy, and a hush falls over the rest of us as the officiant starts the ceremony.

"Welcome, everyone. Please be seated."

The crowd follows the simple instruction, and I glance to my own beautiful bride. She's tearing a little, looking on at her baby sister and her soon-to-be husband, but when she looks up at me, I wink.

Her cheeks flush and her heart thrums—I can see the change in the pulse in her neck. Today and every day, we excite each other, and that hasn't changed a bit since the day I met her.

I may not have made my move fast enough, but once I did, I knew without a shadow of a doubt, there was no going back.

I had to have her. And I had to have her forever.

Luckily enough, she felt the exact same way, which is why, two months ago on an overnight trip to Vegas for an anesthesiology conference, we decided to get married. Put simply, we couldn't exist another minute without pledging our lives to each other.

We always knew we'd have a reception here, with the boys and our families and the other friends we love, at some point after Brooke and Chase tied the knot, but for making it official?

We couldn't wait.

And I know Sammy is worried about how Brooke will react to the news, but I'm confident in my friend. She'll find it in her heart to forgive us.

"I'd like to thank all of you for being here today to celebrate the marriage of Brooke Baker and Chase Dawson. They've invited you all for a reason—because sharing their most special of days with the people they love is of utmost importance to them."

Sammy's eyes slice to mine, and for the first time today, I start to get a little nervous with her.

"Your role today is to bear witness to their incredible love and to lift them up in their decision to commit to each other forever. Without your support, the best of their love isn't possible."

Oh man. Did Brooke write this stuff personally? Or is it just, like, standard wedding jargon? Because I'm starting to feel a little scared.

Sammy glares at me across the aisle, and I take the coward's way out by pointing toward the bride and groom and mouthing, "Watch the wedding."

She rolls her eyes, and I don't blame her. If I were her, I'd know my game too.

"Now, the bride and groom would like to exchange some personalized vows." The officiant gestures to Brooke to go first.

Her voice is shaky as she unfolds the piece of paper from inside the top of her dress and starts to read. "My dearest Chase. What can I possibly say to you that I haven't already written in a book?"

The whole crowd laughs, including me.

"I'm not sure. But I guess a safe place to start is I love you. Every day, I wake up knowing that if there's one thing I've done right in this life, it's choosing to share it with you. You and our daughter are the absolute light of my life. I hope to be the same to you, and today, I promise you to make achieving that my mission. I will love you and honor you and fight for us every step of the way. You're the man of my dreams, and I'll spend the rest of my life trying to be the woman of yours."

Sammy's face is red with suppressed tears as she deep-breathes in an attempt to save her makeup. I smile at her beautiful face the second her eyes meet mine.

God, I love her so much.

"Chase," the officiant offers, gesturing for the groom to answer his bride.

Chase untucks the small sheet of paper from his chest pocket and then rips it up before taking Brooke's hands in his. All of the guests gasp, but Brooke just shakes her head with a smile.

"What are you doing?"

"Telling you I love you from the heart. You and I both know I could edit my speech until the end of time, but that's not what this is about. This is about you and me, and the fact that we're destined for each other. If I only had the choice to keep one thing in my entire life the same, it would be you. You and Emmy are the reason I exist. The reason I get up in the morning and the reason I sleep peacefully at night." He laughs. "When, you know, Emmy actually sleeps."

I chuckle along with everyone else.

"You're it, Brooke. You're the one. So much so, I'll never need any other number."

But while everyone else's attention is on the bride and groom as they exchange rings and all of the official "I dos," my eyes are back to Sammy, solely fixated on my gorgeous wife.

My wife. Man, I don't think I'll ever get tired of saying that.

Sammy

Three hours into the reception of my sister's imagining, the time of reckoning has finally come.

The bouquet toss.

Not a moment has gone by since the start of the reception that Brooke hasn't taken the opportunity to wave it in my face or taunt me with it or put it in my chair every time I've gotten up, and I'm on the brink of absolute insanity.

"Come on, it's going to be fine," Noah coaches again in my ear. "So what if you catch the bouquet when you're already married? It's not that big of a deal."

"Not that big of a deal?" I nearly shriek. "Brooke caught the bouquet at my wedding and married Jamie not long after."

Noah scoffs. "Coincidence."

"Okay, what about Mo catching it at her friend Belinda's right before her wedding to Vinny?"

"When have you been talking to Mo about bouquet tosses?"

"Noah." I roll my eyes and ignore his question entirely. "It means something. I can't just spit on tradition like that."

"Okay, then just tell her we got married. She'll understand."

"She will *not*."

"Baby, you're killing me here. Should we get a divorce just so you can tell your sister we're not married, then plan a wedding that she can attend and get remarried?"

"No!" I shout, horrified at the prospect of being anything but Noah Philips's wife.

Noah pulls me close and pushes his lips to mine, and I melt into the contact like butter. "Good. Because that isn't an option. I love you, Sammy Philips, and I'm not giving you up."

"I love you too, Noah Philips. But, so help me, if you don't keep your voice down, I'm going to scream."

He laughs and shakes his head as the DJ makes the announcement we've been waiting for. "Okay, everyone. I need all the single ladies to make their way to the dance floor for the tossing of the bouquet."

I quiver under the stress of my nerves, and Noah gives me a little shove to the bum in my sister's direction.

She's beckoning with wide eyes and an excited wave, and I trudge my way to the front of the crowd.

She dances to the strummy music the DJ plays, and everyone shouts as she turns to throw the bouquet.

Three tense seconds pass before she turns back to me and throws it right at me like a baseball player doling out a fastball pitch.

I dodge and weave, shouting as the flowers hit me in the shoulder and fall to the floor like a bird that's been shot from the sky.

The music stops, and Brooke stares, a disbelieving look on her beautiful face.

"Did you just...dodge my bouquet toss? What the hell is going on, Sammy? Don't you want to marry Noah?"

All of a sudden, I can't stand the tension for a second longer.

"Brooke, I'm already married!" I blurt out. There's a moment in time when everything ceases to be, and then...*boom!*

"Are you flipping kidding me?" Brooke screeches so loud that all anyone can do is stare at us.

"Flipping kidding, flipping kidding!" Grant shouts at my side. Noah sweeps in and ushers him away, his sweet lips at my cute boy's ear.

"You got married?" Brooke questions, but her eyes are like tiny lasers as they home in on my face. And her voice, well, it's still really fucking loud. "You got married without me there to see it?"

Briefly, I glance around the room, noting that the entire reception is still looking at us, my shocked parents included, but eventually, I do my best to tune it out and focus on my sister. "Brooke, I'm sorry that I've burst your bubble. I'm sorry that I got married without you there, but I'm not sorry that I got married. I...couldn't help it. I couldn't wait. I just...had to marry Noah. I love him." I shrug. "Can you forgive me?"

Brooke just stares at me. No words. No movement. Just a whole lot of glaring.

Chase approaches her with Emmy in his arms and pulls her into an encouraging hug. "Come on, baby. This is what you've always wanted, right?"

I nod enthusiastically. "It is. It's what you've wanted, Brooke. Remember? Remember how badly you wanted me to see it?"

"I remember," she mutters.

"Oh, and also, remember how scary the thought of wine on your dress was? My blood would definitely be worse."

She narrows her eyes, but I push on.

"So, please, please forgive me."

She considers me for a long moment, and then her face transforms into what I can only describe as a sinister smile.

"Okay, Sammy. I forgive you."

"You do?" I ask shakily, quite suspicious because of the look on her face.

"I do."

"Oh, thank God. I was so worried—"

"But just because I forgive doesn't mean I'll forget." She closes the distance between us to pull me into a hug. "I'll get my revenge."

"What?" I question, leaning back to meet her eyes. "What does that mean?"

"Oh, Sammy." She winks. "You'll see."

Part Three

10 months later…

June

Sammy

"Okay, you guys, I'm off!" I call from my spot in the entryway, dressed and ready to tackle another shift at the restaurant.

But Noah is the only one who walks out to see me off.

Although, both Seth and Grant do shout, "Bye, Mom!"

"Man, I feel so loved right now," I tease, and Noah just pulls me into his arms for a hug and a kiss.

"Have a good night at work. I love you."

"I love you too," I whisper, but he doesn't release me from his embrace. Instead, he holds me tightly for another minute or so.

"Make sure you take care of yourself, okay?" he questions. "Find time to take a break and get off your feet for a little bit. Eat something. Drink water. All the good stuff, okay?"

"I will."

"Promise?" he asks, leaning back to look into my eyes.

302 | max monroe

"Promise."

With one soft kiss to my lips, he lets me go. Though, he does give me a little tap to my ass as I head for the door.

I roll my eyes, but I also giggle and think, *this man is my husband. How did I get so lucky?*

As I head out of our apartment and onto the elevator, an incoming call makes my phone ring from inside my purse, and I pull it out to find an unknown number.

Every once in a while, when Mo tries to call me from La Croisette's office, I'll get this same unknown-number business, so I answer it.

"Hello?"

"Hi, is this Sammy Philips?"

"Speaking," I respond as I step off the elevator.

"Hi, Sammy, this is Natasha Lovingfeld. I'm a reporter with the *New York Tribune*. Do you have a few moments for me to ask you your thoughts on *Cluelessly Yours?*"

"Cluelessly Yours?" I question, ironically clueless as to what in the heck that is.

"Brooke Baker's upcoming novel."

My sister's next book is titled Cluelessly Yours? Hell, I didn't even know she'd managed to get another book written since she released *Best Frenemies.*

"I would just like to get your thoughts on the book," Natasha continues. "And whether or not it lived up to your real life."

Lived up to my real life?

"Oh, and your thoughts on the dedication too," Natasha adds. "When I read it, it nearly brought tears to my eyes."

"Brought tears to your eyes?"

"There's just something so sweet about seeing an author dedicate her entire book to her sister's love story."

Brooke dedicated an entire book to my love story?

How am I just finding out about this? And *not* from my own sister, but from a random journalist I've never met?

"Natasha, I'm so sorry, but I'm going to have to call you back," I state as I pause right at the subway entrance. "Just text me your number, and I'll get back to you as soon as I can."

I don't give her any time to respond before hanging up the call, knowing damn well I won't be calling her about anything. I will, however, call the one person who better be prepared to give me some answers.

"Hey, Sam," Brooke greets on the second ring. "What's up?"

"You know, I just got the most interesting call. From a reporter."

"What? Really?"

"Yeah. A reporter by the name of Natasha Lovingfeld who wanted to know my thoughts on my sister's latest book."

"*Oh...*"

"She also wanted to know what I thought of the dedication. The one that states my sister dedicated an entire book to my love story."

"That sure is interesting..."

"*Brooke!*"

"What?"

"What?" I repeat. "I'll tell you what. You best start fessing up right the F now."

"So..." She pauses, but when a good five seconds pass, an exasperated breath falls from my lungs.

"Brooke."

"Okay. Okay," she responds on a sigh. "So, I might've written an entire book about Noah's and your love story."

"Brooke!"

"I guess you can kind of…sort of…consider this my way of getting back at you for the whole not-inviting-me-to-your-wedding thing."

My eyes are one revelation away from popping out of my eye sockets. "You did this for revenge?"

"Well, that, and the fact that your story was too good not to write about!"

"Oh my God, you're insane!"

"But don't worry, I changed the names," she quickly adds, and I grit my teeth.

"Send me a copy right now."

"Are you sure you—"

"Brooke," I cut her off with a tense jaw. "Send me a copy right now."

"Fine. Fine. Sending it to your email now."

I don't even bother with a response. Instead, I hang up the phone and jog down the stairs to hop on the subway before I end up late to work because my sister is a freaking psycho.

By the time my inbox chimes with a new email from Brooke, I'm walking into La Croisette with five minutes to spare.

I don't waste any time, heading into the back office to download the latest and greatest from Brooke Baker, plopping into the leather desk chair as I do. The instant my download is complete, my Kindle is locked and loaded with *Cluelessly Yours*.

When I open up the first page, the dedication sits front and center.

"To the love story of my sister Sammy Baker-Philips and my brother-in-law Dr. Noah Philips."

And I can't decide if I should laugh or cry. Sure, she may've changed the character names in the book, but the freaking dedication may as well include my home address and social security number!

My sister, ladies and gentlemen, don't let her know too much about your life, or her crazy-writer ass will put you in one of her books...*without* your permission.

I only make it ten pages into *Sara and Nolan's* love story before I realize a few things:

Number one: My sister is an amazing writer.

Number two: Sara and Nolan's love story already has me hooked, and I lived it.

And number three: I'm about to rock my sister's world with a payback.

Phone to my ear, I hear Brooke answer on the first ring, and I instantly know she's been expecting this call.

"Are you mad?" They're the first words out of her mouth.

"Just tell me one thing. When does it publish?"

"In two weeks."

"So, it's too late to change anything?"

"Yeah..." She pauses, and I smile.

"Oh, that's too bad because you don't have the full story."

"What do you mean?"

"I'm pregnant."

"*What?*" she questions on a shout.

"I said, I'm pregnant, Brooke," I tell her again and run a hand over my belly. "A little over eight weeks along. Looks like you're not the only one who is good at keeping secrets."

"Sammy! I swear on everything, you better not be lying to me right now!"

"Oh, I'm not lying. But I do have to go. Love you!"

"Sammy! Sam—"

Then, I hang up the phone.

And the smile that consumes my face? Well, it's equal parts I-just-one-upped-my-sister and I'm-pregnant-with-Noah-Philips's-baby.

Hey, universe! How's that for a happily ever after?

THE END

Loved being inside Sammy and Noah's world? Well, we have good news! You can read about how famous author Brooke Baker fell in love in *Accidental Attachment*!

There's nothing like sending your editor—*and secret crush*—the wrong manuscript. Instead of the book that was due, Brooke accidentally sends dreamboat Chase Dawson the secret romance book she wrote about her crush…*on him*.

Oh yeah, baby, it gets *really* good.

Already read *Accidental Attachment* and Need EVEN MORE Max Monroe while you wait for our next release?

Never fear, we have a list of nearly FORTY other titles to keep you busy for as long as your little reading heart desires! **Check them out at our website:** *www.authormaxmonroe.com*

COMPLETELY NEW TO MAX MONROE AND DON'T KNOW WHERE TO START?

Check out our Suggested Reading Order on our website!
www.authormaxmonroe.com/max-monroe-suggested-reading-order

WHAT'S NEXT FROM MAX MONROE?

Stay up-to-date with our characters and our upcoming releases by signing up for our newsletter on our website: *www.authormaxmonroe.com/newsletter*!

You may live to regret much, but we promise it won't be subscribing to our newsletter.

Seriously, we make it fun! Character conversations about royal babies, parenting woes, embarrassing moments, and shitty horoscopes are just the beginning! If you're already signed up, consider sending us a message to tell us how much you love us. We really like that. ;)

Follow us online here:

Facebook: www.facebook.com/authormaxmonroe

Reader Group: www.facebook.com/groups/1561640154166388

Twitter: www.twitter.com/authormaxmonroe

Instagram: www.instagram.com/authormaxmonroe

TikTok: vm.tiktok.com/ZMe1jv5kQ

Goodreads: https://goo.gl/8VUIz2

Acknowledgments

First of all, THANK YOU for reading. That goes for anyone who has bought a copy, read an ARC, helped us beta, edited, or found time in their busy schedule just to make sure we stayed on track. Thank you for supporting us, for talking about our books, and for just being so unbelievably loving and supportive of our characters. You've made this our MOST favorite adventure thus far.

THANK YOU to each other. Monroe is thanking Max. Max is thanking Monroe. We always do this, and it's because we *love* writing books together.

THANK YOU, Lisa, for being you. You deal with our blonde (blond?) behavior so well, and we're not even blond (blonde?). Also, we're really sorry for the unintended cliffhanger we treated you to, but we had to send at least part of the book to you on time. LOL!

THANK YOU, Stacey, for always making the inside of our books so pretty! And for being so dang flexible with our last-minute asses. We couldn't survive without you!

THANK YOU, Peter, for working your ass off on this cover and making it everything we wanted and need it to be!

THANK YOU, Mel, for taking the giant leap to join our team and for surviving our "blackout" period during the deadline. You'll get used to it, we swear.

THANK YOU, Rick, for handling all the complicated numbery stuff.

THANK YOU to every blogger and influencer who has read, reviewed, posted, shared, and supported us. Your enthusiasm, support, and hard work do not go unnoticed. We love youuuuuuuuuuuu!

THANK YOU to the people who love us—our family. You are our biggest supporters and motivators. We couldn't do this without you.

THANK YOU to our Awesome ARC-ers. We love and appreciate you guys so much.

THANK YOU to our Camp Love Yourself friends! We love you. You always find a way to make us smile and laugh every single freaking day. You're the best.

As always, all our love.

XOXO,

Max & Monroe

Made in United States
Orlando, FL
04 March 2024

44268240R00173